LONE STAR LSC COUNTRY CLUB EST. 1923

Ann Major loves writing romance novels as much as she loves reading them. She is a proud mother of three grown children. She lists hiking in the Colorado mountains with her husband, playing tennis, sailing, enjoying her cats and playing the piano among her favorite activities. Readers can contact her at her author Web site www.annmajor.com.

Christine Rimmer came to her profession the long way around. Before settling down to write about the magic of romance, she'd been an actress, a salesclerk, a janitor, a model, a phone sales representative, a teacher, a waitress, a playwright and an office manager. Now that she's finally found work that suits her perfectly, she insists she never had a problem keeping a job—she was merely gaining "life experience" for her future as a novelist. Christine is grateful not only for the joy she finds in writing, but for what waits when the day's work is through: a man she loves, who loves her right back, and the privilege of watching their children grow and change day to day. She lives with her family in Oklahoma.

Beverly Barton has been in love with romance since her grandfather gave her an illustrated book of *Beauty and the Beast*. An avid reader since childhood, Beverly wrote her first book at the age of nine. After marriage to her own "hero" and the births of her daughter and son, Beverly chose to be a full-time homemaker, aka wife, mother, friend and volunteer. The author of over thirty-five books, Beverly is a member of Romance Writers of America and helped found the Heart of Dixie chapter in Alabama. She has won numerous awards and has made the Waldenbooks and *USA Today* bestseller lists.

ANN MAJOR
CHRISTINE RIMMER
BEVERLY BARTON

LONE STAR COUNTRY CLUB:
The Debutantes

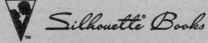

Published by Silhouette Books
America's Publisher of Contemporary Romance

Special thanks and acknowledgment are given to Beverly Barton, Christine Rimmer and Ann Major for their contributions to LONE STAR COUNTRY CLUB: THE DEBUTANTES.

 SILHOUETTE BOOKS

LONE STAR COUNTRY CLUB: THE DEBUTANTES

Copyright © 2002 by Harlequin Books S.A.

ISBN 0-373-48480-1

The publisher acknowledges the copyright holder of the individual works as follows:

JENNA'S WILD RIDE
Copyright © 2002 by Harlequin Books S.A.

REINVENTING MARY
Copyright © 2002 by Harlequin Books S.A.

FRANKIE'S FIRST DRESS
Copyright © 2002 by Harlequin Books S.A.

Visit Silhouette at www.eHarlequin.com

Printed in U.S.A.

CONTENTS

JENNA'S WILD RIDE
Beverly Barton

To everyone
in the Harlequin/Silhouette office in New York:
Thanks for surviving!

Chapter 1

Jenna Wilson felt like doing something wild and crazy, something totally out of character for the sweet, obedient good girl she'd been all her life. As the only child of a wealthy, socially prominent couple who waited until midlife to start a family, Jenna had been spoiled. On the other hand, extra pressure had been put on her to please her parents—something she had obediently done since childhood. Somehow she'd always sensed that her parents' happiness depended upon her actions. A weighty burden to place on a kid's shoulders, but one Jenna had felt even more acutely these past two years since her father's death. Her mother expected so much from her; and God knew she tried to please Nelda Wilson in every way possible. She'd even given up her own plans to attend

Texas A&M in Corpus Christi in order to carry on a family tradition and attend Tensley College, her mother's and grandmother's alma mater. And next month after she graduated, with a double major in History and English, she'd be expected to join all the right clubs, attend all the right parties and begin the extensive search for the proper husband. No doubt her mother would have a hand in choosing her husband; after all, it wouldn't do for Nelda Wilson's daughter to marry beneath her. And what would be so different about her mother choosing her mate? Hadn't her parents always made all her decisions for her? They had chosen her friends, her boyfriends, her high school and college classes and even her extracurricular activities.

God, how she hated her life! She was twenty-one, wasn't she? Legally an adult. She should be free to live her own life, to do whatever she truly wanted to do. Hadn't she promised herself that once she graduated, she would confront her mother and at long last take charge of her own life? And that's exactly what she intended to do.

If only she'd already had that all-important talk with her mother, then maybe she wouldn't be facing the nightmare event planned for May 11. When her mother had told her about the plans for her to participate in the debutante ball at the Lone Star Country Club, why hadn't she vetoed the idea of her "coming out" along with girls several years her junior? Why hadn't she simply said, "I don't want to do it. It doesn't matter that I had to miss out on the ball when

Daddy got sick and died. I'm too old now to be parading around in a big, white pouffy dress. With final exams and graduation so close, I don't have time for this nonsense." But of course she hadn't refused. What defense did she have against her mother's reminder that it was a tradition in her family for the young ladies to be presented to society at this annual ball? For heaven's sake, her great-great-grandmother Rose had been a debutante!

Jenna flopped down on her bed and stared up at the ceiling. Even this apartment and her two roommates, Katie Boyd and Dana Lewis, had had to pass inspection and receive the stamp of approval from Nelda. Both girls were from good families and their mothers were part of Nelda's social circle. It wasn't that she didn't like Katie and Dana—she did. But neither girl was any more liberated than she was. Wasn't that why Nelda had chosen them? Because they were under their mothers' thumbs, just as she was.

So what made Jenna think that she would finally have the courage to break free once she graduated from Tensley? Wouldn't she simply look her mother in the eye, as she'd done in the past, then open her mouth to speak and be struck dumb? Probably. And if that happened, she would wake up one morning a few years from now married to some stodgy banker or lawyer, whom she didn't love, and find herself reliving her mother's life instead of living her own.

Her dreams hadn't mattered to anyone, least of all her parents. Her mother had scoffed at the idea of her attending A&M to seek an art degree, then moving to Chicago or New York, getting her own apartment, working at one of the museums to earn a living while pursuing her goal of becoming a professional artist. Her parents had allowed her to paint as a hobby, but according to them, the only true profession for a lady—even in the twenty-first century—was being a society wife. But Jenna knew she would suffocate and die if she were to live that sort of life.

Oh, what she'd give to break free, to go out and howl at the moon, to kick up her heels and do something—anything—totally outrageous. Tonight. Now. Right this minute! What she needed was just one wild ride of excitement and adventure.

Jenna shot straight up, hopped out of bed and flung open her closet door. Flipping through her wardrobe, she found absolutely nothing that wasn't ''suitable'' attire. For what she had in mind, she'd need something sexy, something that announced to the world that the woman wearing it was ready for a good time. Just as she'd given up on finding something, she spotted a pair of faded jeans that she'd stopped wearing because they were a size 4 and she was now a size 6. Perfect choice, she thought. Skintight, accentuating every curve of her lower body. After yanking the jeans off the rack, she tossed them onto her bed. On to Step Two of her plan.

Rushing out of her bedroom, she called to her roommates. ''It's Friday night and none of us has a date. Why don't we do something together?''

"We are doing something together." Dana, her dark brown eyes half-hidden behind silver-framed glasses, glanced up from where she sat at the small flat-top desk in the living room, charts and graphs spread out before her. "We're supposed to be studying. Finals are coming up in a few weeks and if I'm going to graduate, then I—"

"You'll ace the exams," plump, green-eyed Katie said as she emerged from the kitchen carrying a bowl of ice cream. "You and Jenna both. I'm the one who has to worry. I don't have a 4.0 grade point average."

Patting herself on the chest, as if having heart palpitations, Dana moaned sarcastically. "Oh, no, you have only a 3.8."

"Let's face facts. We'll all three ace those finals and we know it. We've worked like demons for the past few years to keep up our grades to pacify our parents." Jenna went over to Katie and took the bowl of ice cream out of her hand, then placed it on the table atop Dana's papers.

"Hey, watch it," Dana complained.

Jenna reached down, grabbed Dana's hands and pulled her to her feet. As she grabbed Katie around the waist, the girl gasped. Jenna held tightly to both of her roommates. "We're not going to study tonight and we're not going to stay here while the rest of the world is out there having fun. Just because our parents stuck us in a women's college doesn't mean there aren't a lot of men out there."

Dana's black curls bounced around her face as she

shook her head. "I just want to know one thing—what have you done with my friend Jenna Wilson? Are you her clone? Or did you simply take over her body?"

Jenna laughed, loving the very thought that she wasn't acting like her usual logical, well-behaved self. "Come on. Where's your spirit of adventure? Haven't you ever wanted to go somewhere you shouldn't, and do something forbidden, with someone really bad?"

A warm flush colored Katie's cheeks as she smiled. "Yes, I have. But I've never had the guts to do it."

"You've both lost your minds," Dana said, but when she tried to pull away, Jenna held even tighter. When the two looked squarely at each other, Dana conceded, "Oh, all right. Yes. But I'm not the kind of girl who...well, let's face it—I'm the bookworm type, the girl who's had one sexual experience in her whole life."

"That's one up on me," Katie said.

"Me, too," Jenna admitted.

"Oh, great," Dana said. "So what are you suggesting that two virgins and a semivirgin do to get in trouble?"

With a wicked smile on her lips, Jenna danced her friends around the room. "I say let's put on the most slutty outfits we can pull together and drive over to Mission Creek to the Saddlebag Bar. I hear that place is really wild. Lots of cowboys drinking, shooting pool and looking to get laid. We can drink and dance and flirt like crazy."

"And what will our parents say if they find out?" Dana asked.

"Why should they find out?" Jenna said. "Besides, that's part of the fun—doing something that our mothers wouldn't approve of."

"I'm game if y'all are," Katie said.

"Oh, all right," Dana told them. "Count me in."

Brent Jameson downed the last drops of his beer and set the empty bottle on a nearby table before taking his turn in the game he was playing with Clay Hargett, one of the other ranch hands who worked with him at the Carson Ranch just outside Mission Creek. Brent was taking a working holiday away from his job in Chicago as a commodities analyst. His specialty was the cattle industry, but he'd lived away from his hometown of Kansas City, Texas, for ten years and felt he needed a refresher course in being a cowpoke. What better way to stay on top of things in the cattle industry than by doing some firsthand research?

"Six ball in the side pocket," Brent said as he took his shot. He wasn't a professional by any means, but he was a damn good pool player and won more games than he lost up against the guys here at the Saddlebag Bar.

"I see now that I'm going to lose my twenty bucks." Clay smiled in his good-natured, easygoing way.

Brent had found that he enjoyed the hard work and the simple, down-to-earth rest and relaxation guys like

Clay experienced. The physically draining job on a ranch, as well as the rough and ready downtime, was addictive. But Brent knew that nothing could ever be as exciting, as exhilarating, as satisfying as his job and his lifestyle back in Chicago. As much as he enjoyed playing cowboy, it wasn't the life for him. After two weeks on a ranch outside Laredo, owned by one of his father's old friends, he'd moved on to Mission Creek, where he was working incognito on the Carson Ranch. Flynt Carson had been a business associate for several years and readily agreed to hire Brent on a temporary basis.

After his stint in Texas, he'd return to Chicago, to his tailor-made suits, his expensive condo and his sleek, silver Jaguar convertible. The first thing he would do when he went home was telephone one of the lovely ladies he knew. Any one of a dozen would do just fine. Cheryl, with her mane of black hair and legs that went on forever. Or maybe glamorous red-headed Erica, who liked to play rough. Or Stephanie, with the cantaloupe-size boobs, who knew every trick in the book. Oh, yeah. He had his first night back in Chicago planned. He would take the lucky woman to dinner, to the theater and then to bed.

He'd been too long without a woman. Although he was considered something of a playboy, he didn't customarily have one-night stands. He was always careful in every way a man needed to be careful when it came to sex. And that's all it was for him—sex. He wasn't ready for some woman to rope and brand him. Fortunately, he had yet to meet the female who could wrap him around her little finger.

Sinking the eight ball into the corner pocket, Brent ended his third game with Clay, winning their twenty-dollar bet. Just as he shook hands with his opponent, he heard somebody let out a long, low and very loud whistle that instantly gained his attention. He and half the men in the Saddlebag Bar visually searched the room, seeking the object of that hungry wolf whistle.

And there she was. My God, what a beauty. Petite but voluptuous. No more than five-two, with a to-die-for body. Young and luscious. Her skintight faded jeans hugged her trim hips and firm, round butt. A skimpy, white tank top left little to the imagination, revealing the swell of her large, full breasts and the tiny span of her bare waist. Her long, straight, baby blond hair caressed her naked back as she walked.

Just looking at her gave Brent a hard-on.

Jenna had never felt so self-conscious in her entire life. Her heart beat ninety to nothing, pounding so loudly that she could barely hear the band. All sounds blended together into one big roar inside her head. Katie and Dana followed her, somewhat reluctantly. They had ended up taking pieces from their own wardrobes, along with items borrowed from fellow Tensley students, to put together their ensembles. Admittedly, Jenna's outfit was the most provocative, but she loved feeling seductive. Her new and heady sense of power pleased her greatly.

A country and western band played loud, she-done-
him wrong music, which mixed with the drone of talking, laughing and occasional cursing. Smoke created
a thin haze, a transparent gray sheen coating the interior of the roadhouse. Huge ceiling fans swirled and
whined softly. Couples clung to each other on the
dance floor and others made out in darkened corners.
A section just off the dance floor held numerous small
tables, with a variety of customers seated in the
wooden chairs. Men and women congregated around
the four pool tables in the back of the roadhouse and
the crowded bar area was filled to capacity.

When someone let out a loud whistle, Jenna instinctively knew the guy was whistling at her. She'd had
boys following her around like lovesick puppy dogs
ever since she'd outgrown her training bra, but her
parents' tight rein on her social life had curtailed any
chance of romance. That was why she was a twenty-
one-year-old virgin.

Dana grabbed Jenna's arm. "He's whistling at
you!"

"He looks mean and dirty," Katie said. "Oh, gee,
I wish we hadn't come here."

"We should leave now, before we get in trouble,"
Dana said.

"No. We aren't leaving," Jenna told them. "Remember why we came here. Fun. Excitement. A walk
on the wild side."

"I don't think I have a wild side." Dana dug in her

heels—her red, four inch spike heels she'd borrowed from a friend—and refused to budge.

"Have you ever seen so many hot, sweaty men in your life?" Katie scanned the honky-tonk, her eyes wide with wonder, like a kid in a candy shop, overwhelmed by the abundance of goodies.

"There has to be a guy in here for each of us." Jenna surveyed the bar, where the man who'd whistled at her stood. He waved at her and grinned. No, not him, she thought. He wasn't what she was looking for—a little too old, probably thirty-five, and skinny as a rail. "It's just a matter of zeroing in on what we want. We might have better luck if we separate and scout out the area."

"I'm not separating." Dana grabbed Katie's arm and held tight.

A tall, lanky cowboy, with a winning smile and sandy brown hair approached them. He gave Jenna a once-over, nodded and then went straight past her to Katie.

"Hi, there," he said. "I'm Andy Bolden. How about a dance?"

"Uh…ah…" Katie stammered. Her cheeks flushed bright pink.

Jenna jerked Katie free from Dana's tenacious hold, then gave Katie a shove toward Andy. "She'd love to dance."

As Andy led Katie toward the dance floor, Dana stared dumbfounded as her friend disappeared in the crowd. "What just happened?"

Jenna continued searching, her gaze pausing occasionally when she saw an interesting specimen. "Huh?"

"You just sent Katie off with a perfect stranger."

"So what?"

"So...so...oh, I don't know, just so."

Jenna saw him on the far side of the room, near one of the pool tables. That's *him,* she decided. If ever a guy's appearance epitomized the bad boy image, this man's did. Her heart skipped a beat at the thought of just what somebody like that could teach her about life. If she wanted a good time—and she did—he'd be the one who could give it to her. He was tall, a little over six feet, she guessed. With broad shoulders, long, narrow waist and slim hips. Lean and mean. His old jeans fit nicely over his long legs and his white T-shirt molded to his wide chest and big arms.

"What are you staring at?" Dana asked.

"Him."

"Him?" Dana's gaze followed Jenna's line of vision. She drew in a deep breath, then blew it out dramatically. "My goodness, Jen, you've got to be out of your mind. That guy is probably lethal. Just look at him."

"I am looking at him. And he's looking back at me."

Across the crowded roadhouse, Jenna's gaze met and locked with Mr. Wrong. *Mr. Absolutely-perfectly-wrong-for-a-nice-girl-like-me.* She might not have much experience in matters like this, but it didn't take a rocket scientist to figure out that the man found her as fascinating as she did him.

"Go get a beer or something," Jenna told her friend. "I'll see you later."

"Where are you going?" Dana's voice squeaked when she spoke. "And what are you going to do?"

"I'm going over there—" Jenna nodded the direction "—to play a game...of pool."

"Don't do it," Dana said.

Totally disregarding her roommate's advice, Jenna sashayed away, her focus on the ruggedly gorgeous hunk across the room. As she drew nearer, she noticed how black his hair was and that he not only needed a haircut, but he also needed a shave. A five-o'clock shadow darkened the lower half of his face. A sensible tingle of fear radiated up her spine, but she refused to allow the warning to sway her from her objective. When only a few feet separated them, the intensity of his blue eyes—strikingly blue against the tan on his incredibly handsome face—captivated her.

With a boldness she'd never known, Jenna walked right up to him and said, "Hi, there."

An amused smile spread his lips slightly apart, as if he found her amusing. "Hi, yourself."

Butterflies did a wicked dance in her belly. *Say something, you idiot. Don't just stand there.* "How about a game?" she asked.

"You play pool, blondie?" His voice was honey-coated raw and deep, with just a hint of a Texas drawl.

Her father had played billiards with her, teaching

her his favorite game, just as he'd taught her to horse-back ride and shoot a rifle. If she'd had a brother, her father probably wouldn't have bothered teaching her, which made her glad she'd been an only child.

"Would you like to find out just how well I play?" she asked teasingly.

"What do you have in mind?"

He ran his heated gaze over her, from head to toe, lingering at her breasts and then at the apex between her thighs. His perusal was downright suggestive, but instead of feeling insulted or threatened, Jenna felt hot and bothered. What was the word her more experienced friends used? Horny? That was it—she felt horny.

Easing closer, her body almost touching his, she looked up at him. "Just how confident are you that you can beat me?" she asked.

His grin widened, giving her a glimpse of his straight, white teeth. "Do you want to make a bet?"

She ran the tip of her tongue over the inside of her lips, making a complete circle. Her bad boy swallowed hard as his gaze fixed pointedly on her mouth.

"You set the stakes," she told him.

"If I win, you give me a kiss." He continued staring at her mouth.

"And if I win?"

"Name your prize, honey. I'll let you have anything you want."

"Anything?" She couldn't resist the urge to give him the same kind of once-over he'd given her, but when her gaze hesitated at his crotch, she gasped. The guy was already partially aroused. The fit of his clinging jeans left no doubt about it.

Before she knew what was happening, he slid his arm around her waist, pulled her up against him so that their bodies aligned perfectly. With his semihard sex pressed against her, he lowered his head and whispered in her ear. "Eight Ball okay with you?"

"What?" His nearness robbed her of breath, and for just a second it robbed her of her mind, also. "Oh, yes, the game. Sure, Eight Ball is fine with me."

He released her as quickly as he'd grabbed her, leaving her weak-kneed and light-headed. Dana had been right—this guy was lethal. What had she gotten herself into with this sexy cowboy? She had to win their game; otherwise, he would claim his kiss. And something told her that by claiming the kiss he'd take more than she intended to give.

Watching him move like a sleek, dark panther as he racked the balls, Jenna found herself totally mesmerized. She'd never been so instantly attracted to a man, so completely overwhelmed by her own desires. But he seemed totally oblivious to the spell he'd cast over her. He removed a cue from the rack, chalked it and glanced at her.

"What's the matter, honey, change your mind?" His cocky, self-confident smile taunted her.

"No, I—I'm still playing."

Trying to concentrate on the game instead of the

man, she chose her cue, chalked it and faced her opponent.

"No point in lagging," he told her. "As far as I'm
concerned, ladies go first."

Putting on a show of bravado, Jenna sauntered
around the table, psyching herself up for the break,
that all-important first shot. Maybe she could distract
him just enough to impair his game. Saying a little
help-me-dear-Lord prayer, she leaned down, putting
her cue into position, then made a perfect shot, sending
the three ball into a corner pocket. With a sigh of
relief, she glanced at her bad boy, who seemed totally
unaffected by her success. His sky-blue eyes possessed
a devilish twinkle, as if he had a secret she needed to
know, but didn't.

If he thought that first shot was pure luck and nothing more, then she'd have to prove him wrong. Studying the angles, she deliberately brushed against him as
she eased past. She'd have to pocket another one of
the solids, which left her everything from one to seven,
except the three ball.

"Six ball in the side pocket," she said, then with
expert precision, she aimed, shot and could barely contain her exuberance when the six ball landed in a side
pocket.

"You're good, honey," he said. "Looks like
you've got a chance of getting whatever you want
from me."

"Maybe I don't want what you think I want," she
told him, realizing she'd better cool his ardor before

it got completely out of hand. She wanted to flirt, to have a little fun, but this guy was ready to hop in the sack.

"So, sweet thing, tell me, do you live here in Mission Creek?" he asked.

"My name is Jenna. And I was born and raised here. What about you? I haven't seen you around before." Of course she hadn't seen him around. If he was a ranch hand who frequented the Saddlebag Bar, there wouldn't have been a chance for their paths to have crossed in the past.

"I'm new. Came in from Laredo and started working on a ranch here in Mission Creek recently."

Just as she'd thought—a cowpoke. Her mother would faint dead away if she had any idea her darling daughter was in the middle of a pool game with a ranch hand at the Saddlebag Bar.

Jenna called her next shot, then when she hit the four ball into the corner pocket, she couldn't help squealing just a little. She was winning this game, hands-down. So, if you win, what prize will you claim? she asked herself.

She felt him staring at her, studying her. Was he trying to figure out her strategy or was he simply enjoying the scenery?

"Aren't you interested in knowing my name or do you pick up nameless guys in bars all the time?" he asked.

"I don't...I haven't..." When she saw him looking directly at her breasts, she almost yanked the edge of

her tank top higher, but she forced herself not to react.
''Yes, certainly I'd like to know your name.''

''It's Brent.''

''So, Brent, has a woman ever beat you at pool?''

''Nope. Tonight could be a first,'' he replied. ''But
I must admit that win or lose, I think I'll come out on
top.''

She couldn't miss the subtle innuendo; and damn it,
his words fanned the sparks in her belly. The picture
of the two of them lying on satin sheets as black as
his hair flashed through her mind. Brent on top. Big,
hard and commanding. An involuntary shiver passed
along her nerve endings.

''You're awfully sure of yourself, cowboy.''

''Not really,'' he said. ''Just wishful thinking on my
part. After all, how would I know what you might ask
for if you win.''

''Use your imagination.'' She knew she was playing
with fire, but the risk of getting burned seemed un-
important at the moment.

''That's just what I'm doing.'' His eyes narrowed
as he looked directly at her. ''Imagining what it would
be like.''

She took a deep breath before she continued. At that
precise moment she wasn't a hundred percent sure
whether she wanted to win or lose. Concentrate, Jenna,
she told herself. Concentrate.

With one shot after another, she successfully put all
the solids into pockets. One final shot and she would
win the game without Brent even getting a turn. All

she had to do to win was put the eight ball into…she studied her shot.

"Eight ball into the side pocket."

Although she trembled inside, outwardly her hands were steady. Brent watched closely as she chalked her cue and aimed. If she won, she could ask him for anything. A dance. A kiss. A stroll in the moonlight. A wild ride on black satin sheets.

The eight ball rolled steadily toward the side pocket. Jenna held her breath. Then as if an invisible breeze blew the ball off course, it veered slightly to the left, missing the pocket by half an inch.

"Damn," she cursed under her breath.

"Bad luck, honey." He took her cue from her and placed his and hers back in the wall rack, then draped his arm around her shoulders. "How about I buy you a beer before I claim my kiss?"

"Okay." She hated the taste of beer, but she was hardly going to admit that fact to her bad boy.

Brent found them a table, then ordered their drinks. She was halfway surprised when the waitress didn't ask to see her ID. Maybe they weren't very strict about things like that at the Saddlebag Bar.

"So, Jenna, what do you do?" he asked.

"What do I—oh, you mean what do I do for a living?"

"Yeah. You know that I'm a ranch hand."

"I…er…I'm between jobs right now."

"Hmm."

Jenna glanced around, searching for Dana and

Katie. She caught a glimpse of Katie with her long, lean cowpoke, but she didn't see Dana anywhere.

"Looking for someone?" Brent asked.

"A couple of girlfriends who came with me."

"Getting tired of my company already?"

"No, of course not, I—"

The waitress returned with their drinks. "Here you go." She set one bottle in front of Jenna and handed the other one to Brent, obviously flirting with him. Brazen hussy, Jenna thought.

Brent drank half the beer in one thirsty swig. Jenna sipped on the atrocious stuff, forcing herself to swallow it when she would prefer to spit it out.

"You should have told me that you don't like beer."

"I like it all right, it's just that—"

Reaching out, he pressed two fingers over her lips to silence her. The touch of his calloused flesh on her mouth ignited fireworks inside her. How was it possible that this man could do such dangerously marvelous things to her senses with nothing more than a look or a touch?

"Want to dance?" He shoved back his chair and held out his hand.

She took his hand. He led her onto the dance floor. She had never dreamed that walking on the wild side could be so sensually stimulating. Surely he'd ask for his prize now, she thought. What better place to kiss her than while he had her in his arms? They moved with the rhythm of the music, their bodies intimately entwined. She felt hot and cold all at the same time. And the pressure of his hard sex against her belly unnerved her. She'd never wanted anything more in her life than to pay him the debt she owed. Perspiration broke out on her upper lip. Moisture coated her palms. And a trickle of sweat made its way downward between her breasts.

She stared at him, silently pleading with him to kiss her. Now. Oh, Brent, now!

When he rubbed his cheek against hers, rough against soft, she thought she'd scream. Was he teasing her? Tempting her?

"Don't you want to collect your winnings?" she asked, and even to her own ears, her voice sounded breathy.

"More than anything. But not in here. When I kiss you, I want a little more privacy."

"Oh." *Oh, my God!*

"My truck's outside," he whispered against her neck. "How about—"

"Let's go," she said, without giving the consequences a thought.

The parking lot wasn't that well lit and Brent's truck was parked in a dark corner, but she went with him, no questions asked, more than ready to pay her debt. If he tried to seduce her, she wasn't sure she'd be able to resist. And she wasn't even sure she'd want to.

Brent backed her up against the side of the truck, splayed his hands out on either side of her shoulders and stared right into her eyes. "You know I want more than a kiss, don't you?"

Yes, on some instinctive level, she knew. She might be inexperienced, but she wasn't stupid. Brent was older than she by a few years and probably ages older in experience, so who better to initiate her than someone like him. No, not someone like him—only him. She nodded her head, unable to speak. Brent caressed her cheek with the back of his hand. She gasped as tingling sensations zinged through her body.

"Honey, these lips of yours have been driving me crazy. You can't know how much I want to taste them."

When he lowered his head, Jenna flung her arms around his neck and urged him into action. She had expected a rough, tongue-thrusting possession. Instead he gave her gentleness. His mouth took hers firmly yet tenderly, playing with her lips, using his tongue to outline them and taste her essence. She shivered. He groaned deep in his throat. The kiss became the center of the universe for Jenna. Nothing existed except Brent and her and this moment in time. With each passing minute, he deepened the kiss, claiming her more and more, teaching her how unbelievably erotic a kiss could be.

Breathless and aroused, she gasped for air when he eased his mouth from hers and kissed a soft, moist path down her throat and over the tops of her breasts. His big hands cupped her buttocks and lifted her up and against him in a way that told her plainly what he wanted.

"Let's go somewhere even more private." He delved his tongue inside her tank top, between her aching breasts.

"Jenna! Jenna!" Two voices called her name.

She heard her name, but the speakers' identities didn't register immediately. After all, she was cocooned in a sexual fog that blocked out the rest of the world.

"Jenna, thank goodness," Dana said. "There you are."

Dana? What was Dana doing interrupting her like this? Jenna wondered.

"We're ready to go home," Katie said. "We thought we'd never find you."

As Jenna turned to focus on her two roommates who came running toward her, Brent kept his arm firmly around Jenna's shoulders. She didn't want to go home. Not now. Not until later. Much later. She wanted to go with Brent, to stay with him and learn from him.

"You two go on without me," Jenna told them.

Dana reached out, grasped Jenna's hands and pulled her away from Brent. "We can't go without you. We came with you. In your car."

"Didn't I give one of you the keys to my car?"

"No," Katie replied. "You've got the keys. Besides, you can't stay out late tonight. Remember, we've got finals to study for and you have to meet your mother tomorrow to be fitted for your dress for the debutante ball.''

"Finals? Debutante ball?" Brent stared quizzically at Jenna. "Honey, just how old are you?"

"Old enough," she said.

"She's twenty-one," Dana told him. "Just barely."

"You're a college kid," Brent said as the realization hit him. "You sure had me fooled."

"We go to Tensley," Katie said. "A women's college."

"We've never done something like this before," Dana explained. "This is the first time any of us has been at a roadhouse."

"I'll be graduating in a few weeks." Jenna glowered at her friends. "Besides, what difference does it make? I am twenty-one. And that makes me a legal adult."

"Honey, you were passing yourself off as something you aren't." Brent inspected her, this time not pausing at any particular area. "You're certainly a good little actress. And you definitely dressed for the part."

He turned away and headed for his truck. Jenna grimaced. She couldn't let him leave her this way, not without trying to explain.

"Brent?"

He paused, glanced over his shoulder and waited for her to speak.

"I really do want to go with you. We could still—"

"I don't give spoiled little debutantes cheap thrills.

If you want to go slumming, find yourself another cowboy.''

Brent unlocked his truck, got inside and started the engine. Jenna stood in the parking lot and watched him back up and drive off. With anger and humiliation boiling inside her, she turned to her roommates.

"How could y'all do that to me? You ruined everything. I've lost him, and it's all your fault!''

Chapter 2

As the owner of the Mission Creek Creations dress shop for more than thirty years, Margaret McKenzie had been dressing generations of debutantes. Her own grandmother had been a seamstress and owned a dress shop in Scotland over seventy-five years ago. As her mother and grandmother before her, Margaret took great pride in her work. And during the past ten years, since she lost her beloved husband, Kyle, to a fatal heart attack, her dress shop had become the center of her world. With no children of her own, she had turned to her life's work for solace and direction. Then two years ago a special young girl came into her life— Mary Clark, whom she took under her wing after Mary's parents died. She had hired the dear, sweet girl as her assistant, teaching her the dressmaking trade.

Shy, quiet and rather plain in appearance, Mary didn't make friends easily. And despite Margaret encouraging her to date, Mary's lack of self-confidence confined her to a lonely life.

Margaret glanced at her assistant, quiet as a mouse, going about her duties, practically fading into the background and unnoticed by those around her. How Margaret wished that she had been blessed with the magic power to transform the little brown wren into a colorful bird. But her fairy godmother talents were limited.

The front door of the shop opened and in breezed Nelda Wilson and her daughter, Jenna. Now those two were definitely colorful birds. Both beautiful, petite, self-confident blondes, with money, good breeding and social standing in the community. Years ago she had designed Nelda's debutante ball gown and now she had the privilege of creating Jenna's. She had been designing clothes for both mother and daughter for years and felt that she knew them quite well. As well as any servant could know an employer. And that was the way Nelda Wilson treated those she considered socially beneath her—as servants. But Jenna didn't have her mother's cool arrogance. The girl possessed a warmth and friendliness sadly lacking in her parent.

"Good morning, Margaret," Nelda said. "We're a bit early, but Jenna is eager to try on her gown."

"Certainly, Mrs. Wilson," Margaret said. "I'll have Mary fetch it for me and Miss Jenna can put it on for her fitting." Margaret motioned to Mary, who immediately scurried to the storage room.

"I put the finishing touches on the gown last night." Margaret ushered her customers farther into the shop. "Please, have a seat, Mrs. Wilson." She turned to Jenna. "Come with me to one of the dressing rooms. You'll need help getting into your gown."

Mary emerged from the storage room, holding the lovely hand-embroidered, white silk garment on a padded satin hanger. Each tiny, cream flower and delicate beadwork that accented each floral design had taken hours of hand-labor, most of it Mary's.

Margaret opened the pink louvered door, then followed Jenna into the dressing room. While Jenna stripped down to her panties and bra, Margaret removed the dress from the hanger. Only she knew how special this dress was. For only she knew the magical secret that lay hidden within the garment. In the large, airy workroom at her home, she had sewn a little pocket into the folds of the gown and placed three red rose petals inside the pocket. Occasionally and only for certain young ladies, Margaret would do this, making sure the color of the petals specifically fit each girl. Red roses indicated passion. And as she had placed the petals in their secret place, she had made a special wish for Jenna. For it was passion that she sensed in Jenna and it was passion she knew this young woman needed in her life. Passion would lead her to her true love.

Margaret assisted her client into the heavenly creation, one she was most proud of for its beauty and perfection in form and design. An excellent match for Jenna Wilson. As soon as Margaret zipped up the dress and closed the top hook, she opened the dressing room door and shooed Jenna outside to the mirrors.

Most of her young clients were ecstatic the moment they saw themselves in the mirrors, but not Jenna. She stared at herself, forced a weak smile and pivoted slowly so that her mother could inspect her.

"The dress is lovely, Mrs. McKenzie," Jenna said. "Thank you very much."

"You're quite welcome, my dear," Margaret replied. "Creating this dress for you was a pleasure. You look divine in it."

"Yes, she does, doesn't she." Nelda circled Jenna, scrutinizing the gown from every angle. "You've outdone yourself, Margaret. But I believe the waist should be just a little tighter and the neckline lifted some. Jenna is generously endowed so we don't want her displaying too much flesh, do we?"

Margaret waited for Jenna to put up a fuss about her mother's instructions, but the young woman remained silent, almost as if she didn't care. Obviously the debutante ball wasn't the most important thing on Jenna's mind. Now what could be more important to a young woman than the upcoming ball? Margaret wondered.

Jenna wished her mother would leave things alone. The dress was absolutely perfect and didn't need a thing done to it. But Nelda Wilson was an overbearing, bossy woman who always needed things done exactly her way.

The sooner she could get out of this gown and away from her mother, the better. She'd slept fitfully last night, with visions of a cowboy named Brent disturbing her sleep. Even now she could feel his lips on hers, his arms around her, his body pressed intimately against her. Just thinking about him made her go weak in the knees. If Dana and Katie hadn't interrupted them, she'd have spent the night in Brent's arms. This morning she would be a woman—a woman with a past. A one-night stand with a rugged, good-looking cowboy could have been a memory to cherish for a lifetime, especially if she wound up in a miserable, loveless marriage.

"I'll see to the changes," Mrs. McKenzie assured Nelda. "Otherwise, you approve of the gown?"

"Yes, it's an exceptional garment," Nelda said, then without realizing she was being rude to Mrs. McKenzie, she turned to Jenna. "You simply must make a decision about an escort soon. You could have your pick of just about any young man. Why must you be so stubborn?"

"I'm not being stubborn," Jenna said. "I just can't decide which suitable man on the list you gave me is someone I could tolerate for an entire evening."

"Jenna! What a thing to say. Whatever will Margaret think of you?" Nelda looked to Mrs. McKenzie as if expecting her to comment.

"Young people these days. I would never have spoken to my mother in such a fashion."

"Jenna, my dear, why don't you let Mary mark the alterations," Mrs. McKenzie said. "Just go right over there." She then turned her attention to Nelda. "Mrs. Wilson, would you care for some refreshment? We have lemonade and iced tea."

Jenna breathed a sigh of relief, thankful for a momentary reprieve from her mother's constant nagging. She knew that sooner or later she'd have to make a choice about an escort, but how many other debutantes had been given a list of men from which to choose? It wasn't that she didn't like most of the guys on the list. Heck, she'd known nearly every one of them all her life. But if she was going to have to endure this "coming out" ball, she'd really like the privilege of choosing her own date.

And if she could find him, she knew exactly who she'd ask. A long, tall drink of water named Brent. Although he'd looked a bit scruffy last night, she bet he'd clean up real good. Put that man in a tux and every deb at the ball would be drooling over him.

But she could hardly ask him to be her escort when she had no idea where he was. He'd said he was working on one of the local ranches—but which one? What could she do, hunt him down? Go from ranch to ranch asking for a guy named Brent? Maybe that's just what she should do. And she knew exactly which ranch she'd start with—the Carson Ranch. After all, she'd been friends with Fiona and Cara Carson since they were children.

"Would you turn around, please, Miss Wilson?" Mary requested.

"What? Oh, sure." Jenna turned. "How are you, Mary?"

"Me? I—I'm fine. Thank you for asking."

Jenna grasped and lifted a small section of the material where it covered her hip. "Did you do this beautiful embroidery?"

"Yes, ma'am." Mary dutifully kept her head lowered as she made the adjustments for the alternations.

"So, do you enjoy working for Mrs. McKenzie?"

"Yes, very much. She's taught me a great deal."

With a glass of iced tea in her hand, Nelda Wilson left Mrs. McKenzie's side. Lowering her voice to a whisper, but still audible to those near her, she said, "Jenna, you mustn't be too friendly with the hired help."

Jenna gasped. She glanced at Mary, knowing that the young woman had certainly heard Nelda. Mary's shoulders slumped a bit more and her head bowed a little farther. If she rebuked her mother in front of Mary and Mrs. McKenzie, she'd probably only embarrass Mary. How could her mother be so unfeeling?

Thankfully, a new customer entered the shop, taking everyone's attention off Nelda and easing the tension that permeated the room.

"Ms. Delarue. How nice to see you," Mrs. Mc-

Kenzie said. "I have the material for your gown. It came in yesterday."

Gorgeous redheaded Maddie Delarue was not only one of the richest women in Texas, she was the crème de la crème of local society. Everyone assumed she had taken the job as events coordinator at the Lone Star Country Club more as a hobby than anything else. After all, she certainly didn't need the money. Jenna wondered what it would be like to be Maddie Delarue. A woman in her early thirties who answered to no one. Free and totally independent.

"Maddie, darling." Nelda rushed across the shop to greet Ms. Delarue, who was little more than an acquaintance. "How lovely to see you."

Maddie offered Nelda a brilliant smile, one Jenna figured the woman had cultivated at a very young age. No telling how many people fawned over her the way Nelda was doing right now, and being a gracious lady, Ms. Delarue responded cordially.

"Hello, Nelda."

"You simply must tell me how things are shaping up at the country club." Nelda reached out and laid her hand on Maddie's arm. "Are they making any progress with rebuilding the Men's Grill and renovating the damaged part of the club?"

"We're quite fortunate to have Joe Turner as the architect on the project. He's doing a marvelous job, but he can't work miracles. It's going to take time to get everything done." Maddie patted Nelda's arm. "However, Joe has promised Frances and me that the laborers will work overtime to make sure the cranes and the other heavy machinery are removed from the construction site in time for the ball.''

''How is Frances? I simply must call her to see when we can get together for lunch. Hopefully, one day soon. It's so gracious of her to come in all the way from Houston to act as the chairwoman for this year's ball.''

Jenna thought she was going to throw up listening to her mother go on and on, as if Mrs. Donald Adair, of *the* Houston Adairs, was a personal friend of hers instead of a mere acquaintance, as Ms. Delarue was. Why couldn't her mother ever stop trying to impress people, trying to move up the social ladder?

''Mary, would you help me off with this dress?'' Jenna asked, wanting to finish up and leave as soon as possible.

''Certainly, Miss Wilson.'' Mary followed Jenna into the dressing room.

''Please, call me Jenna.''

''I'm not sure that would be proper. Your mother—''

''Is an elitist, a snob and a royal pain in the backside.''

Mary smiled. Jenna laughed.

Hurriedly, Mary helped Jenna disrobe, then took the elegant white gown and placed it on the padded hanger. Just as Mary started to exit the dressing room, Jenna grabbed her arm.

"I'm sorry that my mother said what she did. I know she must have hurt your feelings."

"It's all right. Really. I'm used to being treated that way."

"Maybe you are, but it's not right."

Mary didn't reply as she took the dress with her when she left the dressing room. Jenna donned her white slacks and pale yellow silk blouse, then removed a comb from her straw bag. Using the small, narrow mirror in the dressing room to check her appearance, she combed her hair, which she'd left hanging loose today. She reapplied some rosy pink lip gloss and a touch of pink blush. There, she thought. I'm ready to make a trip to the Carson Ranch and begin my search for Brent. Even if the Carsons didn't known anything about him, she could at least get away from her mother for a few hours and visit with the Carson twins, Fiona and Cara.

The 15,500 acre Carson Ranch was known throughout Texas for its cattle, and the vastness of the property never ceased to amaze Jenna, who'd grown up in town. After all, her father had been a banker, not a rancher. But she considered herself part cowgirl because she not only knew how to shoot a rifle, but how to ride, too. She kept Mariah, the mare her father had bought for her high school graduation present, at the Mission Creek Stables. As she rode Mariah up the road, the huge, twelve-bedroom Carson home came into view.

As the only child of wealthy parents, Jenna had grown up never wanting for anything money could buy. Her mother and father had traveled in the same social circle as the Carsons, so she'd known the family all her life. Fiona had seemed delighted when Jenna called her earlier and invited herself out for the afternoon. She hadn't bothered explaining to her old friend that she was on a mission to find a cowboy named Brent. All she had to do was ask Flynt Carson if he'd hired a new hand recently. Even if Brent didn't work on the Carson Ranch, it was possible that Flynt might know if one of the other ranches had taken on a new cowpoke sometime in the past few weeks.

Jenna had tried—unsuccessfully—to convince herself that the guy from the Saddlebag Bar wasn't the only man in the world who could be her tour guide into the world of unrestricted fun and unbridled passion. The more she thought about Brent, the more certain she was that he—and only he—was the man she wanted, the man she needed.

But even if she found him, she couldn't be one-hundred percent sure that he would cooperate. After all, last night when he'd found out that she was just a college kid, he'd run like hell. Everything had been perfect until Dana and Katie came to her rescue. Damn it, she hadn't wanted to be rescued. She'd come so close to running off with Brent, to getting in his truck and letting him take her someplace very private. The thought of making love with her mysterious cowboy created a heat wave inside her. She hadn't gone to the

Saddlebag Bar actually looking for romance, only a little fun; but meeting Brent had made her realize just what she'd been missing.

Riding off to the side of the half-moon driveway toward the stables, Jenna saw Fiona and Cara as they came running around the house. Cara wore a simple black one-piece bathing suit, but Jenna wasn't sure what you'd call the two small strips of material Fiona wore. A microbikini? Of course she had a great figure, but—

My gosh, Jenna you sound like an old prude.

"Where's your suit?" Fiona asked. "When you phoned to say you were coming out here, I told you we were spending the afternoon by the pool."

"I thought I might borrow one of yours later."

"Fine. Put your horse in the stables and meet us at the pool house." Fiona's dark, shoulder length hair bounced with vibrant movement as she nodded her head in the direction of the pool.

"Uh…why don't you go on and I'll catch up with you in a few minutes," Jenna said. "I really need to speak to Flynt. Is he around?"

"Why do you need to talk to Flynt? If you're thinking about asking him to join us, don't," Fiona said. "He's absolutely no fun."

"Fiona!" Cara scolded. "You shouldn't be that way about Flynt, considering what he's been through. If you'd lost someone you love in such a tragic way, the way he did Monica, you'd be moody, too."

"Oh, all right. I'm sorry. Really I am." Fiona

sighed dramatically. "I know life has been rough for Flynt. I'm just tired of seeing him so unhappy. I wish something wonderful would happen to bring him back to life."

"Go on to the pool, Fiona," Cara said. "I'll see if anybody knows where Flynt is." The minute Fiona flounced off, Cara turned to Jenna. "Want to tell me why you need to talk to Flynt?" Cara asked.

Jenna hesitated. Although Fiona and Cara were six years older than she, they had been friends for ages. She adored both twins. She admired Fiona's outgoing, risk-taking nature, but she related more to Cara, who was a bit shy, and like her, a good girl. *At least I was a good girl until last night,* Jenna thought.

"I need to ask Flynt about the Carson ranch hands. Actually one particular ranch hand."

Cara's sparkling green eyes widened with surprise. "I think you need to explain why you want information about one of our ranch hands."

"Look, just go see if you can find Flynt for me, will you? I'm not even sure the man I'm looking for works here. After I talk to Flynt, I'll tell you everything. I promise."

"Oh, all right. Put Mariah in the stables and then come on out to the pool house. There's at least a dozen bathing suits in there that should fit you. In the meantime, I'll see if I can round up Flynt."

Brent finished giving Mr. Lucky a rubdown. Living in Chicago for so many years, he had forgotten how much he'd once loved riding. Part of the pleasure of living on a ranch was the wonderful sense of freedom a man felt when he was on horseback, out on the range, where the earth met the sky. Since his father's death, he hadn't been back to Kansas City, although he still owned the small ranch there and paid a couple of hands to keep the place up. Maybe one of these days, he'd start taking his vacations on the ranch. That was if he ever started taking vacations. He had become a workaholic, spending ninety percent of his time concentrating on his job, leaving him no time for vacations or for anything more than short-lived, superficial relationships.

Don't think about *her,* he told himself. She was a damn college kid out for a good time. Seven years younger than he was. Getting tangled up with some starry-eyed girl who'd confuse sex with love was the last thing he needed. Sure, he found her attractive. Big deal. He found a lot of women attractive. Yeah, but not like Jenna. He hadn't reacted that way to a woman since he'd been a teenager with overactive hormones and a perpetual hard-on. So she was gorgeous, so she was tempting, so he'd wanted her in the worst way. Get over it! He would never see her again. And he should be thanking his lucky stars that he wouldn't.

After putting his equipment away, Brent headed to the feed bin to get some oats for Mr. Lucky. After he finished up here, he'd go to the bunkhouse and kick back for a while. He needed a shower and a shave, but that could wait until later. Even though this was

Saturday night, he hadn't made any plans, but he knew one thing for sure—he wasn't going back to the Saddlebag Bar. He couldn't take a chance of running into Jenna, and it was just possible that she'd go back there tonight looking for him. After the way she had responded to him in the parking lot last night, there had been no doubt in his mind that she would have left with him. Hell, if her friends hadn't found them and let the cat out of the bag about her being a college girl, they'd have wound up in the sack together.

So, would that have been so bad? he asked himself. Just because she was young didn't mean she was inexperienced, did it? She'd had the look of a woman who'd been around the block a few times. But after meeting her friends, his gut instinct told him that all three girls were innocents. Or if not complete innocents, then pretty green when it came to men.

Brent filled a bucket with oats, then headed back to the other side of the stables, toward Mr. Lucky's stall. Just as he turned the corner, he collided with a woman, who squealed and jumped away from him.

"Sorry, ma'am," Brent said, then took a good look at the woman he'd nearly knocked to the ground.

She stared back at him with a pair of baby blue eyes that sent shock waves through his system. Jenna! My God, how had this happened? How had she found him?

"Brent?" she gasped in surprise.

I'll be damned, he thought. She was as shocked to see him as he was to see her. Brent tipped his Stetson and grinned. "Well, honey, what brings you to the Carson Ranch?"

"I—I came to see Cara and Fiona. They're friends of mine."

"And here I was thinking you'd tracked me down because you couldn't forget me." Was his ego so big that he actually thought she'd been so impressed with the kiss they'd shared that she had come looking for him? Just because that kiss had knocked his socks off didn't mean it had affected her the same way. But he'd bet his last dollar that it had.

"I take it that you work here," Jenna said, a beautiful smile lighting her face.

He had a strong urge to cup her face with his hands, bring her close, lower his head and see if a second kiss would be as good as the first one.

"Yeah, I work here."

She kept staring at him, looking at him as if she could eat him with a spoon. If she didn't stop devouring him that way, he wasn't going to be responsible for what he did next. Didn't she have any idea what sort of effect she had on him?

"I…uh…I'm glad I ran into you." She giggled. "I mean, I'm glad I found you."

"Were you looking for me?"

"Sort of," she admitted. "I was going to ask Flynt Carson if he'd hired a new hand recently."

"So, you did come here hoping to find me."

"Sort of."

"Unfortunately, nothing's really changed, has it?"

He looked her over, from that mane of long, blond hair to the tips of her fancy red boots. "You're still only twenty-one and just a college kid."

"That's not the only thing that hasn't changed," she told him, then boldly moved closer until only a hair-breadth separated their bodies. "I wanted you last night and I still want you."

God help him! Did she really know what she was saying? Maybe he'd been all wrong about her. Maybe she wasn't as innocent as he'd thought. "You could get in a heap of trouble with me, little girl."

"Trouble's what I'm looking for." She laid her hand on his chest, right over his heart.

He covered her hand with his. "Have you got something to prove to somebody, honey?"

"Only to myself." She gazed into his eyes, the look both pleading and encouraging. "So, what do you say? How about taking me out tonight and showing me a good time?"

"I can't think of anything I'd rather do," Brent said, without a moment's hesitation. There was one sure way to find out what he needed to know about Jenna. After tonight, he wouldn't have any doubts. He'd know for certain.

Chapter 3

Brent put up his shaving kit, then reached out on the bed for the chambray shirt he'd just ironed. Tonight he'd find out what sort of gal the luscious Jenna was— sex kitten, innocent or a combination of the two. In retrospect, he figured he should have his head examined for readily accepting her invitation. Common sense should have warned him that a girl that young was nothing but trouble. But this one time his libido had overruled his brain. If ever he'd wanted to get to know a woman...

A loud, resounding knock on the door brought him out of his musings. The bunkhouse room he shared with a hand who'd gone home to Kingsville this weekend was part of a four-room building which provided housing for the employees who lived on the ranch.

Off-days for the hands rotated because a ranch, especially one the size of the Carson's, was a seven-day-a-week operation.

"Yeah, who is it?" Brent asked.

"Flynt Carson."

"Door's unlocked. Come on in."

Powerfully built with sandy brown hair and blue eyes, Flynt reminded Brent a little of the old sixties movie star, Steve McQueen. A rugged man's man. They'd known each other for years and Brent had the greatest respect for his friend. He couldn't begin to imagine the hell Flynt had gone through after losing his pregnant wife in that terrible car crash, so he didn't fault the guy for having turned to the bottle for a while after Monica's death. But even now that he'd straightened himself out, Flynt wasn't the man he used to be. Gone was the good-ole-boy charmer he'd once been.

"I won't keep you long," Flynt said as he approached Brent. "I know you've got a date this evening."

"Is that something you know for a fact or are you just guessing?" Brent chuckled. Flynt didn't. "What's up? Something wrong?"

"Nothing's wrong and I want to keep it that way." Flynt hesitated, as if carefully contemplating his next words. "You see, I've known Jenna Wilson since she was a little girl, which by the way, wasn't that many years ago. Our families have been associated socially for generations."

"Ah…" A tight knot of apprehension formed in the

pit of Brent's stomach. "Are you trying to tell me that she's too young for me or are you warning me off because you're interested in her?"

A pained expression crossed Flynt's face. "Look, Jenna is friends with my sisters and she told Fiona and Cara all about meeting you last night at the Saddlebag Bar and how she asked you out tonight. She came to the ranch today to see if I could help her find you."

"Cut to the chase, will you? I'm beginning to feel like a school kid waiting in the principal's office."

"You have a right to date whomever you please, but... Jenna's not what she seems. Her looks are deceiving. Believe me, before last night, she'd never been inside a roadhouse. Her mama has always kept a tight rein on her. Mighty tight."

"I see."

"I hope you do," Flynt said. "I don't know what's gotten into Jenna, but going to the Saddlebag Bar, picking up a stranger and asking a ranch hand out on a date isn't the norm for her." Flynt searched Brent's face, as if trying to decide whether or not he'd made his point clear.

"I get it. Jenna's a sweet kid and a good girl."

Flynt nodded. "I just don't want to see her getting into trouble."

"Hey, man, that girl is ripe for trouble. If she doesn't find it with me, she'll find it with someone else."

"Then maybe you could give her a little taste of trouble, just enough for her to see that it's not good for her, but not so much that she gets in over her head.''

Brent chuckled. ''Tell you what I'll do—I'll try taking her out for burgers and a movie first. Maybe one date with an older guy—a guy she thinks is a ranch hand—will be enough cheap thrills for her.''

''Yeah, I hope so.'' Flynt headed toward the door, then paused and glanced over his shoulder. ''When you go to pick Jenna up at her house, be prepared for Nelda Wilson's wrath. The woman will have heart failure when she realizes Jenna's date is a ranch hand.''

As soon as Flynt left, Brent finished getting ready, then donned his tan Stetson and picked up the keys to his old pickup truck, one he'd bought at a used-car lot in Laredo. Grinning at the thought of Nelda Wilson's reaction when he arrived at her mansion, Brent walked out of the bunkhouse, then started whistling.

''Who is this young man?'' Nelda asked. ''Where did you meet him? What's his last name?''

''Give it a rest, will you, Mother.'' Jenna peeked out the window to check the drive for any sign of Brent, then she looked at her wristwatch. Seven o'clock. If he didn't show up immediately, he'd be late. What if he'd changed his mind? What if Flynt Carson had warned him off? What if—?

''I don't like your attitude.'' Nelda thoroughly inspected her daughter's attire—jeans, sleeveless red cotton T-shirt and red boots. ''And I disapprove of the way you're dressed. You look like you're going to a rodeo instead of out on a date.''

"I'm dressed just fine. We aren't going to a fancy party or to the opera or the ballet.''

"Just where is he taking you?''

"I'm not sure, but it won't be anywhere that jeans aren't appropriate.''

"What sort of young man takes a girl—''

"Brent isn't a young man. He's a man. Probably nearly thirty. And he's the sort that's used to shooting pool and drinking beer in places like the Saddlebag Bar. After all, he's a ranch hand.''

Jenna wasn't sure where she'd gotten the courage to confront her mother, to be bold and honest about who and what Brent was.

"A ranch hand!'' Nelda clutched her silk blouse, her hand directly over her heart. "I forbid you to go out on this date!''

Jenna saw Brent's old truck a split second before she heard it. She barely suppressed a smile when her mother's eyes widened and her mouth formed a shocked oval.

"He's here, Mother.'' Jenna flew out of the living room and into the foyer. "Don't wait up for me.''

"Jenna Kerr Wilson!''

With her hand on the doorhandle, Jenna hesitated, then turned slowly to face Nelda. "I've got to go. He's waiting.''

"Let him wait. Jenna, I forbid you to leave this

house with a dirt-poor ranch hand. What will people think when they see you with him?''

Decision time. It's now or never, Jenna told herself. If she let her mother continue to dictate her actions, she'd never be able to break free and live her own life. Not even for a little while. *Go. Now. Run. Run before you lose your nerve.*

Jenna opened the door and rushed outside, off the portico and onto the driveway where Brent waited. The minute he saw her running toward him, he jumped out of the truck, rounded the hood and opened the door. Jenna hurried to him, flung her arms around his neck and kissed him soundly on the mouth. There, that would show her mother!

As soon as she let him come up for air, he helped her into the truck. In his peripheral vision Brent noticed the small, slender blonde standing on the portico, a deadly frown on her face. Jenna's displeased mother, no doubt. He slammed the door, then quickly made his way to the other side, hopped in and started the engine. A quick getaway before mama tiger sunk her claws into him.

''Was that your mother staring daggers at me?'' he asked, as they sped down the driveway and onto the road.

''She doesn't like the idea of my dating a ranch hand.'' Jenna scooted across the seat until her body pressed against his, thigh-to-thigh.

Instinctively Brent lifted his right arm and draped it

around Jenna's shoulders. "So, is that what this date is all about—rebelling against Mama?"

"Maybe, just a little bit," she admitted. "But I wouldn't be doing this with just anybody. When I met you last night, something wild and free broke loose inside me and I knew I'd risk anything to be with you."

"Whoa, gal. This is a date. Nothing more. A first date, to be exact. And you should know that I'm not the kind of guy who puts out on a first date."

Jenna burst into laughter. "Oh, Brent, we're going to have so much fun." She snuggled against him and closed her eyes.

Every muscle in Brent's body tightened. The feel of her cuddled against him, all trusting and caring, did a real number on him. He couldn't remember ever wanting to both sleep with a woman and protect her, all at the same time. If he were going to leave Jenna as innocent as she was right now, then this would have to be their only date. Resisting such a powerful temptation might test his willpower far too much. Not only would Flynt Carson take him to task if he hurt Jenna, but his own conscience would be unforgiving.

Brent pulled his truck into the Burger Barn parking area on the outskirts of Mission Creek. A curb service fast-food restaurant, the place was a hangout for local teens and catered to families. As a waitress approached the truck, Brent rolled down the window, then turned to Jenna.

"What'll it be?" he asked. "Hamburger? Hot dog? Barbeque?"

She sat several feet away from him, a sulking pout on her soft, red lips. Taking her to a movie apparently hadn't been her idea of a fun date, nor was bringing her to the Burger Barn. But what else could a guy do with a girl if he was trying his damnedest to be a gentleman?

"I'm not hungry." Jenna crossed her arms over her chest.

"Are you sure?"

"I'm sure."

"How about a milkshake?"

"A cola will be fine, thank you."

The waitress grinned at Brent, who returned her cordial smile.

"What'll y'all have tonight?" she asked.

"Two large colas," Brent replied. "And an extra-large order of onion rings."

As soon as the waitress disappeared, Jenna glowered at Brent. "Onion rings? Don't you care that you'll have onion breath?"

"I thought we'd share." He grinned.

She continued glaring at him. He nudged her arm.

"What's the matter, honey? Aren't you having a good time?"

Narrowing her gaze, she gritted her teeth, then huffed loudly.

"Just tell me one thing—is this the kind of date you

usually have? Do you take all your other women to the movies and the Burger Barn?''

''My other women?'' Brent barely suppressed a chuckle. Who did she think he was—an Arab sheik with a harem of willing females?

''You know what I mean. I could go to the movies and out for burgers with anybody.'' Jenna all but whined. ''I thought you'd take me somewhere fun. Maybe back to the Saddlebag Bar.''

''Honey, it's just a smoky roadhouse, with loud music, drunks and...it's really not a place for a girl like you.''

''What do you know about a girl like me? Who's been telling you stuff about me?''

''Nobody needs to tell me anything,'' he said. ''Don't you think I can see how young you are? And it doesn't take a genius to figure out that you're...well, you're not all that experienced.''

''I thought I had you fooled last night.'' She stared directly into his eyes. ''I did have you fooled, didn't I? If Dana and Katie hadn't interrupted, you'd have taken me with you and we'd have made love.''

''Whoa, there. Even if I'd taken you with me, we might have had sex, but that's all it would have been—a couple of strangers doing the horizontal. Nothing more.''

''Okay, I understand what you're saying.'' She slid across the seat until she was right up against him. ''I am only twenty-one and I am inexperienced. But don't you see—that's why I chose you. Just one look and I knew you'd be a great teacher. I want you to show me, to teach me. I'm sick and tired of being a good girl.''

What a confession! Brent thought. Good God, how did he respond? He could hardly tell her that he'd like nothing better than to instruct her in Elementary Sex 101. If he didn't watch himself, he'd be the one in over his head before he knew it.

The waitress returned with their drinks and onion rings. They sipped on their colas and fed each other the crispy-fried rings. Jenna began loosening up, a tentative smile playing at the corners of her mouth from time to time.

''I'll tell you what I'll do—I'll take you back to the Saddlebag Bar,'' Brent said. ''If you promise me you'll behave yourself.''

''Oh, Brent, I promise.'' She glowed with excitement. ''I won't do anything you wouldn't do.''

Ah, hell!

Jenna belonged in Brent's arms. Dancing to the slow, sweet music, she lost herself completely, becoming one with the big man holding her so close. At first Brent had fought his attraction to her, and she couldn't help wondering if maybe Flynt Carson really had talked to Brent about her. Flynt probably even warned Brent to steer clear of Nelda Wilson's precious daughter. But she wasn't going to let Flynt or her mother or even Brent's reluctance get in the way of what she wanted. It had taken her twenty-one years to grow a backbone and stand up to her mother and by God, she was going to sprout her wings and fly. Fly free. Fly to the moon, with Brent Jameson.

She lifted her arms and draped his neck, then paused, stood on tiptoe and kissed him. Right there on the dance floor, with people all around them. She didn't care who saw them; didn't care what anyone thought. Brent returned the kiss, tenderly at first, but when she ran the tip of her tongue over his lips, he thrust inside her mouth and deepened the kiss. His sex pulsed against her belly. Unconsciously, totally instinctively, she melted against him, wanting more. She whimpered, the sound a plea for him to take them to the next level.

Suddenly Brent ended the kiss, drew in a deep breath, released it, and grabbed her by the shoulders. "Let's sit this one out and get something to drink."

Feeling bereft over his rejection, Jenna turned away from him. Tears welled up in her eyes. How was it that he could end something so utterly wonderful, as if it had meant nothing to him? When she left the dance floor, he followed her, but she didn't want to see him or talk to him right now.

"I'm going to the ladies' room," she told him.

He nodded. "I'll order us another round of root beer while you're gone."

Brent ordered the drinks and waited. He drank half his root beer and waited. He finished off the last drops of his soft drink and waited. Where the hell was Jenna?

He realized that she'd been less than pleased when he'd abruptly ended their kiss. But God Almighty, didn't she realize what was happening? Another couple of minutes and he'd have dragged her off the dance floor, out to his truck and been in her pants before common sense could have stopped him. Yeah, she had a good idea how hot she'd made him. She'd been determined to force him to lose control.

He scanned the roadhouse's interior, searching for his date. When he spotted her, he groaned. Jenna stood at the bar next to a guy who looked as if he was having a difficult time keeping his hands off her. And she was flirting like nobody's business. He knew exactly what she was up to, so he had little choice but to play this game by her rules. For now. If he didn't come to her rescue soon, he'd wind up having to fight the other cowpoke or let the man have Jenna—and that was not an option.

Brent scooted back his chair, removed several bills from his wallet and tossed them on the table. Making a beeline straight for the bar, he knotted his hands into fists when he saw the cowpoke grasp Jenna's shoulder. Increasing his pace, Brent reached the bar area in ten seconds flat, then went in behind Jenna and wrapped his arms around her waist. She gasped. He nuzzled her neck.

"You took a little detour on your way back from the ladies' room, didn't you, honey?"

She relaxed against him, obviously relieved that

he'd shown up when he did. "Sorry, darling. Were you worried about me?"

Brent's gaze lifted and hit head-on with the cowpoke's. In a silent masculine message, he told the other man to back off. Private property. The other guy understood, but hesitated for a split second before he grinned good-naturedly and eased back away from Jenna.

"Come on, honey, let's go," Brent said.

"Nice to have met you, Chuck." Jenna winked at the guy.

Brent grabbed her wrist and hauled her through the crowd and out into the warm April night. He dragged her across the parking lot, slowing only when he realized she was having difficulty keeping up with his long-legged stride.

After he unlocked the truck, he turned around, lifted her by her waist and started to put her into the cab. She grabbed his shoulders and held tight.

"You were jealous, weren't you?" She smiled triumphantly.

"Little girl, you were playing with fire," he said, barely able to contain his anger. "You were coming on to that guy and he thought you were making him some promises. What do you think would have happened if I hadn't interrupted when I did?"

"Would you have fought him for me?"

Brent placed her inside the truck, pried her clutching fingers from his shoulders, then slammed the door.

When he got in on the driver's side, she slid across the seat and wrapped herself around him.

"You would have fought him, if you'd had to." She tried to kiss Brent, her lips making contact with his cheek, then his chin and finally the side of his mouth.

His lips responded involuntarily and before he knew what was happening, Jenna was halfway in his lap and he had his tongue in her mouth, one hand on her hip and the other inside her blouse and under her bra strap.

The laughter of a group of guys emerging from the roadhouse reminded Brent of where he was. With a great deal of effort, he disengaged himself from Jenna and managed to put a couple of inches of breathing space between them.

"What's wrong? Why did you stop?" she looked at him with hungry eyes.

"I'm taking you home."

"Why?"

Grasping the steering wheel, he prayed for strength and patience. And a sense of humor. "Hey, this is our first date, remember? I don't put out on a first date."

His reminder about first date rules gained the desired effect. She smiled. While he had the chance, he started the engine and backed his truck out of the parking lot. Once on the road, he punched the radio button and a local country music station came to life. A Dixie Chicks' number was playing. On the drive to the Wilson home, one of several estates within the city limits, Jenna cuddled against him and hummed along with the music.

Brent pulled the truck into the driveway and stopped. He got out and then helped her down from the cab. As he walked her to the door, hand-in-hand, his noble instincts warred with his male desire. She paused at the double front doors, then stood on tiptoe to kiss him. He gave her a soft, nonthreatening kiss, then pulled back.

"Do you make out on a second date?" she asked.

"Look, Jenna, you're a sweet kid, but this isn't going to work with us."

She looked at him as if he'd slapped her. "I don't understand."

"Honey, I'm the wrong man for this job. Initiating a virgin is a major responsibility. One I'm not prepared for. A girl like you should wait until she's in love and then it would be making love and not just sex."

"You don't want to be my first lover?"

Ah, hell! Of course he did. But he couldn't. "I want you to wait until it's right. Until you're in love. If you think you could handle a one-night stand, then you'd better think again. You couldn't."

Tears glistened in her eyes. Brent felt like a heel. Why was it that if he was doing the right thing—the noble and honorable thing—he felt so damn miserable?

She planted her hands on her hips. "You don't know the—the first thing…about me." Her voice cracked with emotion. "I have every right to sow some wild oats before I settle down. And if you don't want to be the one I sow my wild oats with, then I'll just find somebody else.''

The thought of someone taking advantage of Jenna bothered Brent, but what was he supposed to do? She was daring him. He was in a no-win situation. Damned if he did and damned if he didn't. Run like hell, man, he told himself.

''Then you're going to have to find yourself another man.''

She gasped, as if surprised by his statement. Her piercing glare cut straight through him. ''Fine with me. I'll do just that. I'm sure there are plenty of guys who'd just love to take over where you're leaving off.''

She opened the front door and stormed inside, leaving Brent on the portico. He cursed under his breath. Damn stupid woman! Let her find somebody else. What did he care? He was well rid of the little pest. Better some other guy than him. Right?

Brent marched back to his truck, got in and raced out of the driveway. He drove like a madman down the road, a country song about *she's-with-him-now* blaring on the radio.

Chapter 4

Brent removed his hat, wiped the perspiration from his face with the palm of his hand and looked up at the bright sun. Physical labor took more out of a man than a workout in a gym. It wasn't that he'd gotten soft living in Chicago, but until coming on this research trip, he'd forgotten how downright hard being a ranch hand could be. One thing was for sure—when a cowpoke went to bed at night, he didn't have any trouble sleeping. Being bone tired was conducive to a good night's rest.

The nighttime hours weren't a problem for Brent. It was the long days that gave him trouble. He kept telling himself to forget Jenna Wilson, that she was not his responsibility. Hell, he barely knew the girl. But he couldn't stop worrying about her, wondering what kind of trouble she might be getting herself into, how far in over her head she'd go before she'd wise up.

Brent caught a glimpse of Flynt Carson coming toward him, a sweating cola can in each hand. He hadn't seen the boss man, as the other employees referred to Flynt, since the big date with Jenna this past weekend. Lucky for him that Flynt knew Jenna and had clued him in on the sort of woman she was. Otherwise, despite his own better judgement, he might have rushed into a physical relationship with her because he found her so doggone irresistible.

Flynt walked up to Brent and offered him a cold drink. "Hot for late April, isn't it?"

Brent rubbed the back of his moist neck, then replaced his Stetson atop his head. "Glad I won't be around here in July." He reached out and accepted the cola. "Thanks."

"How much longer do you figure you'll be around?"

"A few more weeks. A month at the most."

"Are you planning on seeing Jenna again?" Flynt lifted the can to his lips and downed a swig. "I thought maybe you might have another date with her since it's Friday night."

"I've decided that the wisest course of action for me is to steer clear of her, if at all possible. She's on a collision course headed straight for disaster. Somebody needs to watch out for her and try to keep her out of trouble."

"Why not you?"

"Whoa there, buddy, no way am I volunteering for the job. I thought maybe it might be something you could do, considering the fact she's a family friend and all."

"Jenna's rebelling against her domineering mother and since I am a family friend, she'd figure out pretty quick that I was keeping an eye on her because Nelda asked me to. I'm afraid my taking on the job wouldn't work."

"Well, if you're commandeering a recruit, count me out. And when you do find somebody, you'd better offer him hazardous duty pay."

Flynt smiled. "If you change your mind—"

"I won't."

Flynt shook his head, then moved on to another subject. "Well, do you think you're learning anything on the ranch that will help you when you get back to Chicago?"

"If nothing else, I'm learning why I left Kansas City and my father's ranch," Brent said jokingly.

"Right before you head back to the Windy City, I'd like for you to have dinner with the family. It won't matter by then that we'll be blowing your cover."

"I'd like that, but until then, I'll eat with the other hands and hang out at the places they do."

"Places like the Saddlebag Bar?"

Brent caught the twinkle in Flynt's eye. "I think I'll steer clear of the Saddlebag for a while, just in case Jenna goes back there looking for me. Tonight I thought I'd head down toward Kingsville. I hear there's a place there called The Rusty Bucket that makes the Saddlebag look like Sunday school. I don't figure I'll be bothered with any little girls there—only experienced women.''

Flynt slapped Brent on the back. "Have a good time. I'd go with you, but a bar isn't the best place for a recovering alcoholic to hang out."

Hearing just a hint of something odd in Flynt's voice—sadness and regret maybe—Brent felt sympathy for his old friend. The man had lost his wife, his unborn child and nearly drank himself to death before he turned his life around. Flynt Carson today bore only a vague resemblance to the old fun-loving Flynt of yesterday.

"You have every reason to be proud of yourself, man," Brent said. "It takes a strong person to fight the battle you've fought and win."

"I'm not sure I've won," Flynt admitted. "Every day's a new battle."

The two stood around drinking their colas and talking, changing the subject to the ranch, the commodities business, the weather. Brent understood that Flynt had said all he wanted to say about his personal tragedies. And Brent didn't want to discuss Jenna Wilson. Hell, he hoped he never heard her name again as long as he lived.

Jenna had moped around her apartment all week. Every minute she wasn't in class or studying she was thinking about Brent Jameson. And sometimes even in class, her mind wandered to the gorgeous cowboy who'd told her to get lost last Saturday night. All those wild, hungry emotions she'd felt couldn't have been one-sided. He'd felt them, too. She just knew he had. So, why had he rejected her? She'd asked herself that question a hundred times, but the answer that kept repeating itself over and over in her head did little to squelch her desire. Her inexperience might have frightened Brent off, but she believed Katie and Dana's assessment of the situation was closer to the real reason he had bid her adios.

"Guys like to do the chasing," Dana had said. "This may be the twenty-first century, but men prefer being the aggressor."

"She's right," Katie had agreed. "You came on too strong. You pushed too hard."

Well, how was she to know that she'd taken the wrong approach with a man like Brent, an old-fashioned rough and rowdy cowboy? After all, her romantic experience had been with boys, not men. Young men handpicked by her mother. Young gentlemen whom she'd found completely boring and unappealing.

Jenna spread out across her bed on her stomach, opened her history book and tried to read. But the words on the page began blurring together and her thoughts drifted from the subject matter straight back to Brent. Maybe it wasn't meant for her to experience a true rebellion. Maybe her short-lived revolution had ended before it had actually begun. But she'd been so sure that Brent was the answer to her prayers. Hadn't he been in the right place, at the right time? But if he was truly her white knight, the man destined to rescue her from her doomed existence, who'd help her spread her wings and fly, then he wouldn't have refused what she had offered. Herself. On a silver platter. With an apple in her mouth.

Damn! If she had it to do over again, she would play hard to get. She'd let Brent do the chasing. She'd let him do the begging.

When the phone rang, she didn't pay much attention because Katie usually grabbed it by the second ring, which she must have done this time. Jenna slammed her history book closed. Who was she kidding? She wasn't going to get any work done tonight. It was Friday night and she couldn't help wondering if Brent would be at the Saddlebag Bar.

Katie tapped on the door and said, "Phone call for you. It's Fiona Carson."

"I'll get it in here," Jenna replied, then reached over to her nightstand and picked up the telephone receiver. "I've got it," she yelled through the door to Katie. "Hi, Fiona."

"Want to know where your cowboy is going tonight?"

"What?"

"Aren't you still interested in roping and hogtying Brent Jameson?"

"Yes, of course I am, but—"

"No buts about it," Fiona said. "I just happened to

overhear the tail end of a conversation between Flynt and him this afternoon. They had no idea I was anywhere around. He told Flynt that he was driving down toward Kingsville tonight to a place called the Rusty Bucket."

"The Rusty Bucket? I suppose it's a bar like the Saddlebag, huh?"

"Yes, but even rowdier. So, you do whatever you want with this information, but a smart girl just might show up beforehand and get herself a few guys hanging all over her before the man she really wants puts in an appearance."

"You know, Fiona, that's not a bad idea." The wheels in Jenna's head turned at breakneck speed. "If I can persuade Katie to go with me, I might be brave enough to try a new plan of action."

"And what might that plan be?"

"Showing Mr. Jameson that I can have a high old time without him. And when he shows up, I'll ignore him. If wants me, then he can pursue me. Not the other way around."

"Hey, when did you get so smart? Sounds like you've figured out how to work this guy. You go, girl."

"Fiona, thanks for calling. I owe you one."

"All you owe me is a progress report."

Jenna giggled. "If I'm lucky, maybe the report will be R-rated."

"If you're really lucky, it'll be X-rated!"

After hanging up the phone, Jenna jerked her skintight size 4 jeans out of her closet, found a semisheer white blouse that was supposed to be worn with a camisole, then called out loudly, "Katie, get dressed. We're going out tonight. And wear something similar to what you wore last Friday night."

Katie flung open Jenna's bedroom door. "Where are we going?"

"To some place down near Kingsville. A roadhouse called the Rusty Bucket."

"Be still my heart." Katie patted the center of her chest. "Are we talking a repeat of last Friday night?"

"Yeah, only better." Jenna stripped out of her navy cotton shorts and gingham blouse, down to her underwear. "And since Dana went home this weekend, she isn't here to give us a hundred reasons why we shouldn't go."

"I'm glad to see that you're over that infatuation with Brent Jameson. I told you he wasn't the only fish in the sea. You'll probably meet another hottie tonight."

"Oh, I intend to meet more than one guy." Jenna pulled on the silky see-through blouse "You drive your car, okay? If my plan works, you'll be coming home alone."

"Jenna!"

Laughing, she plotted and schemed as she fell back on the bed and wriggled into her one-size-too-small Calvin Klein jeans.

A restlessness that he was unaccustomed to hung heavily on Brent's shoulders as he entered the smoky, rumbling den of iniquity known as the Rusty Bucket. He'd been questioning his decision to make this sojourn into the Texas cattle business via working as a ranch hand. In only a few weeks, he'd grown calluses on his hands and backside, his skin was as tan as gingerbread and he'd been celibate for way too long. Although he couldn't deny that the firsthand knowledge he'd gained on the ranch in Laredo and at the Carson Ranch had given him new insight into his work, he had begun missing his normal routine back in Chicago. There was a lot to be said for a cowboy's way of life, but at heart, Brent was a businessman. He belonged in Chicago. Ranching would never be more to him than a hobby, a way to escape—temporarily— from the stress and pressure of a high-powered job in the city.

And tonight especially he missed his social life. Although he'd been opposed to the idea of picking up some woman for a one-night stand while he was posing as a cowpoke, his libido had gone from whispering in his ear to shouting full blast: *You need to get laid!*

Brent made his way to the bar area, found an empty stool and ordered a beer. The way he felt, he could use something stronger, but he would be driving himself home later, so he'd have to watch the amount he drank. Besides, having a good time wasn't dependent on getting drunk. Not for him. Never had been. Never would be.

While he sipped on the cool, foamy brew, a tall

brunette sauntered up beside him, her arm brushing against his shoulder.

"Hi, there, handsome. Buy me a drink?"

The woman possessed a world-weary look, although he suspected she wasn't much older than thirty, if that. She wasn't pretty, but with her slender frame and artful makeup job, she was attractive. In an unsophisticated, country-girl way.

"Sure. What'll you have?" he asked.

"What you're having will be fine."

Brent ordered her a beer, but before he could introduce himself and find out her name, he caught a glimpse of a familiar face. The woman sat talking with a guy a few seats down the bar. Unless he was badly mistaken, the woman was one of Jenna's friends whom he'd met briefly outside the Saddlebag this past Friday night. A knot of apprehension formed in the pit of his stomach. Did seeing her friend here mean that Jenna was at the Rusty Bucket? Or was his vision playing tricks on him and this woman wasn't who he thought she was?

Deciding to investigate, Brent rose from the bar stool. The woman at his side, grabbed his arm.

"Where're you going, sugar?"

"Stay here," he said. "Enjoy your drink. I'll be right back. I think I see an acquaintance that I should say howdy to."

As Brent approached the woman he thought was Jenna's friend, she glanced up at him and smiled. That was her all right. No doubt about it.

"Hi, there, Brent," she said. "What are you doing all the way down here in Kingsville? Get tired of the Saddlebag Bar?"

"Yeah," he replied. "Looks like you did, too. I'm sorry, I don't remember your name."

"Katie," she told him. "Yeah, Jenna and I heard about this place and thought we'd come down and take a look."

"Jenna's here?"

Katie nodded her head, then glanced toward the crowded dance floor. "She's out there somewhere. I swear, every man in the place wants to dance with her."

Yeah, sure. He'd just bet that's what every man in the place wanted. Knowing his own sex as he did, he had a good idea what these guys wanted from Jenna. And it sure as hell was more than a dance.

So why do you care? he asked himself. *You knew that she was looking for trouble and that sooner or later she'd find it.*

He just didn't think she'd find it while he had to stand by and watch—at least watch the initial stage of her downfall. If he were smart, he'd take the been-around-the-block-a-few-times brunette waiting for him at the other end of the bar and get the hell out of the Rusty Bucket as soon as possible. They could stop by a liquor store, pick up a bottle and then find a motel room. By morning, he wouldn't even be able to remember Jenna Wilson's name.

And while his mind concocted the escape-and-forget scenario, his feet led him straight toward the dance floor. He stopped on the outer edge and visually searched through the couples swaying to the moans of a steel guitar. He heard her laughter a split second before he saw her. With her arms draped around her partner's neck, Jenna tossed back that mane of golden hair and laughed giddily. Brent's muscles tensed. The guy holding her was looking at her as if he could devour her whole. Damn!

Brent stood back, watching. And without realizing it, he waited. One song ended and in the brief interlude before the next began, half a dozen guys swarmed around Jenna, each one vying for her attention. And no wonder. Why had she dressed like that? You could see straight through her blouse to her lacy bra. And her breasts were bulging over the pushup cups. Ah, hell, things were fixing to get out of hand. Six young bucks and only one doe. He sensed a fight coming on. And Jenna would be caught right in the middle of it.

Good thing he'd shown up here tonight. Somebody would have to save her cute little butt, and it looked like he was the only candidate for hero. He hadn't been in a fistfight in years and would prefer to avoid one tonight, but he wasn't going to stand by and let some drunk cowpoke put his hands all over Jenna.

What the hell was he thinking? *What's your real motivation? Which is it, Brent—do you simply want to protect her or do you want to take her away from those other guys so you can have her all to yourself?*

The rumblings of battle had begun. A shove here.

A smart-mouthed comment there. Jenna right in the middle, smiling, her blue eyes sparkling with amusement, as her barroom suitors tried to mark their territory. The silly girl giggled when the guy she'd been dancing with grabbed her arm. That's when Brent realized Jenna had been drinking and was slightly tipsy. Great. Not only would he have to deal with a group of testosterone-driven bulls, but he'd have to cope with an inebriated little sex kitten. Neither prospect appealed to him.

A short, stocky, auburn-haired man struck the first blow, sending a pretty-boy blond Adonis to the floor. Jenna screeched and jerked away from her former dance partner. Within seconds, all hell broke loose and a free-for-all fistfight commenced among Jenna's admirers. Through the smoky haze, Brent got a good look at Jenna's face. An expression of shock came first, followed by fright. Wonderful. Now, after she had instigated a riot on the dance floor, she finally realized she was in danger.

Katie ran up beside Brent and tugged on his arm. He glanced at her, then returned his attention to the ongoing brawl.

"Aren't you going to do something?" Katie asked.

Brent glared at Katie. "Do you want me to rescue her?"

"Yes, of course, I do."

"Then tell me one thing—" Brent looked Katie square in the eyes "—did she know I'd be here tonight?"

Katie hesitated, a guilty expression on her face, then she finally admitted, ''Yes, she knew. Fiona Carson overheard you and her brother talking about where you were going tonight.''

''So, this little scene was staged for my benefit?''

''Yes, but we…she had no idea it would get out of hand this way. Honestly.''

''Katie, do you have the car keys?''

''Car keys?''

''To Jenna's car.''

''We came in my car.''

''Ah, I see. Well, you can get yourself home, right? I'll take care of Jenna. That's what she wanted, isn't it?''

Katie hung her head.

Although he felt a bit like a puppet with his strings being pulled by a foolhardy young woman, Brent trouped across the dance floor and through the throng of onlookers. He was a man on a mission. When he heard Jenna scream, he picked up his pace and rushed toward her. Her suitors were so busy trying to beat each other's brains out that they paid no attention to him. He walked straight to Jenna, who smiled the moment she saw him and waved her arms, signaling him to come get her.

Doing his best to avoid getting accidently socked in the nose, Brent sidestepped the fighters. The minute he came near, Jenna threw herself at him, but being unsteady on her feet, she tripped, which tossed her toward Brent's knees. He leaned over, grabbed her around the waist and tossed her over his shoulder. She wriggled and squirmed.

"Put...me...d-d-down. I caaan walk." She slurred her words, enough to indicate she was drunk.

With Jenna over his shoulder, Brent exited the dance floor and headed for the door. He wanted to get out of this place before the brawlers realized some other guy had walked off with their prize. The minute the night air hit them, Jenna squirmed more and more. Without giving his actions a thought, Brent reached up and popped her on the butt. She let out a squeal.

Brent unlocked his truck, opened the passenger side and put Jenna on the seat, then hurried to the other side and got in. As he inserted the key in the ignition, he caught a glimpse of her in his peripheral vision. She swayed back and forth. Damn! He reached over, buckled her seat belt and set her up straight.

"I knew you—you'd..." Her words trailed off.

"Come to your rescue? Save you?"

She lifted her arm, stuck out her index finger and plopped it down on Brent's nose. "I'm not the ag-aggress...I'm not the one doing the chasing."

"Do you have any idea how close you came to getting yourself in a heap of trouble? The kind of trouble you'd regret for the rest of your life?"

"Are you...taking my...taking me home?"

"Yeah, honey, I'm taking you home."

Jenna smiled, a lopsided, tipsy grin. "I told Katie. Knew you would."

She fell asleep. Or passed out. Brent shook his head,

put the gears into Reverse and backed up, then exited the parking lot. He'd take her home all right—straight to her mother. It was high time Jenna and Mrs. Wilson worked through whatever problems that were causing Jenna to rebel. Because next time Jenna decided to put herself in harm's way, he might not be around to save her from herself.

Chapter 5

Brent pulled his truck up in front of the Wilson mansion shortly before midnight. The outside security floodlights lit the exterior of the house, but the inside looked dark, as if no one was at home. He dreaded facing Mrs. Wilson, but he was doing what he thought best for Jenna. If she were his daughter or his kid sister, he'd want someone to watch out for her, bring her home and force her to face parental wrath. Jenna might be twenty-one, but she'd been acting like a foolhardy kid lately. He got out of the truck and went around to open the passenger side. When he shook Jenna gently, she moaned and curled around the seat belt that held her in place. He shook her again. Her eyelids fluttered.

"Come on Sleeping Beauty. It's time to face the wicked witch."

"Huh?"

He reached inside, undid her seat belt, then ran his hands under her and lifted her up and into his arms. Sighing contentedly, she wrapped her arms around his neck and laid her head on his shoulder. She was a little thing, but every inch of her body was firm and sturdy. Heaven help him, he had to stop thinking about her body. He reminded himself that he was playing the good Samaritan tonight. When he reached the double front doors, he maneuvered Jenna around so that he could ring the doorbell. He waited. No response. He rang the bell again. Still nothing. Didn't a place like this have any servants, at least a housekeeper?

"What 'cha doing?" Jenna asked, her eyelids lifting slightly and her lips forming a sleepy smile.

"Trying to get somebody to come to the door," he told her.

"Where are we?"

"At your house. At your mother's home in Mission Creek."

"She's not here. Gone to Houston with friends…to the ballet. She's staying over…overnight."

"Damn." He cursed under his breath. "What about the housekeeper or—"

"Weekend off."

Great. Now, what was he supposed to do? "Do you happen to have a key to the house with you?"

"Sure I do." Jenna yawned.

"Where is it?"

"In my pocket. Key to my house, key to my apartment…my credit card and a hundred dollars."

"Which pocket?"

"Side pocket."

Brent set her on her feet. Still a bit wobbly, she kept her arms around his neck. "Get it for me," he said.

She shook her head, flinging her long blond tresses about her shoulders. "You get it."

He huffed loudly, then rammed a couple of fingers down into one side pocket, found it empty and repeated the move on the other pocket. As he discovered the keys, the credit card and the money, he also discovered the softness of her hip and as he dug deeper into her pocket to shove the items up and out, he felt her pelvic bone. Sweat popped out on his brow. Hurriedly, he pulled the items out of her pocket. With her still clinging to him, he tried one of the keys in the lock. Presto, the door opened. He shoved the other items into his shirt pocket, then guided Jenna through the front door. The security system alerted him that he needed to punch in a code before the damn thing went off. He felt along the inner wall for a switch. Found it. A crystal chandelier illuminated the grand marble-floored foyer.

"What's the code for the security system?"

"The code? Uh, it's three-two-two-nine."

He punched in the code, then breathed a sigh of relief when the green deactivated light came on.

"Where's your room, honey?" he asked.

She swayed into him and wrapped her arms around

his waist, then stared up at him. "Are you going to take me to bed?"

"Yeah, that's exactly what I'm going to do."

"Aren't you going to even kiss me first?" She puckered her lips.

Brent chuckled. Drunk. Disorderly. And cute. Actually, the word adorable came to mind, too. He pushed back a loose strand of shimmery hair that had fallen over her left eye.

"Do you think you can walk up those stairs?" he asked.

"Why don't you carry me?" She nuzzled his chest and then his belly. Her fingers reached for the top button on his shirt.

He had to put a stop to her shenanigans right now.

He jerked her up and into his arms, then climbed the stairs. The sooner he got her into bed so she could sleep it off, the better for both of them. He wasn't the type of man who took advantage of a woman, especially not one who'd had too much to drink. But a normal man could take only so much temptation before he succumbed.

After he reached the landing, he paused. "Where's your room?"

"Third door on the right."

He forged ahead, flipped on the light switch in her room and stopped dead still. This wasn't a young woman's room; this was a little girl's room. Antique white furniture, handpainted with delicate floral designs. A canopy bed with an eyelet lace bedspread and matching curtains at the windows. Stuffed animals and dolls adorning a wall of shelving. Damn! Poor Jenna. No wonder she was trying to rebel. Apparently Nelda Wilson had tried to keep her daughter a child. Why on earth hadn't Jenna rebelled before now? For the first time since he'd met this flirtatious, little renegade, he understood what she'd been up against. This room spoke volumes.

"Brent?"

"Huh?"

"I—I think I'm going to be sick."

"What?"

"I drank too much beer and I had a couple of mixed drinks, too, and... Oh, God, put me down. Now!"

He set her on her feet. She raced through her bedroom and flung open the door to the adjoining bathroom. He heard her heave, then empty her stomach. Poor kid. He wondered if this was the first time she'd ever been drunk. Probably.

He fished in his shirt pocket for the items he had removed from her jeans pocket before they'd entered the house. After retrieving the two keys, the credit card and the forty dollars apparently left out of the original hundred, he laid them on a white antique desk in the corner.

Jenna moaned, then retched again. Brent entered the bathroom just as she finished throwing up a second time. On her knees in front of the commode, Jenna glanced up at him. Tears misted her eyes.

"Not a very pretty sight, am I?"

He lifted the hand towel by the sink, dampened it, then squatted down beside her and washed her face. "Feeling any better?"

"Some."

"What you need is a good night's sleep."

"Please, don't leave me."

"Do you think you're through in here?" he asked. She nodded.

He helped her to her feet; she clung to the edge of the sink. He removed a paper cup from the dispenser above the sink, filled it with water, then held it to Jenna's lips. "Here, rinse out your mouth."

She did as he'd instructed. "Thanks."

He caressed the side of her face. Sweet Jenna. He guided her back into her bedroom. "Want to put on a gown or pjs?"

She shook her head. "I can sleep in my clothes."

He pointed to a spot on her blouse and another on her jeans. "You've soiled your clothes, honey. Let me find you something else to sleep in."

Jenna began tugging on her sheer blouse, but in her slightly disoriented state, she found it difficult to undo the buttons.

"Let me help." Oh, yeah, he'd help her undress. No problem. But who was going to help him keep his hands off her?

Steeling his nerves to act as a nursemaid, Brent removed Jenna's boots, blouse and jeans, which left her in nothing except a pair of red bikini panties and a lacy red bra. He swallowed hard. Talk about temptation personified.

Leading her by the hand, he took her over to her bed, turned down the cover and helped her in. She reached up for him. Tenderly, he pushed her hands away.

"Go to sleep, Jenna."

"Aren't you coming to bed with me?"

He grinned. Even now the little hellion had a one-track mind.

"You're in no condition for anything except sleep."

"You won't leave, will you?"

"No, honey, I won't leave."

Smiling sleepily, she burrowed into the mattress, seeking and finding a comfortable position. "Kiss me good-night."

Brent leaned over and kissed her on the forehead. She sighed contentedly. How the hell had he gotten himself into this situation? Why hadn't he been able to leave her to her fate instead of rushing to her rescue at the Rusty Bucket? *Because despite your determination not to fall for this little filly, you've got the hots for her. And for some damn reason, you've taken on the role as her protector, which puts your position as her wannabe lover at odds with your guardian role.*

Glancing around the room, Brent spotted a chaise longue upholstered in some sort of pink satiny material. If he was going to stay the night to keep watch over the sleeping princess, he could choose between the floor and the chaise. Despite the fact that his feet hung off the end, he chose the chaise.

Jenna woke with a start. Where was she? Why was her head aching? Sitting straight up in bed, she glanced around the moonlit room. Her room at home. The room that hadn't been altered since she was ten. But what was she doing here? Taking a look at the clock on her nightstand, she noted that it was four-thirty. How long had she been asleep? She had no idea. She scooted to the edge of the bed, slipped off the side and stood on unsteady legs. Everything around her was spinning like crazy. She closed her eyes, inhaled and exhaled slowly, then opened her eyes to find that the dizziness had subsided. Scanning the semidark room, she saw a large hulk resting on her chaise longue.

Brent Jameson!

She groaned softly, as her slightly fuzzy brain recalled last night's events. She and Katie had gone to the Rusty Bucket, where she had flirted and danced and drank, in preparation for Brent's arrival. Undoubtedly by the time Brent had showed up, she'd already had too much to drink. She vaguely remembered a fight breaking out and Brent lifting her up and over his shoulder. *Her hero.* Hadn't she wanted him to be jealous, to whisk her away from her other admirers? Yes, of course, but in her grand scheme, she'd been sober. What did they put in those beers at the Rusty Bucket anyway?

Jenna supposed she'd made a total fool of herself last night. Understatement of the century. But at least her plan had partially worked, hadn't it? Brent was here in her room. He'd spent the night. Of course in her original plan, they had shared a bed.

After tiptoing to the bathroom, Jenna closed the door behind her, then stripped out of her bra and panties. She felt grubby and sticky and... Oh, God, she'd puked in front of Brent. He'd seen her with her head hung over the commode. How totally embarrassing!

She turned on the shower. The warm spray felt wonderful. Taking her time, she lathered and rinsed her hair and her body, then stepped out onto the tile floor and reached for a couple of towels hanging on a wall rack. After wrapping the smaller one around her damp hair, forming a turban, she took the larger one and dried herself, then draped it around her, covering her body from breasts to hips. Hurriedly, she brushed her teeth and rinsed with mouthwash.

Although she had a headache, she was at least clean, alert and thinking straight. So, why waste a golden opportunity? Brent was here, in her bedroom. No time like the present to salvage the moment, so to speak. He must care about her, at least a little, or he wouldn't have rescued her, brought her home, taken care of her and stayed the night.

You can do this, she told herself. How hard could it be to seduce a man in your own bedroom? Bolstering her courage, she sauntered over to the chaise longue, eased down and on top of Brent and kissed him on the cheek. He grunted, coming awake slowly. She kissed him again, this time on the mouth.

"What the he—" He sat up so quickly that he almost toppled her off and onto the floor. The turban around her head loosened, then fell off, cascading her long, damp hair down her back. She grabbed his shoulders and held on, straddling his waist as she landed in his lap. "Jenna?"

Snuggling herself up against him, she put her arms around his neck and kissed him again. And much to her surprise and delight, he kissed her back. Reveling in the sensations bursting inside her, she cooperated fully when he took charge, thrusting his tongue inside her mouth and cupping her hips with his big hands. Giving herself over completely to him, she readjusted her body so that the apex between her thighs fit perfectly over his erection.

Brent groaned, deep in his throat, then plunged his hands up and under the loose towel that barely covered her. As he caressed her naked buttocks, she whimpered. Spiraling out of control quickly, she rubbed herself against him, like a purring cat slinking around her master's leg. Somehow she'd known it would be like this with Brent, all hot passion and hungry desire. She'd dreamed of how it would be, how she'd feel, the way he would react. Even though the idea of a wild fling, a rebellious adventure to test her ability to break free of her mother's overbearing control had instigated her pursuit of Brent Jameson, none of that mattered now. He was no longer only a means to an end. As crazy it might sound to anyone else, Jenna realized that she was falling in love with this very unsuitable cowboy. And never having been in love before, her emotions were on a roller-coaster ride of excitement and uncertainty.

Brent kissed and licked a path down her throat and over the swell of her breasts bulging from beneath the terry cloth towel. Her nipples tingled. He nuzzled the towel lower and lower, until it dropped to her waist. The moment his lips touched one tight, aching nipple, she cried out with the pleasure-pain that radiated from her breasts throughout her body.

"Make love to me," Jenna whispered, her voice hoarse with longing.

He froze. He lifted her up and off him, then set her on the chaise longue as he stood. She gazed up at him, puzzled by his actions. When she reached out for him, he held up his hands in a stop gesture.

"Brent?"

He took a deep breath. "It's not that I don't want you, honey. I do. More than you know."

"Then wh—"

"We're playing with fire. And if you play with fire, it's only a matter of time until you get burned."

"I don't care." She held open her arms to him, unashamed that she was practically naked. "Let's jump in the fire and burn together."

"I can't do this, Jenna. I'm not that big a heel. I have a feeling that you want something from me that

I can't give you. For me, it would be just sex. Is that what you want? All you want?''

His words sobered her in a way all the cold showers and cups of hot coffee couldn't have. If he had asked her this question on the first night they met, she could have given him an unequivocal positive response. But not now. Sex wouldn't be enough. She wanted more. She wanted love.

"I guess there have been a lot of women in your life." Suddenly feeling exposed and vulnerable, Jenna pulled the towel up and around her breasts.

"Some," he admitted.

"And you've never been in love?"

He shook his head.

"And you don't feel anything for me?"

"I feel attraction and lust. You're a beautiful, desirable woman and it's not easy for me to walk away from you." His lips lifted in a cockeyed grin. "I hope you appreciate the amount of self-control it's taking for me to give up something I'd very much like to have."

"You don't have to say—"

"I meant it, honey. Every word."

Heat crept up her neck and flushed her cheeks. "Before you leave, I need to thank you for coming to my rescue last night at the Rusty Bucket. I only remember part of what happened. I'm not used to drinking and…well, thanks, Brent."

"My pleasure, Miss Jenna." With a sweep of his hand, he bowed graciously, then leaned over and kissed her cheek. "Keep on rebelling, honey. Just find a safer way to do it. And if you decide to go to another roadhouse seeking excitement, give me a call. I'll take you and keep an eye on you." When she gasped with delight and smiled at him, he amended his statement. "Just as friends. Nothing more. I'll act as your bodyguard."

Her smile vanished; she nodded. "Just as friends."

Brent squeezed her chin playfully, as one might touch a child. "Promise me that you won't go off and do anything crazy without me."

"I...okay, I promise."

"Good girl."

With that said, he turned and left her bedroom. For several minutes she didn't move. Not until she heard the roar of his old truck. Then she stood, walked across the room and flopped down on her bed. The tears came easily. Brokenhearted tears. She had come so close to becoming a woman—Brent's woman. Why hadn't she told him that if they'd made love, it would have been nothing more than sex for her, too? If only she had lied to him, he'd still be here, in bed with her, making love to her.

Just as friends. His words played over and over in her head. *Nothing more. I'll act as your bodyguard.*

Jenna pummeled her fists against the tangled covers, venting her anger and frustration. All her daring plans to walk on the wild side had gone haywire. She hadn't meant to fall in love with anybody, least of all some cowboy hunk with an honorable streak a mile wide.

What was she going to do now? She needed a new plan of action. A winning strategy to accomplish a far more important goal than breaking away from her mother's iron-fisted control. Besides, if she got what she wanted, then she could kill two birds with one stone: be free of her mother's domineering hold and capture Brent Jameson's heart now and forever.

Chapter 6

Nelda Wilson stormed into Jenna's apartment. Katie and Dana made themselves scarce in a big hurry. Jenna wished she could scurry away to safety along with them. But she couldn't. She had to face her mother's wrath. She had to stand up for herself. After all, did she really want to spend the rest of her life letting her mother make all her decisions? No! Most definitely not! If things worked out between Brent and her, she'd have no choice but to confront her mother, to stand up to her and tell her that she intended to spend the rest of her life with a ranch hand who drove a beat-up old truck and probably didn't have more than a few hundred dollars to his name.

"What's gotten into you?" Nelda tossed her alligator-skin bag down on the coffee table. "Have you lost your mind? You cannot continue carrying on the way you have lately. Did you think that people wouldn't talk, that no one would find out that you've been gallivanting around with that worthless cowboy?''

''That cowboy has a name. It's Brent Jameson. And he is not worthless.''

Nelda huffed. ''Have you slept with him?''

''That's none of your business.''

''Of course it's my business. You're a child and I'm your mother.''

''I am not a child. I'm a woman. I'm twenty-one.''

''You're making a fool of yourself and of me. I suppose you know that, don't you?''

''That wasn't my intention.'' Jenna's abdominal muscles twisted painfully into tight knots. Dealing with her mother had all but given her ulcers as a teenager. She'd found it easier to acquiesce to Nelda's wishes than to endure the wounds from battle after battle. But she could not—would not—back down, not this time. She had found something worth fighting for—Brent.

''The debutante ball is in two weeks and you still don't have a date. Two months ago I gave you a list of young men from which to choose. I expect you to make a decision and call one of them—today!''

''The debutante ball! The debutante ball! Is that the only thing you can think about? I didn't want to participate in that society nonsense in the first place, but I agreed just to please you. Because believe it or not,

Mother, I do care about pleasing you. I just wish you cared half as much about what matters to me.''

"How can you think that I don't care about what matters to you? You're my only child. I love you. I want only the best for you."

"You want what *you* think is best." Nausea churned in Jenna's stomach. She felt a strong urge to give in to her mother's demands, to just call Tommy Johnson or Charles Wayne or anyone on "the list." What did it matter who her escort was for the ball?

"What's best for you—and you know it—is to stop all this foolishness, choose a date for the ball and put your life back on track. You'll be graduating from Tensley the week after the ball and you can have a glorious summer at the country club, with young men and women who are your social equals."

"I'm inviting *Brent* to be my escort for the ball and nothing you can say or do will change my mind."

Nelda gasped. Two other rather conspicuous gasps came from the kitchen, and Jenna realized that her friends were eavesdropping on her battle royale with her mother. Dana and Katie were rooting for her, hoping she would not surrender. After all, if Jenna could go against her mother's wishes and not back down, then there was hope that Dana and Katie could do the same with their parents.

"I forbid it." Nelda shook her index finger in Jenna's face.

"Are you going to forbid me to marry him, too?" Where had that grand announcement come from?

Jenna wondered. Oh, well, in for a penny, in for a pound.

"Marry him!" Nelda screeched the words. "Has that cowboy asked you to marry him?"

"We've discussed how we feel about each other. And—and about our future." Okay, so she was telling a little white lie. Surely lighting wouldn't strike her dead for such a tiny falsehood.

"Where did I go wrong?" Nelda wrung her hands, heading straight into a melodramatic performance. "I've been a good mother. Your father and I gave you everything money could buy. You were always such a sweet, obedient little girl. I never dreamed the day would come when you would treat me this way. When you'd walk all over my feelings so heartlessly."

She'd heard it all before. Numerous times. Whenever she dared to imply that she might go against her mother's wishes, she got the drama queen guilt trip from Nelda. And it had worked beautifully in the past. But not now. Everything within Jenna screamed to be free.

"I'm going to ask Brent to be my escort to the ball," Jenna repeated. "And I intend to continue dating him." *Just as friends. Nothing more.* His words echoed inside her head. Yeah, well, she'd see about that. It might take some time, but eventually she'd prove to him that his feelings for her were as strong as hers were for him.

Nelda grabbed her purse from the coffee table, marched to the door, then glanced over her shoulder.

"Mark my word, you will regret this. And when that man breaks your heart, you'll come to your senses."

Hurricane Nelda blew out the door with more damaging winds than when she'd arrived. The moment the door slammed shut, Jenna dropped into the nearest chair and drew in a deep calming breath, then released it slowly. Dana and Katie came rushing out of the kitchen, quickly hovering over Jenna.

"I can't believe you did it," Dana said.

"I can." Katie grinned. "She's in love. A woman would do anything for the man she loves."

"How does Brent feel about you?" Dana asked. "Has he told you that he loves you?"

"Not yet," Jenna admitted. "But he will. Once I see him again."

"And when will that be?" Dana eyed Jenna skeptically. "He hasn't called you for a date or anything, has he?"

"No, but he told me that the next time I wanted to go out honky-tonking, to call him. He doesn't want me getting into trouble. So when I see him tomorrow at the Carson Ranch, I'm not only going to ask him to take me out on some fun dates, but I'm going to ask him to be my escort for the debutante ball."

"What if he says no?" Katie asked.

"He won't. I'm going to make sure of that."

Katie and Dana looked at each other, wide-eyed and mouths agape. Jenna laughed, feeling confident since she'd faced her mother without folding up like a paper fan. All she had to do now was bring Brent around to her way of thinking.

Brent had spent the morning and half the afternoon out mending fences, along with Tubby Wells and Clay Hargett. The other two hands had taken the truck and headed back to the ranch, leaving Brent to check the remaining fencing in the south pasture so they'd know where to start tomorrow. The huge orange sun hung low in the western horizon, its heat sweltering for springtime. Putting Mr. Lucky into a slow gallop, Brent headed toward the natural pond, fed by an underground spring, not far away. When he'd passed the watering hole this morning, he'd thought about coming back by for a dip later on. And right now he could almost feel the chilly water cooling his body.

Partially secluded within a semicircle of trees and bushes, the pond could be seen from only one angle. Brent led Mr. Lucky over to the pond to drink his fill, then hitched him to a nearby tree. Alone and unlikely to be bothered by another living soul, Brent tossed his Stetson hat on the grass, then hurriedly stripped off his clothes. Buck naked and feeling cooler already, he dived into the pond, swam across its surface, then found a shallow spot and sat. With the water lapping around his shoulders, he tossed back his head and laughed.

A part of him was going to miss the ranch life. And if he were totally honest with himself, he'd have to admit that a part of him was going to miss Jenna Wilson. She'd started out as thorn in his side, and mostly that's what she still was. But that darn irritating female kind of grew on a guy. As much as he'd tried not to think about her, his mind had other ideas. He found himself thinking about her way too much. When he'd told Flynt Carson that he had volunteered to be Jenna's bodyguard, if she decided to continue her rebellion, Flynt had thanked Brent for taking on the responsibility. But Flynt had sensed that something more was going on, more than Brent simply agreeing to look out for Fiona and Cara's young friend.

"Why did you change your mind?" Flynt had asked.

"I don't want to see the kid get hurt."

"And that's all there is to it? That's the only reason you're playing knight in shining armor?"

"Okay, so she gets to me…a little. I'd hate to see her sow her wild oats with somebody who'd take advantage of her."

Flynt's eyebrows had lifted and his eyes had widened in a uh-oh expression.

"It's not like that. I swear. I'm only going to be around a few more weeks and I'm hoping that'll be long enough for her to finish her war of rebellion without acquiring any permanent scars."

Brent leaned back into the water and began a slow backstroke. High in the sky, a hawk circled and then disappeared. Billowy white clouds swirled leisurely about in the big, blue sky. Relaxed and cooling off fast, Brent closed his eyes. Jenna appeared in his thoughts. Jenna wrapped in nothing but a towel, that towel slowly slipping below her breasts. Groaning, Brent opened his eyes. Damn, he had to stop thinking about her as a sexy woman. It wouldn't do for him to guard her from other men only to wind up taking advantage of her himself.

Just a couple more weeks in Mission Creek, working as a ranch hand, and then he'd be back home in Chicago. Back to the job and life he loved. And back to women who knew the score and didn't need his protection.

Fiona had told Jenna that Brent had been working with some other hands out in the south pasture, doing fence repair, and that the other guys had already returned to the ranch. That meant Brent was still out there. Alone. She'd waited around for him to return, but after fifteen minutes, she'd gotten impatient and, with Fiona's urging, had decided to ride out to the south pasture. She'd been searching for any sign of Brent for nearly twenty minutes when she saw his horse tied to a tree. She heard the sound of splashing water before she actually saw Brent frolicking in the pond.

She dismounted and tied Mariah's reins to the tree next to Mr. Lucky, then turned to call out to Brent. Just as she opened her mouth, Brent rose from the pond, water rippling from his powerful muscles, over his broad shoulders and down his ripcord lean belly. Jenna sucked in her breath. Unaware that he was being watched, Brent stood in the shallow end of the pond, his magnificent body glowing bronze in the late-afternoon sunlight.

He was naked.

Jenna swallowed hard as she watched him, awed by his beauty and by his impressive masculinity. Everything feminine within her reacted to all that overwhelming virility. To her way of thinking, Brent was the perfect male specimen.

This moment was a gift. And unexpected present from fate. And she wasn't stupid enough to reject a golden opportunity.

"Hey, there, cowboy," she called. "Mind if I join you?"

Brent turned toward the sound of her voice, and the look of surprise on his face quickly turned to embarrassment. Putting his back to her, he headed for deeper water, then immersed himself and swam several yards away from her.

Once he'd reached a safe level and had stood, only his upper torso visible above the pond's surface, he asked, "What are you doing here?"

"I came out to the ranch to take you up on your offer." She removed her hat and tossed it on the ground next to his, then she shucked off her boots and socks.

"You could have just telephoned."

"I could have, but I preferred seeing you in person. It's been days and days since I've seen you." Jenna stripped off her blouse and jeans, leaving her in her bra and panties.

"What are you doing?"

"What does it look like I'm doing?"

"Don't take off anything else," he told her.

"I can't skinny-dip with you if I leave on my clothes."

Jenna unhooked her bra, then did a little striptease, easing the straps down her arms in slow motion.

"Jenna, honey, don't. Keep your—"

She flung the bra on the pile of clothes.

"Oh, hell," Brent groaned.

Jenna slipped off her panties, dropped them on the ground and wadded into the pond. Brent closed his eyes. She laughed, knowing what effect her nude body was having on him. Surrounded by the pond's cool water or not, he wouldn't be able to control his reaction.

"I thought we'd agreed to be friends," Brent said, his eyes shut tight.

"We are friends," she replied. "Who says friends can't go skinny-dipping together?"

Jenna swam toward Brent. He swam away from her. He made it to the far side of the pond before she caught up with him. With his back to the four large boulders that lined that side of the pond, Brent turned to face her as he treaded water to keep afloat.

"I don't think this is a good idea," Brent said.

"What isn't a good idea?"

"Don't play games with me, Jenna. You're out of your league."

"Okay. You're right." She swam closer. "I want you to take me someplace fun this Friday night and Saturday night. And it'll be my treat. I know ranch hands don't make a lot, so—"

"Fine. I'll pick you up Friday night and you can pay for our night out. And we'll paint the town red again Saturday night. Now that that's settled, why don't you get out of the pond, put your clothes on and ride back to the ranch?"

"I have another question to ask." She swam over to him, slid her body against his and smiled when he groaned.

"What—what question?"

"Have you heard of the annual Lone Star County Debutante Ball?"

"Can't say that I have." He reached out under the water, grabbed her waist and tried to push her away, to put some space between them.

She pressed closer to him, her breasts rubbing his chest, as she bobbed in the water, her face only inches from his. "Well, it's this big shindig at the country club and I'm one of the debutantes, so I need an escort and I'd like for you—"

"You want me to escort you to your debutante ball?"

"Yes. Please."

"Jenna, I don't think that's a good idea."

"Yes it is. Besides, it's something one friend would do for another, isn't it?"

"When is this ball anyway?"

"May 11."

"I don't know. Let me think about it and get back to you."

"Don't take too long to think about it."

Jenna lifted her arms out of the water, flung them around Brent's neck and laughed just before they sank beneath the surface. Brent grabbed her and brought her up with him, both of them gasping for air.

He shook his head, flinging droplets of water in all directions.

"What am I going to do with you?"

"Why don't you think about it," she teased. "I'm sure an idea will pop up."

After shoving her off him, Brent swam away, back toward the shallow end of the pond. Jenna huffed loudly, then followed him. As he rose from the water, she grabbed his arm and before he had time to react, she kissed him. To her delight, he didn't push her away again. Instead he returned the kiss and kept kissing her until she was breathless, but then he ended the kiss and helped her out of the pond. With rivulets of water cascading off their naked bodies, Brent eased Jenna onto their pile of clothes, then came down over her. She loved the feel of his big, powerful body on top of her and the way he touched her, with such gentle thoroughness.

As pure sensation controlled her body, she wanted

to plead with him to make love to her. At this precise moment she realized that she was madly, wildly, completely in love with Brent Jameson.

Suddenly Brent jerked her blouse from the pile of clothing beneath them, flipping her over on her belly in the process. He lifted himself up and off her, then popped her on the hip with her blouse before he tossed it to her.

"Put on your clothes, honey."

Confusion muddled her thought process. Wasn't he going to make love to her? She'd been so sure he wouldn't be able to resist her.

"Brent?" She held open her arms to him.

He reached down, grabbed her hands and lifted her to her feet.

"Let's get dressed, then we can ride back to the ranch together."

"But you didn't...we didn't...don't you want to—"

He grabbed her shoulders and shook her soundly. "Yes, I want to, but I'm not going to. Not today. Not this weekend. Not ever."

"But...but..."

"Take our relationship on my terms or leave it," he told her. "I can be your friend, your date, your protector, but that's it. I shouldn't have touched you today. It won't happen again."

Brent picked up the rest of her clothes, handed them to her and then retrieved his own. Jenna dressed hurriedly, a sense of bewilderment fogging her mind. He wanted her, and they both knew it. So, why was it so difficult for him to admit that he loved her?

She wouldn't consider what had happened today a failure, only a postponement of the inevitable. Time was on her side. With each encounter, their relationship moved to a new level, whether Brent wanted to admit it or not. Who knew what might happen on their Friday night or Saturday night date? He might continue to resist her, but it was becoming increasingly difficult for him to reject her. If she could make slow but steady progress, Brent might even propose by the night of the debutante ball. Wishful thinking on her part? Maybe. But maybe not. Jenna had never wanted anything in life more than she wanted Brent. She refused to allow this minor setback to discourage her.

"I'll take our relationship on your terms," she told him. *And I promise that I won't ask you to make love to me ever again. No, Brent, my darling, I'm going to be patient and wait for you to ask me.* And she knew that he would.

Chapter 7

Jenna had told Brent that these past ten days had been the most wonderful and exciting time of her life. He had seen her practically every day since he'd rescued her at the Rusty Bucket, and he'd lived up to his word to be her protector. She'd shown up at the ranch several times. Once with a picnic basket and a quilt. He'd taken a great deal of good-natured kidding from the other hands about that. Weekend dates hadn't been enough to satisfy her, and if he were totally honest with himself, they hadn't been enough for him either. He had found that Jenna Wilson was addictive. He had even dropped by her apartment for dinner a couple of evenings. Katie and Dana had been conspicuously absent both times.

It wasn't easy keeping things platonic between

them, but whenever he was tempted—which was every time he was with Jenna—he reminded himself that he could withstand temptation just a little while longer. A few days after the debutante ball, he'd be back in Chicago, and Jenna would settle down to her former levelheaded self. At least that was what he hoped. And what Flynt Carson hoped. In the beginning of this rather unusual relationship with Jenna, he'd been able to convince himself that he had appointed himself her guardian as a favor to Flynt, whom he owed for letting him work at the Carson Ranch. But it was becoming more and more difficult to continue lying to himself.

He liked Jenna. Liked her a lot. She was a complex and complicated lady. There was a great deal more to her than the young woman who used all her wiles on him, sometimes trying his patience almost beyond reason. Jenna was not only beautiful, but she was exceptionally bright. And she had a fabulous sense of humor. But what surprised him most was discovering how much they had in common. They shared similar interests in books, music and dozens of little things— everything from their love of hot, Texas chili to their penchant for modern art. And Jenna had dreams for her future, plans for a life away from Mission Creek that her mother did not support. Jenna was as ambitious as he was. One more common bond.

Brent had never met anyone quite like his wild-child debutante. He hadn't exactly agreed to be her escort to the upcoming ball, but he hadn't out and out refused her. After all, what would it hurt for him to hang around an extra few days and be her date for the big event? It would make a perfect ending for their relationship. Escorting her to the ball could be his parting gift to her.

Flynt Carson had thanked him for keeping tabs on Jenna, telling him that he took it as a personal favor. He hadn't admitted to Flynt just how difficult it was to remain nothing more than friends with her. After all, he was only a man, and knowing Jenna was his for the taking created a heck of a lot of mixed emotions in him. On the one hand, he suspected that she fancied herself in love with him, and therefore he didn't dare lead her on by making love to her. But on the other hand, what if when he left town, she turned to some other guy on the rebound and this guy was a real sleazeball?

Tonight they had driven to Laredo, then crossed the border into Mexico and found a cantina with a reputation as the wildest, hottest spot anywhere in and around South Texas. They had danced and caroused and drank margaritas, all the while soaking up the local color. Two fistfights had taken place in the parking lot and one inside the *La Casa Rojo*. Drug addicts making purchases seemed unconcerned about being caught. One couple had sex in a darkened corner, as if anyone passing nearby couldn't see what they were doing. Several prostitutes picked up clients in the bar and took them upstairs to the rooms over the roadhouse.

What had promised to be just one more weekend exploration into the unknown for Jenna had turned into exposure to a world far darker and more dangerous than she'd expected. Brent sensed how uncomfortable she was now—now that the adrenalin rush of excitement had worn off and reality had set in.

"Had enough of this place?" he asked.

She nodded. "It's pretty bad, isn't it? A lot worse than the Saddlebag Bar or the Rusty Bucket."

Brent paid their bill, then guided Jenna through the crowd of sweaty drunks and glassy-eyed junkies, keeping his arm firmly and protectively around her. He wasn't armed; didn't usually carry a weapon on him. But right now, he wished he had a gun. There was a rifle in the truck, but the truck was outside in the parking lot. He'd been crazy to have stayed here for a couple of hours. The minute he walked into this joint and saw what it was all about, he should have taken Jenna away.

Two smiling Mexican youths blocked the exit. Damn! Brent cursed under his breath and silently called himself a fool. The two leered at Jenna, then said something graphic in Spanish. Brent knew just enough of the language to understand their words had been insultingly sexual. Brent tightened his hold on Jenna and stared menacingly at the two guys, hoping his superior height and age might intimidate them just enough so that he could get Jenna past them. Their smiles vanished, but they didn't budge. Brent thought about what he was going to say, translating from English to Spanish in his mind, then he told them exactly what he'd do to them if they didn't allow the lady and him to pass without any trouble. He might have butchered the language, but he got his point across—he would kill to protect the lady or die trying.

First one and then the other man slid away from the exit. Brent rushed Jenna outside before he released a relieved breath.

"Come on, honey, let's go to the truck and get the hell out of here."

"That was scary." Jenna clung to Brent as they ran across the dimly lit parking lot. "What did you say to them to make them back down the way they did?"

"You don't want to know."

A loud clap of thunder rumbled in the distance and faraway lighting streaked the eastern sky. A springtime thunderstorm, Brent thought. And since they were going back to Mission Creek through Laredo, they'd be heading straight into the storm.

Brent helped her into the truck, then got in, started the engine and raced out of the parking lot and onto the road. Jenna slid across the seat until she was at his side, then she cuddled up against him, her hands clutching his arm.

"Do you think you've had enough of wild and wooly roadhouses?" Brent asked.

Jenna shuddered. "I think so. I had no idea places like that existed. I thought the Rusty Bucket was bad. Just goes to show I don't know as much as I thought I did."

"We've got a long ride back to Mission Creek. Why don't you put your head on my shoulder and take a nap?"

She kissed Brent's cheek. "You're wonderful. You know that, don't you?"

"You're pretty wonderful yourself." He spread out his right arm to encompass her shoulders, then pulled her closer.

She laid her head against him, shut her eyes and sighed.

A long, dark stretch of road spread out before them. And the farther east they went, the worse the thunder and lightning. Less than twenty-five miles on the other side of Laredo, the bottom dropped out. The rain came down in heavy sheets, obscuring Brent's vision. The howling wind bombarded the old truck, making it difficult for him to keep the vehicle on the road. Lightning danced all around them, thick, heavy bolts of electricity streaking the black sky and striking the earth indiscriminately.

A deafening clap of thunder roused Jenna from her nap. "My heavens! I can't see anything out the windshield, can you?"

"Not much," Brent admitted. "That's why I've slowed down to a crawl."

"How long has this been going on?"

"Not long. Five minutes or so. If it doesn't let up soon, I may have to pull off to the side of the road."

"Maybe it's just a pop-up shower." Another terrifying streak of lightning hit the earth close by. Jenna gasped.

"Check the radio. See if you can get a weather report for us."

She turned on the radio and scanned through the stations. Static mangled the transmissions, making it difficult to understand what was being said. A word here and there. Storm. Caution. Warning. Take cover. She kept turning the knob, trying to find just one station without static. Finally, she returned to the station that came through a bit clearer than the others. The best she could make out a gully-washer was in progress, with heavy rain, a severe thunderstorm and possible hail.

"I don't think it's going to clear up any time soon," she said.

"Yeah, I'm afraid you're right." Brent slowed the truck from thirty-five miles an hour to twenty-five. The windshield wipers click-clacked back and forth, but fought a losing battle with the rain. "I wish we could find a place to pull in. I know we passed several gas stations and a couple of minimarts coming this way. But I have no idea exactly where we are."

Up ahead a flashing light appeared through the thick sheet of rain. At this distance Brent couldn't tell where the lights were coming from, but they seemed to be to the left of the road. Let it be a 24-hour service station or a cafe, he prayed. Someplace they could pull in, get out of the truck and stay for a few hours until the storm moved on.

"Look, Brent!" Jenna shouted. "Up ahead. On the left. It's a sign of some sort. It must be a minimart or something."

As they crept nearer to the sign, Brent was able to make out the flashing neon letters. *M-o-t-e-l.* He slowed almost to a standstill, then turned left, hoping he was headed into the parking area.

"It's a motel," Jenna said, peering through the windshield. "Twin Pines Motel."

Brent killed the motor, then turned to Jenna. "You wait here and I'll see if they've got a couple of rooms. We can stay the rest of the night and head back to Mission Creek in the morning."

While Jenna waited, she thought about their trip across the border. She'd already grown tired of walking on the wild side. But she'd pretended to want more and more excitement because she had been afraid that if she admitted the truth, Brent would think he'd done his job as her protector and stop seeing her. After what nearly happened at the *La Casa Rojo* tonight, she knew she'd be happy to never see the inside of a roadhouse again. Just thinking about those two guys who'd tried to stop them from leaving sent nervous chills along her nerve endings. But Brent had been so brave—and fiercely protective. She knew just enough Spanish to say hello, goodbye and where is the rest room? But she hadn't needed to know the language to realize that Brent had threatened those men's lives. And they had sensed how serious his threat was.

When Brent jerked the truck door open and jumped inside, a gush of cool wind and chilling rain came in with him. "They had only one room available. They're filled to capacity since so many folks have stopped here because of the storm."

"One room's fine with me." She couldn't suppress a girlish giggle.

"Don't get any ideas, honey. We're taking shelter from the storm and nothing else."

"Whatever you say."

He held up a key. "We're in Room 5." He cranked up the motor and carefully eased the old truck along the one-story concrete building until he found an empty parking place. "We'll just have to get out and hunt for our room."

She nodded, then when he opened the door and jumped down, she slid under the steering wheel and hopped out of the truck right behind him. Brent quickly locked the door and grabbed Jenna's arm.

Making a mad dash up the sidewalk, they ran past Rooms 3 and 4. Brent inserted the key in the lock of Room 5, flung open the door and ushered Jenna inside; then closed, locked and bolted the door.

Once inside the warm, humid, dark room, Brent felt for the wall switch, but found none. The blinking neon sign shining through the open blinds covering the wide window gave off a minimum of light through the rain; but enough so that Jenna could make her away around the room until she encountered a lamp on the nightstand. When she flipped the switch, the forty-watt bulb shined eerily through the orange and yellow striped shade. Brent and Jenna stared at each other, then burst into laughter.

"We look like a couple of drowned rats," he said.

A horrendous clap of thunder boomed nearby. Jenna gasped. "This has to be the worst storm ever. I've never seen such wide bands of lightning. And it's raining so hard, you'd think it was coming a flood."

"My bet is that there's flash flood warnings out." Brent inspected the room, then eased open the bathroom door and peeped inside. "Not exactly the Ritz-Carlton, but it's clean and dry. And there are plenty of towels in the bathroom. Why don't you go on in first and dry off? You can hang your things on the shower rod and maybe they'll be dry by morning."

"Okay. But, Brent?"

"Huh?"

"What am I going to wear after I take off my clothes?"

He cleared his throat. "Yeah, that does pose a problem."

"I don't mind parading around in my birthday suit."

"Well, I mind," he told her.

He opened the tiny closet and took a look inside, then reached up on the shelf and grabbed a cotton blanket. He tossed it to her.

"Here, wrap up in this."

She caught the blanket, then scurried into the bathroom. It took her less than five minutes to strip, hang up her wet garments and wrap the threadbare cotton blanket around her. The thing was so big that it wrapped around her twice and dragged the floor. Picking up the end as if it were a bridal train, she opened the bathroom door and emerged in a regal march.

Brent chuckled. "Very fetching, my dear."

Jenna sucked in her breath. He'd already removed his boots, socks and wet shirt, which he'd hung on a hanger in the open closet. Oh, mercy, he was so gorgeous. Her hands itched to touch him, to caress those broad shoulders and wide, hairy chest.

"Bathroom's all yours," she said.

"Thanks."

While he was in the bathroom, she closed the window blinds, then turned down the bed, fluffed the pillows and made a very important decision. Jenna pulled the condom, which had been in the back pocket of her jeans, from inside the blanket, where she'd placed it between her breasts. She opened the nightstand drawer, dropped the condom inside and closed the drawer. After unwrapping the blanket from around her, she folded it neatly and laid it on the far side of the bed, next to the wall, then she crawled in and pulled the covers up to her neck. Lying there with her damp hair spread out on the pillow, she waited for Brent.

How could he resist her tonight? Hadn't Fate arranged everything just for them? The thunderstorm. The last available motel room, with only one bed.

Brent came out of the bathroom, a white towel draped around his waist. A flush of pure sexual longing heated Jenna from head to toe, peaking her nipples and moistening her femininity. He walked over to the bed, stopped at the foot and studied her for couple of minutes.

"It's kind of warm for you to cover up head and ears," he said. "Besides, if I'm going to make a pallet on the floor, I'll need the spread and the blanket."

"You're going to sleep on the floor? Why? There's plenty of room in the bed. It's a king-size."

He shook his head. "Bad idea, honey. You've been behaving yourself lately, so don't go back to misbehaving tonight."

"What if I promise to stay on my side of the bed and not touch you?"

"I'm not sure I can trust you." Brent looked at the bed, then at the floor and back at the bed.

"I promise that I won't jump you and I won't ask you to make love to me and I—"

"If you come near my side of the bed, I'll toss you out and you'll be the one sleeping on the floor."

"All right," she agreed. "If I come near you or touch you, you can throw me on the floor."

Brent turned off the lamp, then slipped his legs under the covers. Still sitting up, he grabbed the top edges of the spread and blanket, then tossed the extra cover to the foot of the bed. Jenna clutched the remaining single sheet, holding it at her neck. Brent folded his pillow in half, then laid flat of his back, leaving his chest uncovered.

"It's warm in here," he said. "I don't think we'll

need more than this sheet. The guy at the desk said the air-conditioning unit in this room doesn't work. Good thing the rain has cooled things off a lot.''

"I'm not hot," Jenna said. "At least not weather-wise."

"Jenna," he cautioned her.

"Good night, Brent." She flopped over onto her side, putting her back to him.

"Sleep tight, honey."

"Mm-hmm."

She would ignore him, then pretend to be asleep. After that she had to figure out a way for Brent to realize she was naked. And she had to do it without touching him.

Brent lay flat of his back, his gaze riveted to the ceiling. Shadows danced across the surface whenever the neon lights outside flickered, creating varying shades of light and dark through the cracks in the closed blinds. Jenna lay quietly, at least three feet separating them, her back to him. He couldn't believe she'd given up so easily. He'd thought for sure that she'd be all over him by now. What was the matter? Was he disappointed?

Breathing in and out slowly, he shut his eyes and prayed for sleep. The longer he lay beside her, the more he realized that getting into this bed in the first place had been a big mistake. Just knowing that she was within arm's reach, with nothing but a tattered old blanket covering her luscious body had his mind reeling with lascivious thoughts. Fantasize about her all you want, he told himself, but don't touch her. If he touched her, for any reason, he'd be lost. His sex grew hard and heavy. He silently cursed himself for ever getting into this situation in the first place. Meeting Jenna at the Saddlebag Bar a few weeks ago had disrupted his plans and wreaked havoc on his life. Once he'd realized that he was trapped in Jenna's web and had become determined to be her protector, he should have broken free and run like hell. Run all the way back to Chicago.

Suddenly a loud chinking sound brought Brent out of his musing state of mind. He rose to a sitting position. Jenna roused, turned over and lifted her head.

"What's that noise?" she asked.

"I think it's hailing."

"That's awfully loud for hail," she said. "It must be the size of golf balls to make that much noise."

Brent flung back the sheet, got up and headed toward the window. Only when he was halfway there did he realize he'd lost the towel covering him when he'd gotten out of bed. Damn! *Okay, so what do you do now?* he asked himself. Hoping the darkness in the room would conceal his nudity, he moved to the side of the window, lifted the edge of the blinds and glanced out into the night.

"It's hailing all right," he said. "My old truck is taking a beating. Looks like the hail is nearly half-dollar size."

"I thought so."

Realizing that her voice came from directly behind him and not from across the room, Brent spun around to face her. His mouth fell open. His heartbeat accelerated. And his sex jutted forward. Heaven help him. Jenna was naked. Beautifully, gloriously naked. The dim light from the flashing neon sign formed shadows that silhouetted her body.

How much temptation was a man expected to resist? He had fought a good battle for weeks now, warning himself not to let his baser instincts take over. Hadn't he protected Jenna, kept her safe, done Flynt a favor and denied himself what he really wanted? And he did want Jenna. Desperately.

"You shouldn't," he said. "We can't."

"Why can't we?" she asked, her voice seductively low. A sultry whisper in the darkness. "We're both consenting adults."

"It would be sex. Are you willing to accept that?" A part of him wanted her to scream no, but another part of him—the selfish, horny bastard part of him—longed for her to say yes.

"I want you, Brent. Anyway I can get you."

Releasing a quiet huff, he forked his fingers through his hair and glanced down at the floor. He'd been at war with himself for weeks now, battling his own desire. But the war was over. He just didn't know whether he'd won or lost.

He lifted his gaze to meet hers. "I don't have any protection."

"I do."

''What?''

''I put a condom in my pocket...just in case.''

''Jenna...Jenna. What am I going to do with you?''

''Whatever you want to do. I'm all yours.''

He made the first move. He touched her. A tender caress across her cheek with the back of his hand. She swayed toward him, but didn't press up against him.

The hunger inside him swelled and expanded until he was ravenous, his need riding him hard. He was powerless to stop the inevitable. With the warm, humid darkness cocooning them, Brent reached for her and brought her into his arms, taking her swiftly and completely. They grasped each other, their naked bodies touching, rubbing, blending together in sexual pleasure. With one hand clutching her hip, he lifted the other to cup her head. Leaning down, he claimed her mouth. She held him to her, accepting his marauding lips, giving herself over to the moment.

Kissing, caressing, making guttural mating sounds, they released the pent-up desire that had been building for weeks. Brent lifted Jenna up and into his arms, then carried her across the room and laid her on the bed. She looked up at him in the semidarkness and held open her arms. He accepted her welcoming invitation, coming down over her, bracing his big body with his hands so that he wouldn't crush her. Instinct urged him to take her now, to part her legs and thrust into her. He ached with the need to be inside her.

But some small measure of sanity remained, not yet

controlled by pure masculine passion. ''Where's that condom?''

''Nightstand drawer.'' Jenna lay beneath him, her fingers exploring his shoulders, her breasts rising and falling provocatively with each breath she took.

Lifting himself up onto his knees, Brent twisted just enough to reach the knob on the drawer, then jerked the drawer open and grabbed the condom. As he unwrapped the shiny cover, his hands trembled the way they had when he'd been a teenager and had used a condom for the first time. Damn, why was he so nervous? Because this was Jenna. Because he wanted her more than he'd ever wanted anything in his life. And because she was a virgin.

After sheathing himself he turned back to Jenna and the look in her eyes stopped him cold. She stared at his sex and then up at his face, an expression of uncertainty combined with adoration in her eyes.

''Honey, are you sure about this?''

She nodded her head. ''I'm sure. But please remember that I've never—''

He silenced her with kisses. Soft. Tender. A gentle trail from mouth to cheek. From neck to ear. ''I know. And I promise to make it good for you.''

Jenna's needs came first, before his own. Her satisfaction was all that mattered. At least for now. His fulfillment was a foregone conclusion. Hers was not.

Jenna had dreamed of this moment and yet now that it was happening, it didn't seem real. Lying naked in bed with Brent seemed like a fantasy. And it was. A fantasy come to life.

He explored her body with his hands and his mouth, learning where she was soft and where she was hard, finding the moisture of her mouth and the wet depths of her femininity. Her breasts swelled, her nipples hardened to tight points...and when his calloused fingers flicked and his tongue laved, she bucked up, lifting her hips. His caressing, tormenting motions continued, teaching her the true meaning of wanton desire. Coiled tightly, pulsating with need, her body beckoned his as she flung her arms around his neck. Brent tested her, dipping two fingers inside, before advancing their lovemaking.

"My beautiful Jenna," he murmured as he cupped her buttocks and lifted her to meet him.

She tensed when his sex stroked her intimately, then sought entrance. He waited a moment before easing inside her. She gasped at the sensation of fullness, yet realized he was not completely embedded within her. She kissed him, then licked his lips before plunging her tongue into his mouth. Her actions apparently pushed him over the edge. He tightened his grip on her hips, partially withdrew and then thrust deeply and fully, burying himself to the hilt in her hot, receptive body. Pain radiated from her core to throughout her body. She whimpered. Brent kissed her again and again as he whispered honey-coated endearments, reassuring her, coaxing her, guaranteeing her satisfaction.

He moved inside her, cautiously, then when she breathed deeply and sighed, he set a steady, undulating rhythm. The pain subsided, replaced by sensations that promised pleasure. She listened to his labored breathing, felt his rapid heartbeat and caught glimpses of the intense expression on his face. For the first time in her life, she experienced the joy of possessing power. The power a woman wields over a man who wants her. A spiraling tension built between her legs as he moved up and down, in and out, putting friction on her most sensitive spot. His mouth sought her breast, then sucked greedily, adding fuel to the flame burning inside her.

As her fingers curled over his shoulders, she moved with him. He increased the pace, moving harder and faster. Her whole body tensed, poised on the edge; with one more stroke he pushed her over and into the abyss. Neither body nor mind existed, only sensation.

Indescribable pleasure. Total fulfillment. While aftershocks bombarded her, Brent hammered into her repeatedly. Fast and furious. Then he let out a long, guttural groan as his climax hit him full force. Jenna clung to him, kissing him, loving him more than she thought possible to love anyone.

"Oh, Brent, I love you so much."

He eased off her, pulled her into his arms and caressed the side of her face with his cheek. Sated and happy beyond her wildest dreams, Jenna lay in his arms, her eyelids drooping as relaxation claimed her. Within minutes she was fast asleep.

Chapter 8

They had made love again at dawn, with the pink glow of a new day seeping through the thin blinds. He had taught her how to pleasure him as he did her, without risking consequences, since they had used their only protection hours before. And once again she had told him that she loved him and he had kissed her, held her, but had not responded verbally to her confession of undying love.

At eight o'clock he had woken her and told her to hurry and get dressed. He'd been fully clothed.

"I got coffee and cinnamon rolls out of the machine in the office," he'd told her.

They had eaten quickly, neither of them saying much of anything. She'd waited for him to mention what their lovemaking had meant to him, but he had acted as if nothing extraordinary had happened between them, as if they'd done nothing more than sleep during the night. Confused by his attitude, she'd kept quiet then and even later as they headed back to Mission Creek. Brent had turned on the radio, letting the loud music fill the cab. And she had been aware of the fact that he wouldn't look directly at her.

Why was he acting so distant and uncaring? She refused to believe that he had used her and was now discarding her. Brent loved her. She knew he did. He had been a tender yet passionate lover, initiating her into the rites of womanhood with pleasure and fulfillment. As long as she lived she would remember what it felt like to make love with Brent Jameson.

When he pulled the truck into the parking slot in front of her apartment, Jenna thought surely he would explain himself, but he didn't.

"Brent, what's wrong?"

"Nothing, honey. It's just that you promised me you wouldn't think what happened between us was anything more than sex and I expect you to keep that promise. I want to believe that when you told me you loved me, it was just because I'd given you pleasure and you felt that it was what you should say."

"Oh, I see." A thousand pound weight pressed in on her, breaking her heart and threatening to cut off her life's blood. Pain unlike any she'd ever known saturated every inch of her body and flooded her mind. "Of course. It was only sex."

Brent reached across her, without touching her, and opened the passenger door. "I...uh ...I hope you've sown enough wild oats with me to satisfy you. You should get back to being Miss Jenna Wilson, social butterfly and Mission Creek debutante."

She nodded and forced a weak smile to her lips. Inside she was dying. Slowly. Painfully.

"Look, honey, I know I sort of said I'd take you to that deb ball, but I—er—I'm not going to be around then."

She stared at him, wondering who this man was sitting next to her. It couldn't be Brent. The man she loved. The tender, caring lover who had taken her to heaven twice in the past eight hours.

"I'm heading out of Mission Creek tomorrow," he said. "I got a better offer and I'm moving on."

"Goodbye, Brent. It's been..." She jumped down out of the truck and ran as fast as she could. She had to get away from him before she made a complete fool of herself. *Oh, God, you idiot, you've already made a fool of yourself!*

"What happened?" Flynt Carson demanded. "Why are you in such an all-fired hurry to go back to Chicago?"

"Let's just say that I've done all the damage here that I can do."

Flynt laid his hand on Brent's shoulder. "I thought you were going to stick around long enough to take Jenna to the deb ball."

"Plans change." Brent shrugged off Flynt's hand.

"When a man gets in as big a hurry as you're in, he's usually running scared. So, what's going on? Are you growing a little too fond of Jenna and you're leaving before you're unable to resist her?"

"Yeah, something like that."

"Are you leaving her heart intact or are we going to have to pick up the pieces?"

"Look, just find her an escort for the ball, will you?"

"Sure. No problem. There are dozens of guys who'd love to date Jenna."

Yeah, he didn't doubt that for a minute and the thought bothered him more than he wanted to admit. She'd been his, heart and soul as well as body. He didn't like the idea that any other man would ever have with her what he'd had.

Brent finished packing, zipped up his bag and held out his hand to Flynt. "Thanks for everything, man. Look after her, will you? Make sure she doesn't get into any more trouble."

"Sure thing. And if you want to call me to check on her…"

Brent forced a grin, then shook his head. "A clean break is better for both of us."

* * *

"Of course you'll attend the ball," Nelda said. "Flynt Carson has assured me that he'll have a suitable young man come by tomorrow evening to pick you up. He told me that he had the perfect person in mind."

She had tried to convince her mother that the last thing on earth she wanted to do was attend the ball. She was hurting in every way a woman who has been rejected by the man she loves can hurt.

"Mother, you don't understand what it's like to be in love with a man who doesn't want you."

"What makes you think that I don't understand?" Nelda took Jenna by the arm, led her over to the sofa and sat beside her. "When I was eighteen, I fell head over heels for one of the hands on my daddy's ranch."

"Mother! I had no idea."

"It didn't work out, of course. He wound up breaking my heart. But I met your father, married him and we had a very good life together. So, you see, in the long run, it was for the best."

Jenna hugged Nelda, feeling for the first time that she'd gotten a glimpse at another side of her mother. A side she never knew existed. "I'm sorry that you got your heart broken."

Nelda patted Jenna's cheek tenderly. "And I'm sorry that you got your heart broken. I could say that I told you so, but I won't. Attending the ball would be the best medicine for your heartache. You can't let that good-for-nothing cowboy ruin your special night.''

"All right, Mother, I'll attend the ball.'' There was no way she could tell her mother that Brent Jameson had ruined more for her than the debutante ball. He had broken her heart, crushed her dreams of love and taught her that she'd been a fool for expecting a happily ever after ending to their romance. "Call Flynt and tell him to arrange for that suitable young man to meet us at the country club. I do not want a date, just an escort.''

"All right, dear, whatever you want.''

"Thank you for being so understanding.''

Nelda cupped Jenna's chin. "I'm sorry that I've been so demanding, especially since your father died. I promise that I'll try my best not to run your life, but you must promise me that you'll be patient with me. I can't change overnight.''

"I promise.'' Jenna hugged her mother again. "We'll both do our best to keep those promises.''

The ballroom was on the third floor of the country club, with a double row of windows across the front that looked out over the driveway and gardens. A balcony off the ballroom, filled with potted plants and settees, provided perfect secluded spots for couples who wanted a little privacy.

Jenna fidgeted as she waited on stage with the other debutantes, all of them lined up in their expensive white dresses. *Little innocents being presented to society,* Jenna surmised cynically. A lively rendition of the national anthem and *Texas, Our Texas* kicked off the ceremonies. A salute to the flag followed, then Mrs. Donald Adair gave the welcoming address.

Where was her escort? Jenna wondered. Flynt had promised that he'd arrive on time. Flynt hadn't even given her mother a name; he'd just told that it was someone Jenna knew and liked and would recognize immediately. Why all the secrecy? Oh, God, she hoped it wasn't Ernest Townsend. If it was, she'd be miserable, but her mother would be ecstatic. The Townsends were old oil money and Ernest was also an only child. Surely Flynt wouldn't do that to her. But what if it *was* Ernest?

Okay, so she was going to be the only deb without an escort, without a young man to join her at the dinner table. She could live with the embarrassment if her mother could. At least Uncle Lyndon had flown in from San Antonio to lead her out. She knew Nelda had twisted her older brother's arm to persuade him to fly in for the occasion. Tonight Jenna missed her father terribly, but at least she wouldn't be the only deb with an uncle, brother or stepfather standing in for a nonexistent dad.

Since the debs were presented in alphabetical order, Jenna waited nervously, with Uncle Lyndon at her side, as she counted the minutes until this part of the night's events ended. Finally the list of names made it down to the *W's*.

"Judge Lyndon Walker Kerr presenting Jenna Kerr Wilson," the announcer said into the microphone.

Her uncle took her arm in his. As he led her out, she looked into the audience and her gaze met her mother's. For that one sweet moment she was glad to be there, because the happiness radiating from Nelda made all the misery worthwhile. Another generation of her family had been properly presented to society.

After everyone made it through the reception line, a fancy steak dinner was served by black-jacketed waiters. Nelda glanced at the empty seat beside Jenna.

"I don't understand what happened," Nelda said. "Flynt promised me your date would be here on time. I'll have to find Flynt later and give him a stern reprimand."

After dinner came a video presentation of the debs' individual good works during the past year and the cake-cutting ceremony. Jenna dreaded her turn, but when it came, she stepped up to the microphone and expressed her heartfelt gratitude to her mother and then to all those who had helped make her debutante year a marvelous, unforgettable time. Such a bald-faced lie. She just kept smiling.

At long last, the band played the first waltz and Uncle Lyndon led her onto the dance floor for the customary father-daughter dance. Jenna kept telling herself to just hang in there. A couple more hours and she could go home, but for now she had to keep up the happy facade for her mother's sake. As the first song ended, Uncle Lyndon gazed over Jenna's shoulder. She felt someone's presence directly behind her. Was it her long-lost date showing up finally? At this point, she didn't even care if it turned out to be Ernest Townsend.

"Sorry I'm late," a familiar voice said. "My plane was delayed."

Jenna whirled around to face the tall, handsome cowboy who had left her brokenhearted only a few days ago. But tonight he bore little resemblance to a ranch hand. This impeccably groomed man looked right at home in an Armani tuxedo. "Brent?"

"Hi, honey. I guess I missed most of your big night."

"What—what are you—?"

"I'm your date. Flynt Carson arranged for me to be your escort tonight." Brent looked at her uncle. "Sir, may I have this dance with your niece?"

Lyndon nodded, apparently relieved not to have to dance again. "Certainly, young man."

Brent led her into the next dance, holding her close. He nuzzled her ear. "Do you think you can forgive me for being such a stubborn idiot? Honey, I ran like a scared rabbit, afraid of being caught and caged. I've never felt about anyone the way I feel about you. It took me only a few days back home in Chicago to realize that I couldn't live without you."

"Oh, Brent. Are you saying that you…that you love me?"

He waltzed her about the room. "I'm crazy in love with you, Jenna Wilson, and if you'll let me, I'll spend the rest of my life making you the happiest woman in the world."

"I suppose you know that sounded like a proposal."

"Consider it just that."

He grasped her wrist, then led her off the dance floor and out of the ballroom. Finding a secluded settee on the balcony unoccupied, he eased her down onto the velvet sofa, then knelt on one knee before removing a small velvet box from his tuxedo pocket. When he flipped open the box, a two-carat, emerald cut, yellow diamond winked at her.

Jenna gasped.

"I love you, Jenna. Will you marry me?"

She flung her arms around him. "Yes, yes, yes. A thousand times yes."

He rose from his kneeling position, sat beside her and slipped the brilliant diamond on the third finger of her left hand. "Do you like it?"

"Like it? I love it. But, Brent, how on earth can you afford something this expensive? And what did you mean about going home to Chicago? I thought you were a Texan."

"I am a native Texan," he told her. "But I live in Chicago. I'm a commodities analyst who specializes in the cattle industry. I took some time off to work, incognito, on a couple of ranches to get in touch with my roots and do a little hands-on research.''

"You aren't a cowboy? You're a commodities analyst?''

"I'm a rich commodities analyst. That's how I could afford the ring.'' He nodded to her hand. "Do you think you'd mind leaving Texas to live in Chicago? I've got friends who could probably get you a job at one of the museums downtown.'' He cupped her face with his hands. "Remember telling me that you wanted to paint? As your husband, I'd support you in every way to help you achieve your career goals.''

She kissed him, not caring who saw them or what anyone might think or say. When they were both breathless, they came up for air.

"I can't believe this. After I thought I'd lost you forever, you've come back and are making all my dreams come true.''

"This is just the beginning. The best is ahead of us. Our wedding. Our honeymoon. The rest of our lives together.''

She clasped his hand. "Brent, I'd like to wait until after we tell my mother that we're getting married before you explain to her who you really are. I know it's mean of me to want to hear her fuss and fume for a few minutes. But it serves her right. Besides, once she knows that you're rich and successful, she's going to be overjoyed.''

"What about you? Are you disappointed because I'm not really a cowboy?"

"Ah, but you are a cowboy at heart. You're my cowboy." Jenna stood, tugged on Brent's hand and said, "I should dance a few more dances before I leave. But after that, we can go to my apartment. Dana and Katie went home for the weekend, so we'll have the place all to ourselves."

Brent followed her into the ballroom. "Do you have something particular in mind for later?"

"I'm interested in taking another wild ride on my favorite cowboy," she whispered. "Before I become an old married lady and settle down with my husband in Chicago."

He swept her onto the dance floor, holding her securely within his embrace. "Jenna, honey, your wild ride is just beginning."

REINVENTING MARY
Christine Rimmer

For Vilma...

Chapter 1

"How about a nice, tall glass of cold tea while you wait, Mr. Campbell?" asked Margaret McKenzie.

Mary Clark, cowering behind a 50%-off rack in the ready-to-wear half of Mission Creek Creations, hunched down a little lower and whispered prayerfully, "No, no. *Please,* say no..."

"Cold tea sounds wonderful," James Campbell replied.

Mary winced and scrunched down even farther behind the rack. "Say, *I'll get it myself,*" she chanted low, willing the big, handsome man in the pink brocade chair to repeat after her. *"I'll get it myself, I'll get it myself...."*

But the object of Mary's impossible months-long crush said no such thing. And Margaret—Mary's boss and dearest friend in the world—advised brightly, "Mary will get it for you—Mary?"

To Mary, the silence that followed was truly deafening. And acutely painful. No escape, she was thinking, not this time.

That one other time he came in the shop, back in January, she'd been quicker. She'd darted into the stockroom and stayed there until he was gone. She'd been lucky; no one seemed to notice her absence.

But today, clearly, her luck had run out.

"Mary?" Margaret called again, a faint note of concern creeping in.

Ridiculous, Mary thought. I am ridiculous.

Adjusting her glasses more firmly on the bridge of her nose and then nervously smoothing her hands down the front of her gray skirt, Mary straightened from her crouch, thinking, *As if he'll even notice me. As if he even knows that I exist.*

A customer near the shoe display a few feet away gave Mary a distinctly puzzled look as she emerged from behind the sale rack. Mary slanted the woman a sheepish smile and then hurried to answer Margaret's call.

"She must have gone in back," Margaret was saying as Mary popped around the end of the half-wall that marked off ready-to-wear from the Mission Creek Creations originals side of the shop.

"Uh. No. I'm right here." Her voice was tight and absurdly squeaky—but at least she'd managed to get the words out.

"Ah." Margaret smiled benignly. She seemed completely unaware that her assistant had been huddled behind last season's leftovers, hoping against hope to avoid the possibility of coming face-to-face with the man who haunted her dreams. "There you are. Will you get Mr. Campbell a glass of cold tea?"

"Oh. Yes. Right away." Whew. A little breathless-sounding, and far too eager, maybe. But not bad. She'd got the words out good and clear, at least. No convulsive swallowing or odd squeaky noises.

Maybe he wouldn't think her a total idiot, after all.

Well, of course he wouldn't. How could he? He didn't even seem to know she was there. He was smiling that wonderful, warm smile of his—at Margaret. Mary was a *function* to him. Invisible. Someone to ring up purchases, to serve him his tea.

And that was fine with Mary. It was. Truly…

"Sugar?" Margaret offered.

"No, thanks," he said in that deep, sexy voice of his. "Just the tea is fine."

Right then, the louvered doors of one of the dressing cubicles swung wide and Julie Campbell, James's younger sister, floated out wearing a strapless white ball gown with a bodice of lustrous silk and a skirt like a cloud.

Margaret sighed. "Ah. Just lovely…"

"You look gorgeous, Jules," said James with satisfied a nod.

It was a dress made specifically for dancing the night away. Julie would wear it to the Lone Star

County Debutante Ball, a gala event held in May every year at the posh Lone Star Country Club.

The pretty eighteen-year-old blushed and twirled in a circle, and layers of sewn-in crinolines fanned out beneath a froth of organza, like the petals of a blooming rose. "Oh, Mrs. McKenzie! I love it! I do!"

Though she was just three years older than Julie, right then, Mary Clark felt like a crone. A terminally shy old maid—too thin, too plain, too utterly, completely bland, someone who would never in a million years dance the night away at the debutante ball.

Margaret was frowning in the direction of Julie's feet. "Where are your shoes, hon? Did you bring them?" Julie Campbell had bought her shoes at the shop, too, the last time she came in to be fitted. They were by a certain very exclusive designer, and Mission Creek Creations was the only place in town a girl could buy them.

Julie giggled. "They're in the dressing room. I got so excited, I came running out without putting them on—just give me half a second." She whirled back into the dressing room and emerged a moment later. "Okay." She lifted her skirt enough to show off a pair of beautiful white satin T-strap sandals. "James. Aren't they gorgeous? They're Gabrielle Amalfi, did you know?"

"Impressive," James said in an indulgent tone.

Margaret commanded, "Here, now. Step up on the platform in front of the mirrors, and let's take a look at that hem."

Still laughing, Julie twirled her way over to the three-way mirror—and Mary remembered that she was supposed to be serving up that glass of cold tea.

Mary scurried to the refreshment table situated in the front corner of Margaret McKenzie's store. There was ice in the bucket and cold tea in one of the two silver urns.

Mary picked up the silver tongs and transferred ice from the bucket to a tall glass. Next, she poured the tea.

And then she couldn't help wondering, what about lemon? Would he want lemon? The bright yellow slices looked so inviting....

But no. He'd said just the tea. Better to simply give him what he'd said he wanted. She certainly wasn't about to trot back over there and *ask* him about it— to risk squeaking at him or finding herself speechless before him.

After all, so far, so good. He didn't even know she was there. And wasn't that just what she wanted?

Mary took the cold glass firmly in one hand, grabbed one of the small pink napkins with the other, sucked in a deep breath and straightened her shoulders. Then she turned, pointed herself in James Campbell's direction and launched herself toward his side of the room.

He was still sitting in the wing chair, watching Margaret pin up that endless froth of organza and crinoline. When Mary got to him, she dared to cough— very discreetly, of course.

He glanced her way with an easy smile. ''Great.''
He held out one incredible, large, finely shaped hand,
a hand with shiny brown hairs dusting the back of it.

Mary gulped and passed him the tea. His fingers
brushed hers—the lightest breath of a touch—and he
had the glass. She gave him the napkin, too.

''Thanks,'' he said.

Her skin seemed to burn where it had made contact
with his. Her heart felt as if it had stopped dead in her
chest.

And James Campbell had already turned away.

That evening, after locking up the shop, Mary and
Margaret rode home together, as they often did, in
Margaret's van. Their two-story wood frame houses
sat, side-by-side, on tree-lined Rose Street right in the
heart of the South Texas town of Mission Creek, not
all that far from the shop, which was on Main. Margaret lived in the house she'd once shared with her
dear, departed husband, Kyle. Mary's house had become hers when her parents died.

Mary helped Margaret carry in the gowns they'd
brought along to work on that evening. Then Margaret
invited her to stay and share the evening meal.

Mary happily said yes. Sometimes it did get a little
lonely, all on her own in the house where she'd grown
up. Her mother, Anne, had died of cancer two years
ago. Her poor daddy had followed shortly after—technically of a particularly virulent respiratory infection.
But Mary knew better. Justin Clark simply didn't want

to go on without his beloved Anne. Mary's mother and father had been like two sides of the same coin, utterly in love and completely devoted to each other. Mary had grieved to lose them, but somewhere in her heart she'd always known that when one went, the other wouldn't be long in following.

After the meal, the two women sat in Margaret's comfy living room with its big, soft floral-patterned sofa and matching easy chairs, turning hems and sewing beadwork, adding the little hand-stitched touches that made a Mission Creek Creations gown so special and so prized.

Mary had worked for Margaret since she was barely sixteen, when she would put in a few hours at the shop in the afternoons and on weekends. Margaret had had a difficult time, at first, talking the tongue-tied Mary into taking a job where she had to deal with the public. And convincing Mary's overprotective mother to let her precious homeschooled daughter work in a *shop*— now *that* was a feat. Mary's father knew how to manage money. He'd seen to it that there would always be enough. If Mary lived modestly, she'd never actually *have* to work.

But short, round, sweet-faced Margaret could be very determined when she set her mind on a goal.

And Mary had always loved being with Margaret. Around Margaret, somehow, she never got tongue-tied. She never burned with embarrassment, never felt awkward or the least shy. Margaret understood the Clark Curse, as Mary's mother used to call it, that

curse of never quite feeling as if you can cope in a
social situation, never quite feeling *good* enough,
somehow. The curse of sweaty palms and a constricted
throat. Mary's father had been burdened with that
curse and so had her mother, though her mother wasn't
even a Clark by birth. They both considered it a miracle that they had found each other, two agonizingly
shy individuals—he, an accountant, she a brilliant, extremely introverted poet. And they always said it was
no surprise that their only child turned out every bit
as timid and retiring as her mama and her dad.

As they worked, Margaret talked of the day just
past. Was it Mary's imagination, or did her friend
seem to dwell on the subject of James?

"I do admire that young James Campbell." Margaret took three tiny, perfect stitches in a satin bodice,
glanced across at Mary, then bent her graying head to
the satin again. "Not only tall and handsome and so
intelligent with a great sense of humor, but also a truly
good person. Did you know he's taken complete responsibility for Julie in the past year, since that awful
accident?"

Mary *did* know. The majority of Mission Creek's
well-to-do mamas took their darling daughters to Margaret's shop. Those mothers did like to talk. They
loved to discuss the local eligible males—of which
James Campbell was definitely one. Mary had heard
all about how James's parents had been killed in a
pileup on I-35 during a weekend trip to the Dallas area
thirteen months ago.

Margaret clucked her tongue. "There he was, fresh out of law school, just getting ready to start up his own practice, and he loses his parents—and ends up his sister's sole guardian."

Not long after the accident that claimed the lives of his parents, James had hung out a shingle around the corner from Margaret's shop. He walked by the shop all the time, going to and from his office—which was how Mary had noticed him in the first place. She had found herself staring at him as he strode by the wide shop windows, thinking how handsome he was, how self-possessed, how calm and self-assured. *Everything* she wasn't.

Mary knew the first time she saw him that he was a "catch," the kind of man all the mamas in the shop would be talking about. And of course, she had been right.

Margaret had more to say. "I think it's so sweet and admirable, the way he's stepped in to sponsor his sister for the debutante ball, the way he was so thoughtful and came in today, for her final fitting. Julie said he's even volunteered to play chaperone this year.

"And he's such a considerate man, too. He insisted on paying in full today, though the dress won't be ready to pick up until Thursday." Margaret paused, took a few more stitches, then looked at Mary again. "And he's so very handsome too, don't you think? More than one local beauty has set her sights on him, from what I hear."

"I'm not surprised," said Mary mildly, determined

to give no clue of what was really in her heart. What she felt for James Campbell was her own special secret. She would share that secret with no one, not even her dearest friend in the world. "He seems to be a very nice man."

Margaret said nothing, just kept looking at Mary— a very strange look, Mary thought, a much-too-knowing look.

Mary frowned. "What? Is something wrong?"

Margaret set down her sewing. "Can you believe it? This year's ball is Saturday. Only five days away."

"Well, I know that, Margaret."

Margaret stood. "Come with me."

Mary's glasses had slid down her nose. She pushed them back into place and peered suspiciously up at her friend. "Why?"

"I have something to show you."

"Well, now, this is some pretty tricky beadwork I'm doing here and I'd like to get it finished before I—"

Margaret took the dress right out of Mary's hands. "No excuses. Come on." Margaret tossed the dress across the sofa. "I mean it. Now."

When Margaret got that tone, there was no arguing with her. With a sigh, Mary got up. "Where to?"

"To my workroom."

When they reached the door to the big room at the back of the house, Mary's friend said, "Close your eyes."

"Oh, Margaret. Is this really necessary? I really don't think we need to—"

"Don't argue."

"But—"

"Close your eyes."

"Oh, all right."

She felt Margaret's hands on her shoulders, guiding her. "Stand right here."

Mary grumbled out another grudging agreement. She heard the door swing open and the click of a light switch.

"Okay," said Margaret. "Go ahead. Look."

Mary opened her eyes and found herself staring at a dressmaker's dummy in the center of Margaret's workroom. The dummy wore the most incredible dress Mary had ever seen—and working for Margaret, Mary Clark had seen any number of beautiful gowns. It was a curve-hugging floor-length slip dress, the fabric unbelievably supple, like something poured rather than woven, of an impossible, truly marvelous color: white and silver and opalescent simultaneously. Margaret had flipped on a small spotlight above the gown and it shimmered and gleamed, so perfect it seemed it could not be real.

"Margaret." Mary breathed her friend's name in pure admiration. "You have surpassed yourself."

"You like it, then?"

"*Like* it? It's a dream, a wish, a *prayer* of a gown."

Margaret laughed. "Oh, Mary. You sound like your mother, like a poet, I swear."

"Who, Margaret? Who's the lucky deb?"

Margaret only said, "Try it on."

"Oh, no, I couldn't do—" Right then, halfway through her sentence, Mary understood her friend's intention. She gulped, pressed her hand against her throat, and backed up a step. "You're not serious."

"I am. I made this dress for you. It's perfect for you. It *is* you, Mary. It's the you no one ever gets to see."

Mary was shaking her head. "But I don't understand. Why? I have nowhere to wear it."

"Oh, yes, you do."

Mary backed up another step. All at once, her heart was racing and a thousand little butterflies had gotten loose inside her stomach. "Oh, Margaret. No. That's crazy. I couldn't. Never in a million years…"

Her friend only smiled.

"Margaret. Listen. A girl needs a sponsor. And an escort. And besides, I'm too old."

Margaret pursed up her mouth. "Oh, of course. Twenty-one. Positively ancient."

"You know what I mean. All the girls do the deb thing when they're eighteen or nineteen. It's a whole *process*. I can't just…*crash* the deb ball."

"Tell you what. Just try on the dress."

"Oh, Margaret…"

The problem was, Mary couldn't seem to stop looking at that dress. Every time she glanced away, she just had to look back. Astonishing. The way it shimmered—like something alive—in the light from above. It seemed, somehow, to beckon her.

Margaret stood at her shoulder and spoke softly, coaxingly. "Just try it on. You know you want to."

"Oh, Margaret..."

"Just try it on."

That night, at home in her bed alone, Mary couldn't seem to keep her mind on the novel that had held her spellbound the night before. The pages kept blurring, fading away. Without even realizing she was doing it, she let her eyelids drift down and relaxed into the pillows.

And there, on the dark screen of her own eyelids, she saw herself. And not just her everyday, ordinary *boring* self. No. She saw herself as she had looked in Margaret's workroom that night, wearing that fabulous, silver-white dress.

She simply could not get over how perfectly it fit her. And how totally it transformed her.

Like magic. Yes. Exactly. The dress was magic. It wove a spell so powerful, it could make even Mary Clark into someone beautiful.

Margaret had whispered that she could fix Mary's hair for her, and do her makeup, as well. And now she thought about it, why couldn't she just go without her glasses? She *could* see without them—more or less, anyway.

She really did look so different in that dress. Like someone else altogether. With the right hairstyle and makeup, no one would recognize her. It might be her chance for...

What?

She wasn't sure. To be a new woman, maybe. Someone lovely and special—if only for one night.

And James would be there, playing chaperone, Margaret had said so.

Mary's eyes popped open. Her glasses had slid down to the end of her nose. She shoved them back in place with her index finger and sat straight up in bed.

What was she thinking? It was impossible. She could never crash the Lone Star County Debutante Ball...

In the house next door, Margaret sat up late, adding one more special touch to the silvery gown, sewing three white rose petals, symbols of innocence, of secret love, into a hidden pocket in the hem, cleverly tucking them away so that Mary would never even know they were there.

Chapter 2

James smiled fondly down at his baby sister. "Having a good time?"

"The best time of my life." Jules grinned at him as he whirled her beneath the crystal chandeliers in the upstairs ballroom of the Lone Star Country Club.

"That was some program, I have to say."

Jules laughed. The carefree sound pleased him. "Mrs. Adair promised us this would be a night that none of us would ever forget."

"Sounds more like a threat than a promise to me."

"Well, with Mrs. Adair, sometimes it's hard to tell the difference." Frances Adair, wife of Donald Adair of the Houston Adairs, had chaired the deb ball that year. And she took the job seriously. This year's ball was a lot more than just a formal dance. It was, according to Mrs. Adair, a "rite of passage."

"A debutante ball," Mrs. Adair had declared at one of the sponsors' meetings, "is not just an excuse for a girl to dress in a lovely white gown and get lots of attention, as too many, unfortunately, seem to think. A debutante ball is an introduction of a young lady fully into society. A debutante ball tells all and sundry that this girl is now a young woman, a responsible member of her community—and of course, that she will be expected to behave as such."

The ceremonies had begun with rousing renditions of the national anthem and *Texas, Our Texas* as performed by all the debs, lined up in their big white dresses on the bunting-draped stage at the upper end of the ballroom. After the anthem and the song came the salute to the flag.

Next up, the welcome address—given by Mrs. Adair herself. Then the introduction of distinguished guests, including the parents and families of the debutantes. After that, a slide show of deb biographies, followed by the presentation of the debs themselves.

And that was just the beginning.

Black-jacketed waiters served a fine steak dinner. Reverend Fallworthy of Mission Creek First Baptist delivered the blessing.

After the meal, they enjoyed a lengthy video presentation of the various good works performed by the debs during the past year. Then came the cake-cutting ceremony. And finally, each deb stepped to the microphone to express her gratitude to everyone who had made her deb year such a wonderful, fulfilling, memorable time.

Now, at last, the band played and everyone was allowed to dance and have a good time.

James whispered in his sister's ear, "Did I mention I love your dress?"

She whispered back, "Some big brothers always know just the right thing to say."

He pulled away enough to see her shining face again. "You look beautiful. I mean it." He watched the sadness darken her eyes. And he knew she was thinking of their mom and dad, gone for more than a year now, thinking of how this night would have thrilled them. Their mother, Evelyn, would have cried for happiness, and their father, James, Sr. would have shed a tear or two himself—and claimed it was only his allergies kicking up.

"They're here in spirit," James said softly. "Watching over you. And they are very proud."

"Think so?"

"I know so."

The song ended and Jules's escort, her high school sweetheart, Toby Bartholomew, appeared to reclaim her. The band started up again—a fast number this time. Jules picked up her skirts and she and Toby danced away into the crowd.

James made his way to the punch table and served himself a glass of something pink with hunks of rainbow sherbet floating in it. One sip and he decided he would head downstairs to one of the club's bars for a real drink. No one would miss him. Technically, he was a chaperone, but that was merely a formality, a bow to tradition. Mrs. Donald Adair had a real fondness for tradition.

However, this *was* the twenty-first century, and all the debs had reached the age of consent. And should one of them require the intervention of a chaperone, well, each deb did have at least one adult family member in attendance.

James set down his too-sweet drink and started for the nearest exit. He got about five steps when soft fingers closed over his arm.

"James Campbell, I've been wonderin' if you were *ever* going to ask me to dance." Susie Andersen had silky blond hair, a pretty face and curves in all the right places. She was also very grown-up for her eighteen years. The predatory gleam in those china-blues of hers said it all: if he would only pursue her, she'd find a way to get herself caught.

"Hello, Susie." He took the small hand that had grasped his sleeve, wrapped it snugly around his arm and led her out onto the crowded dance floor. She moved into his embrace as if taking up residence there.

He supposed he should have welcomed the feel of her voluptuous little body rubbing way too intimately against his.

But James had grown somewhat weary of pretty, spoiled rich girls coming on to him. Since high school, he'd hooked up with a number of the county belles— women closer to his own age than sweet little Susie here. But otherwise, very much the same: pretty and so feminine. Girls who looked good on a man's arm and even better on the tangled sheets of his bed. They were high-maintenance women. They wanted compliments and thoughtful gifts and to be the center of their man's world.

With them, a relationship was like a game—an important one, with extremely high stakes. They played that game for all they were worth and they expected their men to do the same.

Recently, in the last year or so, after he'd lost his folks and found himself thinking more and more about what really mattered in life, James had started to realize that the relationship game bored him silly—at least as it was played by the pretty, spoiled daughters of the Mission Creek elite.

James smiled to himself. He was twenty-six. A little young to be so jaded.

But lately, he'd been thinking a lot about how empty the house would seem when Jules went to Austin for college in the fall. He'd been hoping that maybe, soon, he'd find someone he could *talk* to, a real companion, a friend as well as a lover.

Susie sighed and looked up at him dreamily. "You are a wonderful dancer, James. A girl feels like she's floating right off the ground with you."

He grinned and told her how good she looked in a bikini—among the slides earlier, there had been one of her and two other debs back when they were toddlers, splashing in a wading pool.

"I was only two then. You should see me now."

"Is that an offer?" As soon as the question escaped his mouth, he wondered why he'd asked it. It got to be kind of by rote after a while, he supposed. He knew every move in the game and he played it without a second thought.

"Oh, yes," she whispered. "It's most definitely is an offer…." That gleam in her eyes was harder and brighter than ever.

And the song came to an end. Deck Holloway, quarterback on the Mission Creek High football team—and Susie's escort, if James remembered right—came striding toward them.

"Here's your date," James said mildly, feeling nothing short of rescued by the younger man.

Susie let out a little huff of breath. "Oh, don't worry about Deck. I'll get rid of him and we can—"

James peeled her hand off his shoulder and stepped back. "Thanks for the dance."

"But—"

"Hey, Deck. How's it going?"

"Just fine thanks, Mr. Campbell. Come on, Suze. Let's dance." Deck grabbed Susie's arm and hauled her off into the crowd.

James shook his head and turned for the exit again, promising himself that he would not, under any circumstances, dance with another deb that night. He would go downstairs to the quiet, dim bar off the lobby and he would order a bourbon and branch water and he would sip it slowly and he would think about what he really wanted in a woman, about friendship and someone to talk to and—

Right then, he saw her.

She stood just beyond the entrance to the ballroom, in the wide aisle that led out onto the moonlit balcony and the curving staircase to the lobby below, the most beautiful creature he'd ever set eyes on. She was tall, very slim and striking, with small, perfect breasts and a long, sinuous waist, a woman for whom the word "elegance" might have been coined. Her features were delicate, fine-drawn—except for the wide, tender mouth and the huge cat eyes. Her dark hair had been smoothed up into a sleek twist and the gown she wore clung to every singing curve, glittering and gleaming like new snow under a winter moon.

So much for trying to find a woman he could *talk* to, James thought wryly. A woman who looked like that didn't have to be able to talk.

She stood alone. He couldn't decide if she looked charmingly unsure as to what to do next, or if she merely waited for something to happen. Or for someone—her escort maybe—to come and claim her.

What the hell was she doing here? He knew all the debs and she wasn't one of them.

But then again, who cared where she'd come from? She was here, at the Lone Star County Debutante Ball. And he intended to meet her.

Now. Before whoever had been foolish enough to leave her waiting alone had a chance to come back and sweep her away from him.

He started toward her, weaving his way through the crowd. It wasn't that far. It only seemed to take forever to make it to her side.

But at last, he was there.

"Were you waiting for me, maybe?" he heard himself ask. Damned if she wasn't even more beautiful close up, her skin translucent, with the lightest dusting of adorable freckles at the bridge of her nose, her eyes a rich and golden brown.

She blinked, as if she hadn't really seen him until he spoke. And then—oh God. She smiled. "As a matter of fact, yes, I was."

She carried a small beaded evening bag on a platinum chain in one hand. He reached for the other hand, which was cool and smooth and sent a flash of heat arcing through him as he imagined those slim fingers sliding over his skin.

Since she didn't object, he dared to tuck that hand into the curve of his arm. "I'm James Campbell."

"Yes," she said, in a tone that teased. "Of course you are."

He stared right into those fabulous cat-slanted amber eyes, waiting for her to say her name. She did, after a moment, though somewhat reluctantly, he thought.

"Olivia." She gave him no last name. Fine. He didn't need it right then. He'd get it out of her soon enough.

"Olivia." He found he liked the feel of her name on his lips. It was a romantic name, he thought. A little old-fashioned and yet also sophisticated. Mysterious, too. Like the woman herself. "Dance with me, Olivia."

"I would love that."

People were staring—probably wondering the same things he wondered: where she had come from, who she really was.

And how he had gotten so lucky.

He thought of that missing escort of hers. The man would come back and find her gone. Then the poor guy would have to go looking for her.

Too bad, James thought. His loss—and my gain.

"This way." He led her through the wide-open doors into the ballroom. The bandleader must have read his mind. A slow number started up just as he walked her out onto the floor.

She turned into his arms and once he had her there, he realized he was going to find it difficult to let her go. There could be a problem, when that fool who had brought her here showed up.

But no. He was a reasonably civilized man. He could let her go when he had to—for tonight, anyway. He'd get her number before she escaped him. He'd call her tomorrow and they'd take it from there.

She lifted her head from where it belonged—on his shoulder—and looked into his eyes. "What is it? You're scheming."

"More like planning."

"Planning what?"

"You have a last name?"

She hesitated again. Then whispered, "Leigh."

"*L...?*"

"*E-I-G-H.*"

"Olivia Leigh." For a moment, he was certain he knew that name—but then the tenuous thread of recognition broke. He told her, "I like it, your name. I like the sound of it—and I'll need your phone number."

She laughed, a laugh both musical and husky. "I don't think it's really a question of need."

"The hell it's not."

"You have nothing to write with, nothing to write *on.*"

"So? I'll remember it, don't worry."

That amber gaze scanned his face, seeking...what? He couldn't have said. At last, with a sigh—and without giving him what he sought—she laid her head near his heart again.

"You're not getting away from me until I get your number," he murmured into her shining hair.

"Oh, James..." She rubbed her cheek against his shoulder. "I have no desire to escape you."

It was so exactly what he wanted to hear that he didn't push her further right then. They merely danced, their bodies so temptingly close, touching, then sliding away, driving him a little bit crazy, making him hunger for what he knew damn well he wouldn't be getting that night.

His luck held out. The next song was a slow one,

too. He kept her in his arms and they danced another dance.

As he led her around the floor, it came to him that everything he knew about her so far pleased him. He liked the sound of her laugh. And the scent of her, which was fresh, faintly floral. Dewy and sweet—but not *too* sweet. He liked her voice, a little deeper than the average woman's voice. A little husky. If a caress had a sound, it would be this woman's voice. He liked her eyes, her wide mouth, her long, slim body and those beautiful uptilted little breasts.

He wanted her. A lot. It was that kind of blind, groping wanting that a guy rarely felt after his first agonizing high school love affairs. A wanting so acute, it hurt.

He was aroused, had been since that moment she first turned and entered his arms. Luckily, his tux jacket kept the world from knowing how he felt. And he took care not to pull her too close, not to let her know for sure how powerfully she affected him.

The second song ended. And a fast number began.

He stepped back enough to lift an eyebrow at her. "How about if we sit this one out?"

"Yes."

"Something to drink?"

"No, I'm fine, thanks."

He let her move free of his embrace, but kept hold of that slim, cool hand. "This way." He set off toward the main doors that led out of the ballroom again, planning to lead her onto the balcony where they could find a quiet corner under the stars.

He got about five steps and then he almost plowed into Maddie Delarue, the club's events manager.

"Hello, James. Going to a fire?" Maddie was gorgeous, redheaded, still single in her early thirties—and extremely rich. Planning and coordinating the various entertainments at the club was more of a hobby for her than anything else. She certainly didn't need the job. But she did take it seriously. She'd worked almost as hard on the ball this year as Mrs. Adair herself.

"Just headed out to the balcony," he said. "Nice to see you, Maddie. You've done a great job tonight." He clutched Olivia's hand tighter and tried to feint around the redhead.

But Maddie slid a step to the right and blocked his path. "I don't believe I've met your friend." Maddie wore a knowing grin and those bright blue eyes of hers gleamed with questions.

James resigned himself to a quick introduction. "Olivia Leigh, Maddie Delarue."

Maddie offered her hand. Olivia took it, rather stiffly, James thought. Maddie said, "Your name is familiar." She frowned and peered at Olivia more closely. "*You* look familiar. We've met, haven't we?"

"No, I'm sorry. I don't think so." Olivia blinked— and yanked her hand free of his grip. "Oh! Who's that?" Her tone was brittle, aggressively false. "I believe it's Teddy Youngblood." She stared, wide-eyed, toward the main exit from the ballroom. "You'll both excuse me? I just *have* to say hello."

And before he thought to stop her, she was picking up that shimmery skirt and striding swiftly away from him on those long legs of hers.

Maddie chuckled. "She's moving pretty fast, James. Better get going or you'll lose her—oh, and I'd keep her away from Frances Adair. The girl is stunning, but she's not a deb and she's not in a deb's family. Which makes her something of a gate-crasher, now doesn't it? And Frances has been known to bite the heads off of gate-crashers, if you know what I mean."

James heard only half of Maddie's advice. He'd already turned to chase after Olivia before she could vanish from sight.

Chapter 3

He caught up with her right beyond the ballroom doors, midway between the spot where he'd first laid eyes on her and the curving staircase that led down to the lobby. He grabbed her arm, but gently.

She allowed him to catch her, freezing in midstride, hovering undecided for a moment—then, at last, turning toward him, her sleek head bent a little, her gaze cast down.

He moved in closer, spoke for her ears alone. "Sorry. I think Teddy Youngblood has vanished into thin air. Teddy's a strange one that way."

She made a low noise in her throat. "Very funny."

"There is no Teddy, is there?"

She slowly shook her head.

He put a finger under her chin and got her to meet his eyes. "Why did you run off like that?"

"I should have kept going—and you should have let me go."

"Not a chance. And that doesn't answer my question."

"Oh, please. You already know the answer. I don't belong here. I never should have come."

He captured her hand again, wrapped it securely around his arm. "But you *are* here. You *did* come."

"It was a crazy idea."

"I disagree. From where I'm standing, it was a great idea."

"You think so?"

"I know so."

"You...you mean that?"

"I do."

She looked so lost—and yet hopeful, too. Vulnerable, he thought. And that surprised him. In his experience, beauty and frank vulnerability rarely went hand-in-hand.

He led her past the inviting conversation areas in the aisle, toward the wall of high windows and graceful French doors opening onto the balcony that overlooked the grand front entrance to the clubhouse below.

Outside, the night was warm and windless. Not a cloud marred the dark beauty of the wide dark sky. James found a small round iron table in a cozy corner next to a potted palm. He slid into one chair, she took the other.

He was careful not once to let go of her hand. They

ended up leaning close, elbows on the table, hands meeting in the middle.

"Tell me," he said. "Did you come here tonight with someone?"

The puzzled way her smooth brows drew together gave him his answer before she even said a word. "With a date, you mean?" He nodded. She swallowed, then straightened those fine white shoulders. "I came all on my own."

He said exactly what was in his mind. "I'm glad."

"Well." Her incredible face showed pure pleasure. "Then so am I. But I really shouldn't stay very long."

"You've barely arrived. No more talk about leaving. Not for at least an hour or two."

"But I—"

"No, I mean it. Let's talk about you." He cleared his throat. "So tell me. Do you live here—in Mission Creek?"

"Oh, James." Her mouth twisted with distress. "You can't ask me a lot of questions. If you do that, I won't answer. And if you *keep* doing that I'll have to—"

He squeezed her hand. "Don't say it."

She looked at him for a very long time, then she whispered, so softly, *"Don't say it. Goodbye is not a word we know. Between us, there is only, and always…hello."*

He sat back in the chair. "It's a poem, right?" She tugged, as if to pull her hand from his. But he didn't let go. "It's beautiful."

She looked away. In the moonlight, he could see a faint blush on her cheeks. ''It's corny, I know. Old-fashioned.''

He leaned near again, dared to brush the back of his knuckles along the velvet skin of her white neck. She shivered slightly at the touch, which pleased him. Greatly. ''Olivia, don't apologize for the things you love.''

''I'm not apologizing. I'm only…embarrassed, I guess.''

''Why?''

Her eyes were very dark right then, that mouth he wanted so much to kiss drawn down. ''I'm not what you think, James.''

He smiled at that. ''To tell you the truth, I don't know quite *what* to think. And you know what else?'' Now her mouth quivered in a smile half-born. ''Go on,'' he coaxed. ''Do it. Smile all the way.'' And she did. He let out a long breath. ''You are so beautiful.'' He groaned. ''Now, *that* was original.''

She laughed her wonderful husky laugh. ''Some things don't need to be original.''

''Oh, no?''

''No. For some things, all you really need is to mean them sincerely—and what else?''

He frowned, not following.

She helped him out. ''You said that you didn't know what to think, about me—and then you said, 'And you know what else?'''

''Oh. Right.''

"Well?" She made a face. *"What else?"*

He turned her hand over, opened the slim fingers, traced a heart in the center of her palm. "I don't even care—that I don't know what to think. I saw you. And all at once, this perfectly ordinary world was magic."

Her eyes seemed to glow from within. *"Then there was you. Finding me. Magic. Wonder. Eternity."* A small, abashed sound escaped her. "Oh, God. I did it again."

"Keep doing it. It's fine with me." He looked up at the wide starry sky. "We'll just sit here forever, all right? You and me, under the stars. You'll quote me every poem you know. We'll talk and we'll laugh and—"

"You talk," she said. "Please."

"About what?"

"Yourself. Your life. What you long for, what you dream…"

He gave a shake of his head. "You don't want to hear all that."

"Oh, but I do, James. I want to hear it all, everything about you. But mostly, the important things."

"Like…?"

"Favorite color?"

"That's important?"

"Oh, yes. To me. But then, I have to admit. It's *all* important. Every detail. Whatever you're willing to share with me."

"Well then, I'd have to say…the color of your eyes."

"Brown?" She wrinkled up that delicate nose.

"No, not merely brown. Golden-brown, honey-brown. The softest, most *unusual* brown."

"Hmm." She considered a moment, tipping her head to the side. "Unusual brown. That's good. I like that. Tell me about your work."

"I can't."

"Oh, come on. Of course, you can."

"No. You might start telling lawyer jokes. I hate lawyer jokes."

He waited for her to say, *Oh, you're a lawyer, then?* or something along that line. But she said nothing of the kind, which seemed strange—until he realized that maybe it wasn't strange at all. Maybe she didn't *need* confirmation about the kind of work he did. Maybe she already knew.

She put her other hand over their joined ones. "I give you my solemn vow. No lawyer jokes."

So he told her—of his one-man practice, of his secretary whose name was Mona Letterby. "That Mona. A remarkable woman."

"In what way?"

"The word *efficient* must have been created with her in mind."

"And?"

"And what?"

"I can tell by your tone. Something about her bothers you."

"Well, there is one drawback to the perfect Mrs. Letterby."

"And that is?"

"No sense of humor. None. Sometimes I even wish she'd tell a lawyer joke if it would mean she'd crack a smile now and then." He leaned closer again. "I'll tell you a secret."

"Oh, yes. Do."

"Mrs. Letterby intimidates me."

"She does?"

"Yeah."

"How so?"

"I'm afraid I won't live up to her expectations for me."

She looked so sweet and sympathetic—for a moment. Then she made a scoffing sound. "You're exaggerating."

"Well. Maybe a little."

"You wish your secretary would give you a grin now and then, but she's great at her job and she doesn't scare you in the least."

"Have me all figured out, do you?"

"Well, I know you're not the type a snooty secretary can push around. You wouldn't *hire* a snooty secretary."

And how do you know all this about me? he wanted to ask. But he knew, if he did ask, he wouldn't get any kind of real answer. She'd brush it off as teasing— or she'd clam up again.

He supposed he wouldn't particularly mind the first possibility, but he didn't want to take a chance on the second.

"Tell me about your family," she said.

So he gave her the facts. "I have one sister. This is *her* night. She's eighteen and she's a winner—dean's honor list this year, headed for the University of Texas in the fall. I'm her guardian now." He paused. "My parents died last year. A car accident."

"You miss them a lot." It wasn't a question.

He looked down at their joined hands and then up again, at her. "It's strange—when you love someone and then they're gone. The spaces they leave are the hardest to take. The spaces they filled. I mean that literally. I mean things like the *rooms* they were in a lot."

"Oh, I know, I honestly do." Her eyes stared straight into his. "The rooms they loved and lived in are suddenly truly empty rooms. And why is it that their favorite perfumes and aftershaves tend to linger, somehow, never really vanishing completely, so you always have that faint reminder of all that you've lost? Oh, and the places where they liked to sit—their seat at the table, a certain chair at the window—the sight of those places, months or even years after they're gone forever, can break your heart all over again."

She had it right. Just the way it was. He said, "I moved back into my parents' house when they died. It seemed better, for my sister, to have that consistency. She'd lost her mom and dad. I didn't see why she had to lose her home—not yet. She had her senior year ahead of her, and then her college years. Not that long, really, and she'll be out on her own anyway. But for that first year after Mom and Dad were gone..."

"Oh, yes. That was good of you. Sometimes the memories are hard to take, of living where you lived with them. Still, I'm sure it's been better for her, to be in her own home, to have that, at least, remain the same."

She did understand. Too well. He dared to ask, "Was it your parents that you lost?"

That tender gaze slid away. He thought with a sinking in his chest that she would start saying she had to leave again. But then her glance shifted back, met his. He felt a soft sort of jolt—a sensation of connection, as if they were touching on some deeper level than just their joined hands. "Yes. My parents. They were...so much in love, always. It's hard to explain, how much they meant to each other. You know Kurt Vonnegut?"

"The writer?"

She nodded. "He wrote this story, *Mother Night,* about a man who posed as a Nazi while spying for the Allies in the Second World War. This man was totally, completely in love with his wife. He called what they were to each other 'a nation of two.' My parents were that. They didn't need anyone else, as long they had each other. They loved me, very much. But I was definitely *extra* to them. Something precious, but not absolutely necessary, the way they were to each other."

"But that's good, I think—don't you? I think the most important relationship in a family is the one between the husband and wife. That ought to be the center, the primary relationship.''

''Yes.'' She frowned, thinking. ''I do see what you mean. And I agree with you. But maybe my parents were a little...extreme that way—like the man and his wife in *Mother Night*.''

''Extreme?''

''They were...dependent on each other, I guess you could say. I mean, sometimes, for them, it was like the rest of the world didn't even exist. They could relate to each other, but not really to anyone else.''

''How long ago did they die?''

''My mother went two years ago, my father three months later. I think he was happy to go. He missed her so much.'' She looked away, but only briefly. Then her eyes found his again. *''And when I go, come with me. No need to linger here. Alone with all we might have said, hearing the echoes of our laughter. Tasting the memory of our tears...''* She shivered a little.

''You're cold?''

''No.'' She drew in a long breath, looked up at the sky. ''What a night. A perfect night for the debutante ball.''

Her head was tipped back and her long white throat gleamed in the darkness. He wanted to put his mouth there, to taste her skin, to feel the tender flutter of her pulse against his tongue.

She lowered her head. She was looking in his eyes again. ''What do you dream of, James Campbell? Late at night, in your room in the house where you grew up. When you close your eyes, what do you see?''

He smoothed her hand open again and stroked her wrist, her palm, the soft pads of her fingers. ''Nothing all that exciting.''

She laughed, low, for his ears alone. ''Let me decide that.''

''As long as you remember, you were warned.''

''It doesn't matter to me, exciting or not. I just want to hear about your dreams.''

So he told her. ''Sometimes my dreams are worried dreams. That I've lost something and I can't find it and I don't think I'm going to find it—because I don't know what it is.''

''So far, I take it, you *haven't* found it.''

''That's right. So far, I haven't.''

''And what else? What other dreams? Do you ever have dreams of flying?''

''I used to. When I was younger. Not so much anymore. Not in a long time, now I think about it.''

''When you used to dream of flying—did you fall?''

''Never.''

''Did you look down?''

''Not a chance.''

''Maybe that's the secret then, of flying in dreams. Not to look down.''

He twined his fingers with hers again. ''Listen. Hear that?''

''The music, you mean?''

He nodded. "It's a slow song. And I want to dance some more. With you."

For a moment, she was a portrait of indecision, probably fearing the possibility of another encounter like the one with Maddie Delarue.

"If you wait too long," he warned, "the song will end."

That fabulous smile appeared. "All right. Let's go."

They stood as one and went back inside.

When they reached the dance floor again and she moved into his arms, he realized he was happy—happy in a way he hadn't been for a long time. Maybe in a way he had never been. There was so much here. With this particular woman.

Excitement. Understanding. Tenderness. Laughter.

He had wanted her from the moment he first saw her.

But now there was more. Already. In a half an hour at her side. They had danced. And they had talked beneath the stars.

And now he was gone. Finished. Overboard. For the vulnerable Olivia, with her slanted amber eyes and her husky laugh and her tendency to quote wonderful, corny, old-fashioned poetry.

He was gone. And he was glad.

There was no yesterday. And no tomorrow. Only this instant, right now, on the dance floor of the ballroom at the Lone Star Country Club with Olivia Leigh in his arms.

* * *

Mary lifted her head from his shoulder and gave James a tender, dreamy smile. She'd left her glasses in the glove box of her car. Everything beyond two feet away was out of focus. But that was no problem. She could see well enough to get where she needed to be.

She *was* where she needed to be. In James's arms. He held her nice and close and she could see *him* just fine.

And really, what else did she need to see?

Not a thing. Everyone else—the whole rest of the world—could just fade away. That would be fine with her.

She wasn't herself tonight. Oh, no. Tonight she was the beautiful, mysterious Olivia Leigh. She had crashed the Lone Star County Debutante Ball—and she had gotten away with it, gotten just what she came for: the chance to spend an enchanted hour or two dancing in James Campbell's big, strong arms.

The next dance was a slow one. And so was the one after that.

Then James asked her if she'd like some punch. She was a little thirsty by then, so she told him yes.

He led her to one of the refreshment tables lined up near the side wall. "Let's see," he said. "There's something pink. And something purple. And something that looks like it just might be lemonade."

"Lemonade," she said. "Please." He lifted the silver ladle and scooped her up a cupful. She took a sip—and watched as a frown formed between his dark brows. He was looking at something behind her. "What is it?"

"Frances Adair," he said, his fine mouth twisting wryly. "Chairwoman of this year's ball. Headed this way."

Frances Adair. Mary's stomach lurched and her heart seemed to stop dead—then start in again way too fast.

Everyone knew about Mrs. Adair. Everyone talked about how hard she'd worked this year, about her dedication and her respect for tradition. Mrs. Adair would not be impressed with the lovely and charming Olivia Leigh. She wasn't going to grin and see Mary's presence here as a delicious little joke, the way that Maddie Delarue had done.

No. Mrs. Adair would see Mary for exactly what she was—a counterfeit, a phony. A fake.

James took the lemonade from her suddenly nerveless fingers and set it back on the table next to the punch bowl. "Don't even think about it."

"Think about what?"

"Running off."

"I'm not." It was a lie and they both knew it.

He caught her hand and tucked it securely around his arm. "Stick with me. I can handle Frances Adair."

Chapter 4

Mrs. Adair marched right for them, coming to an abrupt stop about three feet away. "James, I wonder if I might have a word with you."

Mary squinted, just a little, trying to see her better. But the woman hadn't moved in quite close enough for Mary's nearsighted eyes to make out any details.

Mary *could* see that the woman had short, dark hair. And she was stocky, like Margaret—but much taller. Five foot ten, at least. Her voice matched her presence. Strong and imposing.

Mary resisted the urge to lower her head and scrunch up her shoulders.

"Frances," James said easily. "What can I do for you?"

There was a silence, a heavy and unpleasant one.

Right then, the band had paused between songs and it seemed to Mary that every last soul in that huge ballroom had turned to stare in their direction, would witness her disgrace.

Then the band started up again and Frances Adair said, "An introduction, I think, to start."

"Fair enough. Olivia Leigh, I'd like you to meet Mrs. Frances Adair." James laid his hand over Mary's and pressed lightly, in a reassuring way. She looked at him, saw his encouraging smile, and made herself smile back. He went on, "Did I mention that Mrs. Adair chaired this event?"

"Yes, James, I think you did." She surprised herself. Her voice was calm. Thoroughly composed. She turned her smile on the big, blurry woman opposite her. "It's great to meet you, Mrs. Adair. Of course, I've heard all about you. Everyone has. You've done a truly outstanding job this year."

"Excuse me? You've 'heard all about me'?"

"Yes. I have."

"Isn't that interesting—considering that I know nothing at all about you."

"Well, there's not that much to know, really...." Mary let the words trail off, thinking how utterly lame they sounded. But what else could she say? She hated to make up a bunch of lies—and she refused, under any circumstances, to reveal her true identity.

"I'll get to the point," said Mrs. Adair with icy contempt. "Ms. Leigh, your dress is white."

It took every ounce of will she possessed. But somehow, Mary resisted the urge to cringe. There was going to be an ugly scene now, she just knew it.

James cleared his throat. "Not *quite* white, Frances. More silvery, I would say."

"White enough. It's traditional, at the debutante ball, that only the debs themselves wear white."

"Oh," said Mary, her heart beating so fast it felt like it might just explode right out of her chest. "I'm so sorry. I—"

"Didn't know?" Mrs. Adair made a humphing sound. "Please. Do you really expect me to believe that?"

No, Mary didn't. She didn't expect the woman to believe anything, she just wanted out of there. She tugged sharply on her own hand. But this time, James was ready for her. He tightened his grip and refused to let go.

"Frances," he said flatly. "If you don't mind, Olivia is my guest."

Mrs. Adair made that humphing sound again. "We both know she's not on the guest list."

"I'm vouching for her." There was steel in his tone now. "She's apologized for her dress. She'll never wear anything close to white at a deb ball again— unless it's her own deb ball. Will you, Olivia?"

Trapped, Mary thought, *trapped and humiliated. What was I thinking? I had to be crazy, imagining I could crash the deb ball, steal one wonderful evening with James and get away without someone challenging me.*

"Olivia?" James said her name softly. With real concern.

It helped, that concern. To think that he cared, that he was sticking by her, facing down Mrs. Adair for her sake.

"No," Mary said. By some miracle, her voice remained calm. "It was a huge error in judgment, on my part, to wear anything even close to white here tonight. And I'll never make that kind of mistake again."

Mary's apology failed to appease the outraged Mrs. Adair. "I want to know what, exactly, you're doing here."

"She's with me, Frances." James's voice was rock-hard, now. "I think that ought to be explanation enough."

The band played on, but Mrs. Adair said nothing for several seconds. Mary understood her silence. She was coming to a decision. Whether to leave it at that, or to order Mary out—which would be a slap in the face to James, a man of substance in the community, well-liked and highly respected by everyone.

Mrs. Adair made her decision at last. "Well." She'd backed off from the brink of fury, but she still sounded severe as a preacher in a room full of prostitutes. "I suppose that's the best I can hope for, at this point."

James said, "All right, then. That's settled."

"You do understand," Mrs. Adair added in a tone dripping with reproach, "I couldn't just let it go without saying something. As the one in charge here, I have certain…responsibilities.''

"It's all worked out," said James. "Olivia, I think I'd like a little fresh air. What do you say to a walk outside? The club grounds are beautiful this time of year.''

"Yes. A walk. Please." A stroll on the grounds, a trip to Timbuktu. Anywhere. As long as it was away from here.

He turned for the exit again, pulling her with him. She hurried to keep up.

James nodded and smiled at people he knew, but he didn't slow his rapid pace to talk to anyone—which was just fine with Mary. Talking to Mrs. Adair had been enough, as far as she was concerned.

They left the ballroom, crossed the aisle to the wide staircase and went down. Then he led her through the club's massive two-story lobby, past the huge central fountain tiled in Texas pink granite. Even moving at such a swift pace, it was a very long walk.

At last they emerged from between the big front doors of the clubhouse, under the giant portico that arched over the curved front drive.

The two doormen saluted. One asked, "How's it going, Mr. Campbell?''

"Fine, thanks," said James.

Mary forced a bright smile for the men. She hadn't had to deal with them when she came in. She'd used a side entrance, through the area adjoining the lobby, what they called the "original clubhouse," former site of the Men's Grill. The Men's Grill had been blown up several months ago—a bomb set by a group of corrupt Mission Creek police officers. The area was under construction now, which meant it was deserted at night and thus had provided Mary an ideal means for sneaking into the exclusive club without being noticed.

James led her out from under the portico and beneath the blanket of distant, silvery stars. "Come on. I'll show you the east gardens. They're incredible. You'll hardly know you're in South Texas. Not a prickly pear or a clump of bunch grass in sight— they're just past the tennis courts. This way..."

But Mary refused to be dragged along any farther. She dug in her heels right there, at the edge of the wide drive, beneath a huge old oak tree. "I'm sorry, James."

He turned to her, his eyes, through the shadows, narrowed and gleaming. "There's nothing for you to be sorry about."

"It's time for me to go."

"No."

"I shouldn't have—"

He put a finger against her lips. "Don't say it." His touch was warm. And gentle as a breath. Tears constricted her throat, to feel that—his flesh pressed to hers. "If you say you shouldn't have come, it's like saying you wish we'd never met."

"No." Mary swallowed, pushing down the dangerous tears. "That's not it. You know it's not. As far as you, and me, well, that's been pure magic. But Mrs. Adair was right. I had no business coming here tonight.''

"Stay.'' His jaw was set. He'd put his hand over hers again.

She shook her head. "I can't. And you have to let go of me. Now.''

A long moment passed. Behind them, from the ballroom, the music poured out into the night, another slow song, one Mary recognized, a song of unrequited love.

He released her and stepped back. "Give me your phone number.''

Oh, how she wanted to do that. She would have risked almost anything to do that—*almost* anything.

But not the inevitability of him learning her real identity.

So far, she'd given him few clues that might lead him to the shy, mousy woman who worked for Margaret McKenzie and could barely bring herself to speak in his presence. If she left now, never saw him again and gave him no way of finding her, chances were excellent he would never have to know that Mary Clark and the fascinating Olivia were one and the same.

And she didn't want him to know. Ever. She wanted to have this too-brief time they'd shared to treasure in her heart for always.

It was enough for her. And it was going to have to be enough for him.

"I can't give you my number, James."

"Why not?"

"Look, I just have to go."

"Damn it, Olivia—"

"Let me go. Let it be."

He only stared at her, that gleam in his eyes suddenly hard and unforgiving.

"Goodbye, James."

Mary stepped around him and set off down the drive beneath the wide canopy of oaks. She'd entered the massive grounds of the two thousand acre country club by a service road Margaret had told her about. And she'd left her car tucked away in a corner of a parking lot not far from the stables. But she wouldn't head in that direction yet—not until she was certain James wouldn't see where she'd gone.

She got about fifty yards when she realized he was coming after her. She could hear his footfalls on the drive. Oh, *why?* Why was he doing that? She'd made it very clear to him. She was leaving. Their time together was done.

She walked faster, refusing to look back.

He picked up his pace, as well.

Her heart beat too swiftly and a dew of nervous sweat beaded her brow. She swiped it away.

What to do now?

No good to halt, to turn, to engage him, to demand that he stop this, that he leave her alone. That would only get them started all over again.

Mary shoved the chain of her evening bag up over

her shoulder, anchoring it there. Then she gathered her skirt in her fists, getting all that silky, clinging fabric out of the way as much as possible. And she walked faster.

So did he, increasing his speed to match hers. She could hear him behind her, moving briskly in her wake. She sent a glance over her shoulder. He paused, a shadowed, blurry figure, perhaps fifteen feet back—and then he kept coming for her.

That did it, the sight of him, relentlessly following her.

Mary clutched her skirt tighter in white-knuckled fists and took off at a run, veering to the left, moving beneath the trees and then out onto the sweet-smelling endless lawn of the Lone Star Country Club, wishing she could see better, scared she would run into something, yet somehow managing to dodge hedges and clumps of bushes when they reared up out of nowhere into her path. She found herself headed for the parking lot, aware somewhere in her frantic mind that James couldn't be allowed to see her get into her car—and yet not knowing where else to go.

He came on behind her, the same as before, quickening his pace to a run—a run just swift enough to keep up with her. Her evening sandals hobbled her. And the grass was so soft. She ran for all she was worth, but she knew it was no good. She would crash into a hedge soon, or trip on her own skirt.

Then she made the mistake of glancing back again, toward the clubhouse lights and the music, toward the man of her dreams, who didn't seem to have the sense to stay where he belonged—in the lovely little fantasy she'd woven around him.

She turned—and tripped, losing her grip on her gathered-up skirt, falling with a sharp cry, facedown in the thick, green grass.

He called to her then, "Olivia!"

She rolled over, got her legs under her and struggled to her feet just as he reached her.

He took her by the arms, a gentle grip, but a firm one, scanned her face through worried eyes. "Olivia, are you all right?"

"Oh, James, why did you follow me?"

His dark brows drew together. "I...I don't know. I just couldn't let you walk away like that, let it end like that, before it's even really begun."

She'd torn the hem of her fabulous dress, but she hardly noticed. James filled up the world for her right then. She looked at him and he looked back—a shared lightning bolt of a look, a look that made the air burn and crackle.

He muttered, "Damn it. Stay, won't you? Just for a little while."

Then he pulled her into his big, strong arms and brought his mouth down to cover hers.

Chapter 5

Never had Mary known such a kiss.

She hadn't even come close. How could she? That kiss was her first. She had never in her life kissed a man. Or a boy. Or anyone, except her father and her mother, on the forehead. Or on the cheek.

Never, ever, full on the mouth.

And James wasn't satisfied just to put his mouth on hers. Oh, no. There was more. So much more.

It was a revelation, that kiss. It gave meaning to words she'd known but, until that precise moment, hadn't really understood.

Words like *desire*. And *lust,* too. Oh. Yes. *Lust.* Definitely.

She felt the hot, probing pressure of his tongue at the seam where her lips met. It thrilled her, to feel that wetness. His tongue was…silky. And yet rough, at the same time. She gasped.

And then she sighed, opening, letting him in.

He made a noise, a low, growling sort of sound. And she heard herself moaning a little, as if in answer to that growl. His arms banded tighter. And his hands caressed her in a hungry, possessive way, molding her waist, sliding up the curve of her spine and then back down again.

She could feel him, down low. She might be a virgin, but she knew what that was down there, knew what it meant, what he wanted of her.

Should she have been shocked?

Probably.

But somehow, she wasn't. Not in the least.

It made her want more.

Made her want to go on kissing him, touching him. To press herself closer to him. His big body radiated heat and need. And she responded with utter, complete abandon, thrusting her small breasts up against his chest, lifting all of herself tight to him, longing to just melt right into him, to fuse her body to his.

Lines from one of her mother's love poems echoed in her mind: *Body to body. Soul on soul. What is this rough and tender magic? This beast between us, shy and bold….*

All at once, he pulled away. She cried out at the loss, at the sudden absence of that incredible kiss.

He took her by the shoulders again, stared into her eyes. She stared back, stunned, thoroughly aroused—

and completely his. His mouth was swollen, his skin flushed. And his gaze claimed her every bit as completely as that kiss had done.

His fingers gripped tighter, digging in just a little. "You'll stay, for a while. Say that you'll stay."

She swallowed, knowing he would expect an answer, yet much too dazed with yearning to actually speak.

"Say it," he commanded.

She blinked, her gaze drawn beyond him, over his shoulder, past the sweep of lawn and the row of oaks and the long, curving drive, to the soaring pink granite front of the clubhouse.

"No," he whispered. "Not back there. We'll go where we can be alone."

Not wise, she thought. Not wise in the least to be alone with him right now.

But then again, what did wisdom have to do with this, with *any* of this, from the wild insanity of her coming here tonight, to the astonishing, erotic kiss they'd just shared?

There was no wisdom in any of it.

And why should there be? Tonight was not in the least about wisdom.

Tonight was magic and wonder. A Cinderella night. Tonight she had shed her real identity like an ill-fitting skin, leaving the stunning Olivia Leigh to take her place, to meet James. And to whirl with him beneath the chandeliers in the ballroom of the Lone Star Country Club, to listen to the secrets of his heart—and to accept his kiss, right there, where they stood, on the sweet wet grass beneath the wide, star-scattered Texas sky.

Wisdom could come later, when she was plain, shy Mary again. There would be years for wisdom—and years to remember this night. Might as well give herself a memory good for a lifetime of dreaming. After all, a chance like this would never come again. After tonight, her dreams were all she would have.

"What are you thinking?" he asked roughly.

She only smiled.

"Say that you'll stay," he commanded again.

Then she remembered Julie. It was, after all, Julie's special night. "What about your sister? Shouldn't you go back to the ball, for her sake? Won't she be worried, when she realizes that you've disappeared?"

"Jules doesn't need me right now. She probably won't even notice I'm gone."

"But what if—"

"Olivia, the ceremonies are over. Jules has an escort, her boyfriend Toby, who brought her here in the first place. Toby will take her home. And we have a live-in housekeeper, so she won't be alone when she gets there—not that it matters, for this one night. After all, Jules *is* eighteen, old enough to be home by herself."

"Still, it seems wrong to—"

"Olivia. Stay."

"You're sure she won't miss you?"

"I am positive. Say that you'll stay."

She'd run out of arguments—and she was glad that she had. "All right. Yes. I'll stay. For a while."

"Good." His big, warm hand slid down her arm. She shivered in pleasure at the long caress. He twined his fingers with hers. "This way..."

And they were off again, racing across the grass. She shoved the chain of her evening bag back up on her shoulder and grabbed her skirt in her free fist, hiking it high to keep it from tripping her again.

Neither of them thought to glance back to the place where he'd kissed her—and it's unlikely they would have recognized anything strange if they had.

Rose petals, after all, are delicate in nature. And by then, Margaret's three petals—white for innocence and secret love, freed when Mary tore the hem of her gown—had been trampled under their careless feet and lay curled to little more than pale, battered slivers on the thick damp grass.

Chapter 6

James led her away from the parking lot, between the lighted tennis courts and the original clubhouse, which was swathed in darkness now. They entered the formal gardens and wound their way through a series of paths lush with blooming roses, tumbling bougainvillea bushes and bright hibiscus, their way lit for them by in-ground lanterns tucked among the greenery. Once or twice, on those paths, Mary heard a woman's laughter and a man's low, answering chuckle. Faintly, she heard voices, too. But they didn't see anyone. And always, on the warm spring night, the music from the ballroom played on, muffled by high, thick walls, yes, but always there, if you listened.

They emerged from the garden onto another stretch of lawn. James pulled her onward, to a wide walk that led up to a gate.

They went through, to a pool area fenced in stone and furnished with rows of cushioned lounges and wrought-iron chairs pulled up to matching round tables shadowed by broad umbrellas.

There was a small building near the fence: the pool bar. The bar was closed and the whole area appeared deserted right then, the lounges all in a line, waiting for lazy sunbathers, the lights at the bottom of the pool shining up into the night, making that eerie, rippling effect as the brightness welled up through the water. More light was provided by round, moonlike globes perched on iron pillars at each of the fence corners.

"Almost there," James whispered. And right then, back in the ballroom, the band started in on something slow and bluesy. James stopped, lifted her hand, brushed the back of it with his lips, making her skin burn where his mouth touched—and her heart stutter in her chest. "Dance with me."

Mary dipped her head in acceptance. And he took her into his arms. They danced, slow and easy, along the wide tiles at the edge of the pool.

Like breathing, Mary thought, her head on his shoulder, a dreamy sigh on her lips. Easy and natural as breathing, to dance with James.

Mary had done very little dancing in her lifetime. Once or twice, her dad had danced with her, in the living room at home. He'd led her across the floor to old standards on the stereo, while her mother watched, tapping her toe, a loving smile on her wide mouth. And sometimes, in her room alone, Mary would dance with one hand against an imaginary broad shoulder and one hand held high, as if cradled in a man's light grip, doing her best to master the basic steps without a partner to take the lead.

James knew how to lead, but he kept it simple, too. He didn't do anything fancy, just a straightforward box step and few waltz-type glides.

They glided past the end of the pool and then he waltzed her in among the deserted umbrella-topped tables. Mary laughed low, delighted, imagining people sitting at the tables, sipping tall, bright-colored drinks garnished with fruit and little paper umbrellas, watching admiringly as James and the lovely Olivia danced by.

The song ended as they danced very close to the pool bar. And he took her hand again, leading her forward toward a green-and-white tent—the round kind, with a high spire on the top—tucked in between the bar and the back section of the stone fence.

"The men's cabana," James explained, and gestured toward an identical tent in the opposite corner. "The women's cabana is over there."

The tent flaps, tied shut, were the kind that could be pulled wide whenever guests used the pool. It was a simple matter to untie them and slip through into a shadowy space furnished with sofas and several chairs, and big, fat pillows everywhere. Mary could make out the shadowy shapes, though poorly, by the light that bled in from outside.

"It's a sitting area, mainly," James explained. "A

pool lounge, more or less, and everybody uses it—
men, women, kids, too—older kids, I mean. There's a
separate pool for the little ones. They call this the
men's cabana because the men's facilities are back
that way.'' He gestured toward the dim area opposite
the way they'd come in. ''A door back there is actually
a gate in the fence and outside the fence are restrooms,
showers, changing areas—all that.''

''You know this club well, don't you?'' she whispered, and then smiled to herself for being so secretive. They were alone here. Somehow, though, the
darkness made whispering seem like a good idea—as
if they were a couple of naughty children, sneaking
around where they shouldn't be.

And then again, why not whisper? They might not
be children, but they *were* somewhere they probably
shouldn't be.

''I practically grew up here at the club,'' James said.
''I've been swimming in that pool out there since I
was old enough to graduate from the little kid's pool
on the west side of the clubhouse. My great-grand-
father was one of the founding members, way back
when Big Bill Carson and J. C. Wainwright kicked in
a thousand acres each to create the club in the first
place. That was a long time ago, before the start of
the feud—you've heard all the old stories, haven't
you? You know about the Carson-Wainwright feud?''

Mary did know. The Carson-Wainwright feud was
the stuff of legend in Lone Star County. Big Bill's
eldest son had loved J.C.'s only daughter, Lou Lou,

and Lou Lou had loved Jace Carson in return. But their great love had gone wrong. Lou Lou Wainwright died a tragic death. And two fast friends became bitter enemies—an animosity that lived on through their children and their children's children.

And beyond knowing the old story, Mary understood that James was testing her, trying to pin her down as a local girl, since a local girl would almost certainly have heard the tale.

But it wasn't much of a trap, really. A girl from out of town might have heard the story, too. So she told him honestly, "Yes. I've heard about the Carsons and the Wainwrights. So sad, really, the way it all got started. All Jace Carson wanted was to have more than his daddy's money to give Lou Lou."

"Don't forget, he did betray her with another woman."

"Yes, he did. But he *was* drunk at the time."

His eyes gleamed with humor. "So. It's okay to betray the woman you love—as long as you're drunk when you do it?"

"That's not what I said. I just meant, well, there were extenuating circumstances. The way I heard it, he was celebrating some successful business deal he'd made and he had more than he should have to drink. And that other woman—what was her name, anyway?"

"Ramona Parks, daughter of Elliott Parks, who was mayor of Dallas at the time."

"Well, I think that Ramona was a schemer. She was

out to trap herself a husband, the way that I heard it. She lured poor Jace into her bed and then—surprise, surprise—turned up pregnant.''

James chuckled. ''And in the end, the truth came out—that the baby she was carrying wasn't Jace's, after all.''

''But the damage had been done,'' Mary said in a mock-somber tone. ''Lou Lou had already drowned herself in despair—which is a little extreme, if you ask me.''

James touched the side of her face with his hand. Heat bloomed at the point of contact. ''You wouldn't…die for love?''

Mary thought of her father, wasting away so quickly, once her mother was gone. Waste. Yes. That was the operative word, though until now, she had never really let herself think of her father's death as a waste. But tonight, posing as Olivia, she seemed to have a fresh perspective on a lot of things. ''No, I wouldn't die for love—or at least, not because my heart was broken. I would…go on. Try to live a full and productive life. I might die to *save* the one that I loved. But life, well, it's just too precious. We should never waste it—or throw it away.''

Warm lips brushed her hair. ''I like the way your mind works, Olivia.''

She laughed. The sound surprised her—surely that laugh could not have come from her mouth. It was low, husky and frankly sexual. She whispered words as bold and teasing as that laugh. "Oh, so it's my *mind* that you're after."

His lips found her temple, lingered there. "I'd say it's the whole package."

"Ah." She pressed herself closer, sliding her hands up over his hard chest to clasp his broad shoulders. "The whole package."

"Yeah. All of you. The way you look, the way you talk. Those poems you keep quoting from—"

"Oh, come on, admit it," she interjected. "You could do without the poetry."

He laughed. "And did I mention your sense of humor?"

"Oh, well, I'm a very funny woman."

"And a certain shyness, behind your eyes. As if there's someone else altogether in there, someone tender and sweet and nervous as a scared kid."

He'd come so close to describing her real self that Mary stiffened.

"What?" he whispered. "What did I say?"

She ordered her body to relax, pressed herself close to him again, because she wanted to—and also, to keep him from dwelling on what might have bothered her right then. "Nothing. Really. I *liked* what you said."

"You did?"

"Oh, yes."

He took her face in both of his big hands, whispered her name—and then he kissed her again, a long, sweet, incredible kiss, one every bit as passionate, as thorough, as the first one. When he lifted his mouth from hers, she swayed toward him, wishing he hadn't stopped, that he would never stop, that they could just go on and on forever, kissing and kissing, until the end of time.

"Come on," he said. "Let's get comfortable." He shrugged out of the fine black tux jacket he wore and tossed it carelessly over a chair. His white dress shirt seemed to glow in the darkness. He pulled off the small black strip of silk at his collar, undid the top two buttons of the shirt and then removed his cuff-links, shoving them in a pocket.

She watched him roll those white sleeves to the elbow, warmth pooling in her belly, a slow, lazy desire claiming her—to run her hand along his forearm, feel the texture of his skin, the muscle underneath.

She did it—so easily. Just reached out, put her hand on his wrist and caressed upward, toward his elbow. Oh, he felt so good, hard and hot, the silky dark hairs lifting as she brushed them against the grain.

He caught her hand before she could pull it away. And he reeled her in to him again.

Another kiss. Their third.

And many more to come. She intended to get a lot of kissing in, before this impossible, perfect night was through. Yes, she decided, they would share so many kisses that she would lose track. Kiss upon kiss upon kiss upon kiss. When the night ended, she would have fifty, a hundred, a *thousand* kisses to remember in the long years to come.

When he lifted his head again, he guided her toward one of the wide sofas. "There are lights in here," he confessed. "But if I turn them on, we're likely to attract the attention of one of the groundskeepers."

"Then don't turn them on. The shadows are nice. And my eyes have adjusted, anyway." That is, as much as Mary's eyes *could* adjust, which wasn't a whole lot. Things would remain pretty much of a blur to her anyway, lights or no lights. Not that she would ever tell him that. As far as he would ever know, Olivia Leigh had 20/20 vision, excellent eyesight to go with her great looks and her fine mind and her naughty-but-utterly-charming sense of humor.

"Sit here."

She took the spot he indicated, on the sofa, brushing her hand briefly against the curving shadow that was the back of it, identifying it: wicker. The cushions were soft and deep and there were throw pillows plumped against the arms and lining the back.

He stood above her, his head tipped to the side in a manner that seemed to say he was studying her.

"What?"

"You look pretty comfortable already."

"Maybe that's because I feel pretty comfortable."

"But there are—"

"What?"

"Those pretty shoes you're wearing."

She bargained, shamelessly, "If I take off my shoes, then you have to take off yours."

"Deal."

They regarded each other. Then she said, "You go first."

"No problem." There was a chair just a foot or two behind him. He sat, untied his shoes, and removed them, pausing when he had them off to ask, "Socks, too, I suppose?"

She waved a hand. "Well, of course."

So he took off his socks, and she wondered why that felt so much more dangerous than when he had only removed his shoes. There was just something so…private, about it. About his being barefoot with her, here in the darkness.

He slid off the chair—and onto his knees before her. "Let me help you."

Her breath got all tangled up in her chest as he lifted her left foot and slid the strap over the curve of her heel. His hand felt so warm and lovely cradling her heel, she almost wished he would never let go. "Pretty toes," he whispered.

And she wiggled them for him. She wore no panty hose—Margaret had seen to that. "You're slim as a willow," Margaret had told her. "And it's a warm night. You don't need stockings. Just skip them."

"You think so?" Mary had asked, unsure.

"Skip them," her friend had said again.

At the time, she'd never imagined what would happen. That she'd end up alone in the pool house with James, and that he would hold her bare foot in his big hands. He set that sandal aside and took her other foot, sliding that sandal off, too, making of the whole procedure something lovely and intimate, deliciously wicked.

That time, before he let go, he slid his hand up the back of her leg.

"Oh!" she exclaimed, a hot little thrill coursing through her at the feel of his palm cupping the swell of her calf. Then she laughed. "I think you'd better come up here and sit beside me." She patted the cushion next to her.

He didn't argue, just swept upward and turned, dropping easily into the place she had indicated. He put one arm along the back of the sofa, and one hand under her chin.

"Another kiss," he whispered.

It seemed like a wonderful idea to her. She offered up her mouth eagerly. He didn't hesitate to claim it.

That time, when he pulled back, he slipped a finger under the gleaming chain of her evening bag. "I think we can do without this." He slid the chain down her arm. She allowed him to take it.

He weighed the bag in his hand. She was close enough to see that he glanced down at it, then back up at her. "I am tempted..."

She took his meaning. "Oh, James."

"There could be important information in here. A phone number, an address. The things I need you to tell me. The things you *haven't* told me."

She tried to tease him from his purpose. "You don't *need* my phone number. Or my address."

But he wouldn't be teased. "Yes, Olivia. I do. There's no other word for it. I *need* them."

She saw she had no choice but to say it right out. "Well, you can't have them."

"Why not?"

Mary sighed. She knew that whatever he did, the bag would not betray her. It contained a comb, a lipstick, a blusher compact, a car key—and nothing more. "Just...please don't."

He looked at her for a long time. She stared right back at him, not giving an inch—not on this issue. Never. She *couldn't*. No matter how angry he became at her.

At last, he turned and set the bag on the side table at the end of the sofa.

He faced her again. "All right. Happy?" He looked anything but.

At that moment, she almost wished she could give him what he asked for—the truth about who she really was.

But then she saw it all, in quick, awful flashes—the way it would be. At first, when she told him, he wouldn't even remember the pathetic little sales clerk who had served him cold tea just a few days ago.

And then, well, he'd insist on coming into the shop in broad daylight. And he would see her as she really was—see Mary.

Oh, God. She was not a person who planned to die for love. But looking at James's face when he saw her as she really was...

That just might do her in.

"I'm sorry," she whispered. "But you said you understood."

"I don't," he said harshly. He reached for her, pulled her to him, a little roughly that time. His mouth was less than an inch from hers, his eyes so hot and dark it made her dizzy looking into them—but she didn't try to turn away.

She *couldn't* turn away.

"You'll tell me how to find you," he breathed the tender threat against her parted lips. "Before tonight is over, you know that you will."

She wouldn't. Tonight was it. All. Everything. "No," she whispered. "I won't."

She saw in those dark eyes that he didn't believe her. He thought that there would—that there *could*— be more.

"Just kiss me, James," she pleaded.

He gave her what she asked for, taking her mouth hard. She moaned—and so did he.

He guided her down among the pillows.

Chapter 7

It wasn't real.

It didn't happen.

Not to her real self, anyway.

It happened to Olivia, bold and beautiful Olivia—but the memory of it would be Mary's, forever.

She would remember.

His eyes through the darkness. The kisses she lost count of, on her mouth—everywhere.

The delicate silk straps of her gown, light as something woven of cobweb, slipping down her arms. The dress itself, skimming down her body, when he took it away. Her own blush—oh, she blushed all over—when the dress was gone. Under it, she had only a strapless silk camisole and tiny bikini panties to match.

Like the dress itself, they were Margaret's doing—

that camisole, those panties. Margaret had presented them, along with the shoes. "Nothing like the right underthings to give a woman confidence, to make her know that she's beautiful all the way to the skin, that even what no one will see is just perfect."

Well, Margaret would never know it. But someone *did* see.

James saw. And what he saw pleased him. Aroused him. Excited him.

He whispered all the right words—that she was so soft, so sweet, so tender to hold—as he took away that camisole and the little panties, too.

She tried, then, to cover herself.

But he caught her hands. "No. Please. Let me see you."

So she let him see. He praised her beauty, and he did it so sincerely, that even if she'd doubted him— which she didn't—she would have been convinced.

He stood. And he took off his clothes while she lay back among the pillows and watched—she was, after all, Olivia, who thought nothing of watching as her lover undressed.

And besides, she couldn't really make out the details that might have shocked poor, plain Mary. His body seemed to gleam, hazily, in the darkness, big and broad. Strong-looking.

Naked, he picked up his jacket from where he'd thrown it earlier, across the chair. He felt in the inside pocket, took something out—a wallet? Yes. And then he took something from inside the wallet.

She understood, then. Protection. Something she probably should have had sense enough to consider on her own. But she hadn't.

The night, after all, was a magical one. Not quite real to her, more like a dream.

And she did get a little confused, now and then, almost believing that she really *was* Olivia, who, judging by her behavior, knew very little of consequences.

No matter what happened, Olivia would pay no price at all for the caresses she and James shared, here in the dark. When the night was over, Olivia would vanish forever, in her white dress and her perfect underthings, leaving Mary to deal with the results of her folly.

But now, Mary didn't have to worry. There would be no consequences. James would make sure of that.

And she wasn't going to let herself think the kinds of things a silly virgin would be thinking now, either—things like how many other women he had held naked in his big arms, how many other times he'd looked in his wallet for the protection he always kept there, just in case.

She opened her arms and he came down to her.

There were more kisses. Secret kisses, kisses in places she had never dared imagine she might be kissed. Those kisses thrilled her. She tried not to cry out too loudly—after all, she didn't want to get caught, naked with James, in the men's cabana. And even more than her fear of getting caught, she didn't want to be interrupted in the middle of this wonder, this magic, this glory, this dark and intimate adventure.

She wanted all of it. And she wanted it in this one night.

When he rose up over her, she felt she was ready, that it might hurt a little, but certainly not too much.

He pressed into her. In spite of her arousal, her untried body burned. She boldly wrapped her legs around him and lifted herself toward him, urging him to do it, to go ahead, to fill her.

He thrust in—and felt the barrier. He made a shocked sound, low in his throat, and he pulled his head back to meet her eyes. He looked...wounded, as if she had struck him, or somehow betrayed him. "Olivia, what...?"

He started to pull out.

She didn't allow it. She wrapped her legs tighter around his hard waist and she bucked up hard against him, letting out a cry as her innocence finally gave way.

They were both still, then. And silent, except for their ragged breathing.

And then, very softly, he whispered, "Why?"

She stroked his silky, sweat-damp hair, pressed her lips to his temple. "You are so special to me. I wanted it to be you. And I'm glad—so glad—that it is."

"You know me." It was half accusation, half question. "Before tonight, I mean. You knew me, knew who I was."

"Oh, James."

"Just give me that. Please. Tell the truth about that."

So she whispered, though she shouldn't have, "Yes. All right. Yes. I'd seen you before. I knew who you were."

"But we've never spoken, right? Never actually met, face-to-face?"

How could she answer that? It just wasn't wise. "Don't," she said. "Please…"

So he took her mouth again, his tongue delving in. And he began to move.

It hurt, but she didn't care. She did her best to move with him. He made love like he danced, simply, gracefully, in a way even an untried girl could follow.

When he finished, he cried out—a low, harsh sound, something ripped up from the depths of him. She held him close, so close, memorizing the scent of him, the flesh and bone of him, the heat and hardness, pressing her down into the cushions.

He lifted his head, sought her eyes, then sighed and rested his damp forehead against hers. "You should have told me."

"I couldn't."

"That's not true."

"If I had, we wouldn't be here, like this, would we?"

He seemed to think that question over, but he never did actually answer it. Instead, he asked, "Did I hurt you?"

"It's all right."

"In other words, I did."

"It was what I wanted."

"To be hurt?"

"No. I...oh, just leave it. Please. Don't ask me to explain."

He was silent. She knew he wanted to keep after her for answers. But then he finally whispered, rather sadly, "All right."

He slipped to the side a little, pulling her with him, settling her in close, getting them as comfortable as possible, given the narrowness of their makeshift bed. For a brief, lovely time, they simply lay there, cuddled close, his strong arms around her, his cheek on her tangled hair, as the sweat of their lovemaking dried on their skin.

But they couldn't stay like that forever, and Mary knew it.

So did James. Too soon, he was moving again, pulling away from her. When he got to his feet, he reached for her hand.

"Come on. This way."

He led her through the door at the rear of the tent, to the dressing rooms and showers. She took note of the exit sign glowing red above another door there, judging that it had to lead to the grounds outside the pool area.

James didn't turn on any lights, which was just fine with Mary. Her natural shyness had resurfaced with a vengeance and she was having some difficulty pretending it didn't bother her to be wandering around the men's dressing rooms without a stitch on. She didn't need the added agony of doing such a thing in the hard glare of overhead lights. It was definitely soothing to her tattered nerves, to see only shadows and the vague shapes of things—and to know that James couldn't see that much more than she could.

He was wonderfully tender with her, taking such pains to get the water the right temperature in the shower, even drying her himself, rubbing her down with one of the club's thick white cotton towels.

But he had a tendency to linger over the whole process. More than once, she urged him to hurry. She'd become so acutely aware that the night was passing, that they'd been lucky so far, but there was always a chance someone might come upon them.

Back in the tent, they put on their clothes, except for their shoes. And James didn't bother with his jacket.

Mary had lost track of most of the pins that had held up her hair. She didn't even try to sweep it up on her head again, just got her comb from her bag and worked out the tangles as best she could, then left it loose on her shoulders.

There was a little blood on the cushions. She happened to touch the sticky spot, by accident, and realized what it was just as she brought her hand up to check.

"It's nothing," James told her. "Don't worry about it."

But then he must have seen from her face that she

simply could not do that—just put that sticky stain from her mind as if it wasn't there at all. So he went back to the dressing rooms to get her a towel.

"Here," she said, when he returned. "Please. Let me."

He gave her the towel, which was dry. For heaven's sake, what good was a dry towel on a bloodstain?

She scrubbed at the spot anyway, thinking of the rich ranchers and businessmen and their wives, members of the country club, sitting on that sofa and guessing what that stain might be.

Then again, maybe they'd have no chance to wonder. She'd heard somewhere that Flynt Carson, the club's current president, had seen to it that they hired a new club manager, a Mr. Harvey Small, who now ruled the place with an iron hand. Everyone said Mr. Small was a real stickler for detail. No doubt the stain would be discovered right away—and the sofa taken off to be cleaned or recovered.

"Olivia," James said, so gently, "You're going to wear a hole in that couch if you're not careful."

She stopped scrubbing and stared up into his shadowed face, thinking how she had to go, very soon. And wondering if, when she told him she was leaving, he would try again to make her stay.

Maybe not, now that they'd done…what they'd done. Now that he'd found out she wasn't anywhere near as sophisticated as she'd pretended to be. Now that she'd left a stain on the couch cushion—and then been so gauche as to insist on trying to scrub it out.

Maybe he'd feel only relief when she left. She certainly wouldn't blame him for feeling that way.

Oh, what had happened to her Cinderella night? It seemed to be going seriously sideways. And it was her fault. She'd blown it. Hadn't run off at the stroke of midnight the way any sensible Cinderella would. Oh, no. She'd had to go and have *sex* with her prince. And now there was this…awkwardness, this feeling of embarrassment, of being more plain Mary than she ever wanted to be in his presence—and much less the glamorous Olivia.

He was holding out his hand.

She passed him the towel and muttered sheepishly, "Best I can do, I'm afraid."

"It's fine." He dropped the towel at his feet with the ease of a person used to having others wait on him, taking it for granted that someone would come along later and pick it up. "Come up here." His deep voice thrummed along her nerve endings.

And she understood. It wasn't the towel he'd been reaching for.

He was reaching for *her*.

She gave him her hand and he pulled her up into the warm, strong cradle of his arms, close enough that she could see his eyes—and the miracle waiting in them.

He still *wanted* her.

She could hardly believe it. She *felt* like plain Mary. But he still saw Olivia. A musing smile played at the edges of that wonderful mouth of his—the mouth that had kissed her mouth, not to mention all those other parts of her body.

"You are just so extraordinary. Never the same, from one minute to the next. Nothing short of wayward, then suddenly, all innocence. And then so worried about a little stain." He brushed at her hair with the backs of his knuckles as her vanished confidence came flooding back, heady and sweet as sparkling wine. "I mean it. That stain is nothing to worry about."

She laid her hands on his shirtfront. "All right. I'm through worrying."

"Good."

She slanted him a look from under her lashes, thinking what she shouldn't think, about how incredible it felt when his lips touched hers. "I wonder..."

"Anything."

"Kiss me?"

"No problem." He speared his fingers in her hair, capturing her face between those fine, tender hands.

He took her mouth. And plundered it.

When he lifted his head, her knees had gone wobbly and her blood pumped hard and hungry through her veins. She saw in his eyes that he was thinking what she was thinking. About the two of them, on that sofa, making love....

Down low, where their bodies were pressed close together, she could feel that he was ready all over again.

He groaned, grasped her shoulders and put her a

little away from him. "No." He seemed to be talking to himself as much as to her. "I'm not a complete animal. Tonight was your first time. And I hurt you, I know I did, even if you never would quite admit it. You're safe from me—for tonight, anyway."

She heard herself murmur in a voice that was all Olivia, "I don't remember saying anything about wanting to be safe."

He laughed then, low and knowingly, and he pulled her close again. She sighed in anticipation of another bone-melting kiss.

But just as their lips met, she heard it: laughter and voices, out by the pool.

Chapter 8

James heard it, too. He lifted his mouth from hers. They stared at each other as the voices got closer.

"Come on, there's no one here." That was a woman's voice, provocative and hopeful.

They heard a man's chuckle. "In there? You're kidding."

"Stay here," James whispered. "I'll get rid of them."

Mary nodded—and knew an instant of devastating loss as he stepped away from her. She longed to reach out and grab him back, to never let him go, to hold him there, in the darkness, just the two of them, alone together, forever.

As her mother had written in a lighthearted mood, *Stay. Just a little. Till forever, and I'll let you go. Or maybe…just a little longer. The day after forever. That's better for me. How about you? Will the day after forever do for you, too?*

Yes. Till the day after forever and not a day, an hour, a minute less. Let that man and woman out there burst in on them and know just what they'd been doing in here. Mary didn't care.

Or rather, if only she really *were* Olivia, she wouldn't care.

But she wasn't Olivia.

And she'd better stop dwelling on silly love poems and get a grip on herself. It had to be very late. And, come to think of it, now she listened for it, she couldn't hear the music from the ballroom anymore.

How long ago had it stopped?

Was the ball over? Had everyone gone home? Oh, she had to leave now. She had to get away.

James turned from her. She let him go, staring after the tall, proud shape of him as he left the tent, her throat tight, her half-blind eyes blurring even further with tears she would not allow to fall.

Goodbye, she thought, biting her lip hard to keep the word from actually escaping. *Oh, James. Goodbye.*

The man and the woman out there would know immediately what he'd been up to—his shirt was half-buttoned and he wore no shoes. But he was one of the confident people, the successful, self-assured people. He didn't give a damn what that man and that woman thought.

Her beaded evening bag caught an ambient ray of

light from some unknown source in the dark tent and glittered at her from the side table as she turned. She grabbed it and raced for the door to the dressing rooms, remembering when she was halfway there that she'd forgotten her shoes.

But she didn't break her stride, didn't even considering going back for them. The shoes were somewhere at the other end of the wicker sofa and James would be returning any second now. She'd just have to leave them. She'd be faster barefooted, anyway.

A true Cinderella, she couldn't help thinking ruefully. One who left both of her slippers behind, instead of just one.

She reached the dressing area and made for the door with the red-lighted exit sign above it. It gave, heavily, when she pushed on the bar-latch and closed silently behind her as soon as she slid through.

She headed straight for the stone fence that rimmed the pool area, following it around to the wide walk that ran along next to what was left of the east wall of the original clubhouse. Better to avoid the gardens, she decided. It would be way too easy, with her limited vision, to get lost in them.

But following the walk worked just fine. And her bare feet made no sound on the cool concrete. Plus, she was in the shadows, less likely to be spotted by any sharp-eyed club member or curious employee who might happen to be out on the grounds at that time of night.

When she reached the front of the construction area,

she veered off across the grass again, poignantly aware of the lack of cover, yet having no other choice, really, but to sprint for her car. She held her skirt out of the way and ran for all she was worth, the breath coming fast and hard in and out of her chest, around the tennis courts, then between them and the stables, to the parking lot.

There were trees around the lot. She hovered in the shadows of one and dug her key from her bag, holding it ready in her hand as she started out again, remaining at the edge of the lot, using the cover the trees provided. The lot was quiet, only a few lonely cars spread far apart. The gravel-spattered asphalt was a lot harder on her poor feet than the grass. More than once she had to hold back pained cries when she stepped on sharp pebbles.

Never in her life had she been so grateful to reach her little white car. She stuck the key in the door, gave a turn—and pulled the door wide, scooping her skirt out of the way, sliding into the driver's seat, and closing the door, shutting herself safely inside.

Still panting hard, she rested briefly, putting her forehead against the steering wheel, thinking, It's okay. I made it. I'm safe.

Her glasses waited in the glove compartment. She flipped it open and got them out. The world swam into focus as she settled the heavy, ugly frames onto the bridge of her nose.

A swift glance around showed her just what she

hoped to see—no one. James hadn't followed her. The lot was deserted.

She stuck her key in the ignition and gave it a turn. The car started right up. She put it in gear and backed out of the parking space.

The other couple, as it turned out, presented no problem. They ducked into the women's cabana on the opposite side of the pool just as James emerged from the men's tent.

He waited for a minute or two, at poolside, making certain the two didn't decide to pop right back out again.

When they stayed where he wanted them, he went back to Olivia—only to find that she wasn't there.

For a number of endless, wasted seconds, he just stood there, staring at the emptiness, half expecting her to jump up from behind one of the sofas, laughing that husky laugh of hers, whispering teasingly, "Scared you, didn't I?"

But she didn't jump out at him. There was no husky laughter, no naughty whisper. Nothing but silence.

He was alone.

He scoured the tent anyway, looked behind every last stick of furniture. Then he went in back, to the dressing rooms, and called for her softly. No answer.

He walked through the dressing areas and the locker room, the showers, even the big empty rest room, calling for her, *willing* her to answer.

But she didn't.

So he returned to the cabana and dropped to the sofa where he'd lain with her, naked, less than an hour before. He sat there for a long time, remembering those incredible eyes of hers, staring up at him, nodding yes when he told her to wait for him here.

Damn her. The little liar.

Gone without a trace. He had only her name—or did he? She'd been so secretive about everything else, why should he imagine she might have told him the truth even about that?

So what did he have of her?

The memory of her kisses, the intoxicating scent of her hair and her soft, soft skin, the sound of her laughter, still echoing in his ears. A few lines of poetry—

No. Wait. Wrong.

He didn't have the poetry. He couldn't remember a single line of it. She'd only said each line once. How was he supposed to remember from that?

James closed his eyes, muttered, stumbling over the words a little, *"Don't say it. There is no goodbye between us. There is…"* He swore low. "No. That's not right." He growled out another oath and slumped back against the cushions. Nothing, he thought. Nothing much at all.

It all might never have happened, might simply be something he'd made up in his mind.

He sat up straight. And then he reached for the lamp on the table beside him, flicking it on.

Yeah. There it was. Right there on the couch cushion. That stain she had tried so damn hard to scrub away.

The stain existed. It had happened, all right.

A hot flash of something like triumph coursed through him. She did exist. They had danced, and talked. And made love. Right here, on this couch.

And so what?

Emptiness chased the hollow triumph away.

She was gone now. And she'd left no way for him to find her. She'd made it painfully clear that tonight was all of it, all he'd ever have of her.

Just one hell of a one-night stand.

He was never going to see her again and he'd damn well better get used to the idea. Time to pack it in. Head on home.

So where had he put his shoes and socks?

He bent over the arm of the couch and spotted them—right next to those fine high-heeled sandals she'd worn.

He shook his head, whispered, "Olivia, Olivia...ran off so fast, you forgot your shoes."

He reached over, hooked the strap of one and dangled it up to eye level. A glittery oval etched in black with a designer name twinkled at him from the high curve of the arch.

"Gabrielle Amalfi," he read.

The same name Jules had used to describe the pretty satin shoes she'd bought at Mission Creek Creations to wear to the debutante ball.

Chapter 9

The next day was Sunday.

Margaret knocked on Mary's door at a little after two in the afternoon. She had on a thick pair of red oven mitts and she carried a covered casserole. She also cradled a bottle of white wine in the plump curve of her arm.

"My special Shrimp Florentine," she proudly announced. "Got a couple of plates and some forks?"

"Oh, Margaret. It smells like heaven. You shouldn't have—"

"I've got hot rolls, too. And a salad. But I couldn't carry everything at once."

"Come on in." Mary stepped out of the way, her stomach growling. She hadn't even thought about eating all day, had been much too busy thinking about other things. And trying *not* to think about them.

But the scent of Margaret's casserole had done the trick. Mary realized she was starving.

"Go over and get the rolls, will you?" Margaret headed for the kitchen. "And the salad. I left the door open. It's all on the kitchen counter."

So Mary ran over to Margaret's and got the rest of the feast. They set Mary's table, uncorked the wine, and sat down to eat.

"Here's to you, Mary," Margaret toasted, raising her wineglass high. "My dear friend who has no idea what a special, special person she really is."

Mary felt herself blushing. "Oh, Margaret. You are so sweet."

Margaret chuckled. "Drink up, now. Go on."

Mary took a sip of her wine. "Um. Delicious." She set down her glass and tasted the shrimp casserole, sighing at the lovely, delicate mingling of flavors. "Now *this* is pure heaven."

Margaret picked up her own fork. But she didn't even manage to take her first bite before she set it down and demanded, "All right. I can't stand it. What *happened?* Tell me everything. Was it wonderful? Scary? Perfect? Awful?"

Mary couldn't help grinning. "Yes."

Margaret scowled. "Meaning?"

"All of the above."

"Did you dance?"

"Yes."

"With…?"

Vivid as if it was all happening again, Mary saw

James's face, his eyes only for her, as they danced. And then, a little later, leaning close across that iron table out on the balcony while they talked and laughed beneath the stars.

And later still, in the tent by the pool, his eyes looking into hers, shocked and a little hurt, at that moment when he realized it was her first time.

Mary set down her own fork, her appetite suddenly gone.

Margaret's eyes had widened with alarm. "What is it? What's happened? Tell me, dear."

"Oh, Margaret..."

"Please. Tell me about it."

So Mary told. More than she should have, probably—though not the whole truth, not *everything* that had happened in the men's cabana. She said that she danced with James and James only, that they talked for hours. That, yes, he had kissed her.

She told about the ball itself: the music the band had played, the decorations—well, what she had been able to see of them, anyway—about how she and James had taken a break from dancing to enjoy a glass of lemonade. About the encounter with Maddie Delarue and the scary confrontation with Mrs. Adair.

And the way she had tripped on the lawn, tearing the hem of her dress just a little, about the way James had caught up with her and kissed her and led her to the men's cabana, where, as she described it, they had "whispered together, sharing secrets." She even told how she'd run out the back at the end, leaving her shoes behind.

"But why?" Margaret demanded when Mary finished. "There was no need for you to run off like that. It's clear the man was completely taken with you. You'll be seeing him again, and soon, I'd bet on it. He'll be dropping by the shop. He's even got a nice little pretext for it—to make sure you get your shoes back."

"He won't be dropping by the shop."

"Oh, well, of course he will."

"Margaret, I didn't give him my name."

Margaret stared at her in disbelief. "But...why not?"

"I just didn't, all right? I just...that was the way I wanted it."

"You spent a whole evening with him and you didn't even tell him your name? Didn't he ask you?"

"I don't know if he asked me directly. I don't remember."

"You know what I mean. What did he *call* you, if not by your name? 'Hey, lady?' 'Hey, you'?"

"No. I, well, I gave him another name."

"What name?"

Mary balked. She knew what her friend's reaction would be when she said the name.

"Well?" Margaret prompted.

Mary gave in and muttered, "Olivia Leigh."

There was a silence. A long one, as Margaret just

gaped at her. Finally, Margaret said, "Well, then. He *does* have a way to find you, now doesn't he?"

Mary poked at the bridge of her glasses, which had slid down her nose the way they were always doing. "Oh, don't look at me like that. He'll never figure it out."

"He could. You know he could. He just might put it together, if he's determined enough. And perceptive enough—and that's why you used that name, isn't it? To test him, to see if he really is the kind of man that you could love?"

"Oh, Margaret, no. That's not so. I didn't test him. I wouldn't do something like that to him. I just…that name came to me. And I gave it to him, without really thinking about it."

Margaret was looking at her fondly—and shaking her gray head. "Well, whether you gave him that name purposely, or it just popped out of your mouth, it *is* a clue to your real identity."

"Not enough of a clue for me to worry about. He's not going to figure it out. It was a wonderful night and I'll treasure the memory of it forever."

"But?" Margaret's mouth was a grim line.

"But now I don't want to talk about it anymore. It happened and it's over and I…I do thank you, Margaret, for making that incredible dress and fixing me up so I hardly knew myself. For making the whole thing possible."

"I don't want your thanks. I wanted to do what I did, and you know it. And I wasn't the one who made it all possible. That was *you,* Mary. You did it yourself and—''

Mary refused to let her get going. ''It was a magical moment in time, and it's over. I don't want to go crazy dwelling on it. I want to…think of it sometimes. But not obsessively, you know? I think it's better if I get on with real life now.''

''But Mary, whatever happened last night, it was every bit as *real* as anything else in your life. You might have called yourself Olivia Leigh, but you *were* there. It *was* you. You were—''

''Margaret. Please. I mean it. It's over and I want to let it go.'' She picked up her fork. ''Can't we just enjoy this delicious meal?''

Margaret sighed—but she kept her mouth shut.

''Thank you,'' said Mary softly.

Margaret forced a smile. ''There you go, thanking me again. You're the daughter I never had, and we both know it. No thanks are necessary between us— and you said you tore the dress?''

''It's only a small tear, at the hem. I'll mend it.''

''Oh, let me.''

''No, Margaret. You don't have to do that.''

''I want to. I'll take it with me today when I go.''

''I am so fortunate to have a friend like you.'' The two women looked at each other across the table, misty-eyed on both sides.

Then Mary straightened her glasses and Margaret picked up her own fork.

"Let's eat then, shall we?" said Margaret. "Before it gets cold."

In the big house on the quiet, prosperous street where he'd been raised, James Campbell kept himself from checking the phone book until four in the afternoon that Sunday.

When he finally gave in and looked, he found no listings for anyone named Olivia Leigh. There was, however, an O. W. Leigh.

James decided he wasn't going to dial that damn number. That resolution lasted exactly eighteen minutes.

The phone rang twice. And then O. W. Leigh actually answered: a man. "O.W.'s for Odell Walter," the man told him.

James thanked him and said goodbye.

The next morning, James carried a brown bag containing a pair of evening sandals to his office with him. When he passed Mission Creek Creations on the way there, he almost stopped and went in, almost marched up to Margaret McKenzie and demanded to know if, just possibly, those sandals had come from her shop—and if so, did she have any way of telling him who might have bought them?

But he ended up walking on by.

It was too much of a stretch to imagine that Mrs. McKenzie might be able to tell him from a pair of shoes where the hell he could find their vanished owner. Wishful thinking to put it mildly. Borderline idiocy to get a little closer to the truth.

And besides, if Olivia had wanted him to find her, she wouldn't have run out on him in the first place.

No.

Better to forget her.

To be truthful—something she *wasn't*—he was more than a little angry with her. She'd made love with him, for pity's sake. He'd been her *first*. Yet she'd refused, repeatedly, to let him have her number. And then she ran out on him, left him cold, after promising—with a definite nod and a yes in those gorgeous cat-slanted eyes—to stay put.

People were whispering about her, about the vision who appeared at the ball, danced only with James, and then vanished, never to be seen again. Even Jules had heard all about the mystery girl. And she'd quizzed him on the subject, too, then rolled her eyes and called him a grouch when he said he didn't want to talk about it—because he *didn't* want to talk about it.

As the days passed, he became more and more certain that he wanted to forget Olivia Leigh. He wanted her out of his mind. And out of his dreams, where, somehow, she seemed to have found a permanent place. Now, in those dreams he had told her about—the seeking dreams, where he looked for something he could never find—he realized what it was he sought: Olivia.

But the dreams remained the same as always in terms of their outcome. He never found her.

And it was all right, he kept telling himself. He didn't *want* to find her. *He wanted to forget her.*

Too bad he couldn't.

And too bad Mary couldn't forget *him.*

Margaret mended the beautiful dress and returned it to her on Monday after the ball. Mary had it cleaned, then stored it in the back of her closet, knowing she would never wear it again. Out of sight, out of mind, she told herself.

But James was somehow a lot harder to put away.

In spite of all her firm promises to herself—to put James behind her, not to obsess over the memory of the too-brief hours they'd shared, she couldn't seem to stop herself from watching for him, couldn't keep her heart from beating too hard at the thought of just catching sight of him through the wide display windows of the shop. Too often—at nine-thirty, at noon, at one, or at five, the times when he passed by, going to and from his office—she would find herself standing right where she shouldn't be, at the window.

And that was exactly how it happened.

On a Tuesday, seventeen days after the ball. At three minutes after noon.

Mary was waiting at the window, hoping to catch just a glimpse of him as he strolled by on his way to lunch. She saw him appear at the edge of the wide glass and her heart lightened with sheer gladness in her chest. And then, as he came even with her, by pure chance, he turned his head her way.

Their eyes met. Locked.

And even in her ugly glasses and her nondescript clothes, even without the magic of that perfect dress and clever makeup, James knew exactly who she was.

Chapter 10

It was the absolute worst moment of Mary's life.

She saw his shock, which turned to something that just might have been joy—and then, all too quickly, darkened to anger.

Oh, no! her heart cried. Please, *no!*

She didn't want him to see her like this, didn't want him to know that the marvelous and complex Olivia Leigh was only that strange, painfully introverted store clerk, Mary Clark.

She whirled from the window, headed for the stockroom. She flew past Margaret, who was straightening the hat display.

"Mary? What is it? What's the—oh, my..."

Mary didn't stay to hear more, though she knew the sound of that "Oh, my," meant that Margaret must have spotted James, that the bell ringing over the door signaled his entry into the shop.

Mary kept moving, made it to the doorway that led to the back of the shop, ducked inside. But she wasn't fast enough.

James saw her vanish through the stockroom door— and he followed right after her, striding past Margaret and a pair of customers at a skirt rack without so much as a glance in their direction.

"Olivia, wait!"

She didn't wait. She kept going. But since he'd come right on into the back room with her, there was really nowhere to go. She dodged around boxes and rolling racks of hanging clothes—and he kept coming, right behind her. She'd almost made it to the exit that opened onto the alley when he caught up with her, grabbing her arm roughly and whirling her around to face him.

"Hold on." He took both her arms in his big hands and he shook her. "Damn it, what's up with you? Why the hell are you always running away?"

His questions came at her like hard, sharp-edged stones. And she couldn't answer, couldn't make a sound—except for one pitiful whimper of misery.

Her distress finally got through to James.

He stopped shaking her. And he stared. It hit him, at last, who she actually was.

Why, she was Margaret McKenzie's assistant. Mary...? He had to think for a moment to come up with a last name. Then he had it: Clark. Mary Clark. A plain store clerk, a woman he'd hardly noticed—

except to think once or twice that the poor creature seemed scared of her own shadow.

This was the girl he couldn't make himself forget?

He let go of her arms. He felt confused, sick at heart— and he was also starting to realize that he had behaved cruelly, that she was painfully shy, could hardly cope with him at his best—let alone when he grabbed her and shook her and shouted questions at her.

He backed off a few steps, to show her she was safe from him, that he wouldn't touch her again. "Look. I'm sorry." Damn. She looked stricken. Her beautiful face behind those godawful glasses was way too pale. "Listen, I didn't mean to upset you. Really. Are you...will you be all right?"

Mary still couldn't make words come. But she did somehow manage one quick, desperate nod.

That nod was every bit as much a lie as the ones she had told the night of the ball. She was not, by any stretch of the imagination, all right.

But if he would just go, just leave her alone, she could begin to pull herself together, to recover from the bleak horribleness of this.

"You're sure? You're all right?" He kept backing away.

Go, she commanded in her mind, though the words still wouldn't come. *Just go! Just leave me alone!*

He got the message. "Yeah. All right. I'm going. But I...I mean it. I'm sorry. I truly am."

And she just stared at him, wordless, through those eyes that haunted his dreams.

What else could he do? He turned and got the hell out of there.

Mary felt relief—for a minute anyway—just to have him gone. And then misery claimed her.

There was a low wooden stool a few feet away. She moved over there and sank down onto it, yanking off her glasses, dropping them to the floor, then covering her face with her hands, wishing she could hide herself that easily, that she could just disappear. Vanish into thin air, never to be seen or heard from again.

"Oh, Mary, oh my dear…" Margaret was standing over her. Even without her glasses, Mary could make out that her friend was holding out her arms. Mary didn't hesitate. She surged up off that stool and into Margaret's loving embrace, the dam of silence breaking in a hot flood of unhappy tears.

"It's all right." Margaret held on good and tight and whispered soothingly in Mary's ear. "You cry. You just cry. Sometimes, crying is the only thing a girl can do."

While Mary cried, James was busy despising himself.

He walked out of Mission Creek Creations blindly, putting one foot in front of the other, hardly aware of where those feet were taking him. He just walked, and he kept walking, down one street and then the next, headed nowhere in particular, the scene at the shop reeling through his mind.

He had shouted at her. And grabbed her. And shaken her. And sworn at her.

And she was...

Only a shy, scared shop girl. Someone he'd never so much as looked at twice. Someone he never in a million years would have guessed might be Olivia—*his* Olivia—the most contradictory, incredible, intoxicating woman he had ever known....

But wait a minute. He had to start facing the truth here. There *was* no Olivia.

Only poor Mary Clark, whom he'd just pretty much terrorized.

Across the street, someone's car alarm sounded. James blinked and glanced that way—and ended up bumping into an elderly lady and knocking her purse to the ground.

She snapped at him. "Watch where you're going, young man."

He got her purse and handed it to her, then backed away from her, apologizing. "Sorry. Really. Wasn't looking..."

"Be more careful."

"Yeah. I will. Sorry."

He started to turn back the way he'd been headed—and discovered he was standing before a two-story brick building with a pair of stone lions guarding broad concrete steps that led up to wide glass doors. He knew the building, of course. It had been there all his life.

The Mission Creek Public Library.

"Olivia," he whispered, not really even realizing he had said it aloud. "Olivia Leigh."

And at that moment, he remembered where he'd heard the name originally.

Damn. Way back when he was a kid. Middle school, wasn't it? Miss Lathrop, his language teacher, had made the class study the poems of a local poet, a woman, Miss Lathrop said, who lived right there, in Mission Creek. All the guys had griped and groaned. Poetry—and *love* poetry, especially—was for wimps and *girls*.

But Miss Lathrop had made them read and discuss those poems anyway. Secretly, James remembered, he had liked some of them, though he never went so far as to confess that fact out loud.

James was already mounting those wide concrete steps. Inside, he went to the circle of computers where they stored the card catalog. He took a chair at one of the monitors. At the prompt for "author," he typed in Leigh, Olivia.

Three titles came up, all of them checked in: *You and Me and Forever, Stay* and *Blue Telephone*.

James got up from the computer and left the big brick building without even looking to see if the volumes were actually on the shelves. He had no intention of borrowing Olivia Leigh's poetry from the library. He was headed for that big, rambling bookstore on Main Street. He wanted copies of his own.

* * *

When Mary had cried herself out, Margaret sent her home for the day. Mary washed her face and put on her nightgown and went to bed, even though it wasn't even two in the afternoon by then.

Misery was a sort of pulse behind her eyelids, a sour, sad taste in her mouth. Maybe she'd stay in bed for a day or two, only get up when she had to.

What did she have to get out of bed for, anyway? To go to work at Margaret's store? Well, Margaret knew what condition she was in. When Mary didn't show up for work tomorrow, Margaret would understand.

Mary didn't want to talk to anyone. She didn't want to see anyone. She just wanted to lie there, with the shades drawn and the lights off, letting time tick by until this awful misery could pass.

She did just that until a little after six, when Margaret got home from the shop—and came knocking at the door.

Mary didn't want to go the door. She *wouldn't* go to the door. Margaret should be more understanding of Mary's misery. Margaret should just go away.

But Margaret didn't go away. She kept on, knocking and knocking, until finally, muttering swear words under her breath, Mary threw back the covers, grabbed her glasses from the nightstand and stomped to the door, putting on the glasses as she went.

She flung the door wide. "What?"

Margaret had that look—her stubborn look. She folded her plump arms over her ample breasts and planted her legs wide apart, someone who would not be budged. "You went to bed, didn't you? You've just been lying there in bed, with all the shades drawn, haven't you?"

"Yes, I have. Now, go away." Mary shut the door—or at least, she tried to. But Margaret put out her hand and caught it before it could close.

"We need to talk."

"No, we don't. I want to be alone."

"Well, too bad."

"Margaret—"

But Margaret wasn't listening. She pushed back the door and she grabbed Mary's hand. "Come with me. Now."

"Margaret, I'm in my *nightgown*, I—"

"Oh, who's looking? I mean it. Come with me."

Margaret already had her out the door. And Margaret didn't stop. She kept going, pulling Mary across the stretch of lawn between their houses, up onto Margaret's porch and on into the house.

"What?" demanded Mary. "All right, I'm here. So *what?*"

"This way." Margaret pulled her onward, down the hall, to her workroom at the back of the house. She flipped a switch on the little panel by the door. A spotlight popped on over the three-way mirror against one wall. "Come *on.*" She led Mary over there, and took her by the shoulders, positioning her so she could see herself in each of the three panes of reflecting glass. "Now. Look. Look in the mirror. What do you see?"

Mary made a growling sound low in her throat. "A skinny woman in ugly glasses and a nightgown, with really messy hair."

"Look harder."

Mary narrowed her eyes and jutted her chin forward. "I still see the same thing."

Margaret spoke softly in her ear. "You see more. Much more. And you know you do."

"Margaret, I—"

"No. You listen now. I've been trying to make you see—really see—yourself for years, and you know it. Sometimes I thought it was never going to happen. But I think we're close now, very close. And I want to say a few things, about your mother. And your father. About the love they shared."

Instinctively, in protection of the habits of a lifetime, Mary tried to cast her gaze downward, lowering her lashes and dipping her chin.

But Margaret, very gently, put up her hands and guided Mary's head back so she was looking right into the mirrors again. "Oh, yes," she said. "It's time you faced it. You know that it is. They were good people, your parents. And they shared a beautiful, private, perfect world, just the two of them. It worked for them. They had each other. And that was enough for them.

"But Mary—they had no right to do what they did to you, to teach you to be the way that they were, to bring you up believing you had no choice but to be that way. It's not true, Mary. You are not your mother.

Or your father. You can make your own way. You can have so much more.''

Margaret took her by the shoulders again and gave a reassuring squeeze. "Come on, look. *Really* look. That's you. Do you see? The scared, shy clerk who works in my shop. And the beauty at the ball. You're both. And you're more.''

''Oh, Margaret—''

''Shh. Listen. I have a secret. I'm going to share it with you. I love all my girls—and yes, I do, I think of them that way, all the girls who come for my dresses, as 'my' girls. But some of them, well, they're extra special to me. And for those—the really special ones—I like to sew a little token, something they'll never even know is there, for luck, for happiness, right into the gown I design for that special girl. For you, it was white rose petals, sewn into the hem. Your special secret charm. White to stand for innocence—and for secret love, too. You lost those petals, did you know that? I discovered they were gone when you gave me the gown to mend—and you know what?''

Mary met her friend's eyes in the mirror.

''It doesn't matter,'' Margaret said. ''It doesn't matter that you lost them. Because the real charm is no secret. The real charm is inside you. You *are* that incredible girl at the debutante ball. That was you, in that dress, so confident and so stunning. You danced and you laughed, didn't you? You carried yourself with pride. And you *talked* with James Campbell. Talked easily. Intimately. You told me you did. And maybe you even shared a few more kisses than you admitted to me?''

Margaret chuckled. ''Oh, yes. I see your blush. I know. I'm a woman. I know how it was...I know how *you* were. Because I know you, Mary.

''And the truth is, now that you've let yourself *be* that beautiful woman, even if only for one night, you can never again deny that she *is* a part of you. You came out of your shell for an evening, Mary. You did it. And you can do it again.''

Mary stared at herself in the mirror. She *was* listening. And she was also admitting the truth at last.

Her dear friend was right.

Margaret sent Mary home to put on some street clothes.

Then, together, they drove back to Mission Creek Creations, where they indulged in an after-hours shopping spree. They dressed Mary from the ground up, choosing clothes that would fit the ''total'' Mary, the woman who was regal and self-possessed—as well as sweet and shy. Mary agreed that she'd visit her optometrist tomorrow. She'd get some more attractive glasses, and possibly contacts, as well.

''Good,'' said Margaret. ''You'll start wearing these new clothes tomorrow, too. You want to look your best. Because James Campbell will be back. Now he knows where to find you, that man will not be able to stay away.''

Chapter 11

As usual, Margaret was right.

James was waiting at the shop the next day when Mary arrived for work. She came in the back door as she always did, to find Margaret holding a box knife, ready to start going through a recent delivery.

"You have a visitor," Margaret said with a grin, tipping her gray head toward the doorway that led to the front of the shop.

Mary knew immediately who it had to be. Her heart kicked into high gear and her cheeks felt a little too warm.

But it was okay. It was manageable. She smoothed her hands down the cream-colored linen sheath that she and Margaret had chosen the day before, wishing she'd had time to get those new glasses she'd planned on.

"How do I look?" she said, low enough that no one but Margaret could hear.

"Just fine," Margaret whispered back, then made a shooing motion with her hands. "Go on now. You go talk to him."

She found him waiting at the counter, a brown bag tucked under his arm. "Your shoes." He handed her the bag.

"Uh, thank you." It came out all right. A little shaky, maybe. But at least she'd spoken up, and she wasn't a mass of tangled-up nerves, wasn't fighting an almost unbearable urge to run and hide.

He looked at her steadily. She did wonder what he might be thinking.

She was thinking that he was the best-looking guy in the world, that she did not for a minute regret their time in the pool house. That, except for the lies she'd told him, she wouldn't have had any of it any other way.

"I've been wondering," he said. "That name you called yourself. Olivia—"

"Leigh," She provided. He nodded. He looked as if he hoped she'd say more. So she did. "It was…my mother's. Well, not her *given* name. But her pen name. She was a poet."

"The poems you quoted were—"

"Hers. She wrote them, to my father."

He cleared his throat. "They *were* beautiful. I meant that, when I said they were."

She felt a smile tugging at the corner of her mouth. "Well, James, you only heard a few lines."

"I liked what I heard."

"Well, then thank you. I mean, for my mother's sake."

He was looking at her so strangely. As if he *admired* her. As if he didn't want to go.

And he didn't.

James would happily have stood there by the cash register in Margaret McKenzie's shop for the rest of the day, staring into Mary Clark's incredible eyes, wondering how he'd ever managed *not* to notice her.

However, he had a practice to run and she had her own work to do. "Listen. About yesterday—"

She put up a slim hand. "No. Honestly. Don't worry about it."

"You're sure?"

She nodded.

And there was nothing more to say, really. "Well, then, I guess I ought to be going."

"Thanks again." She held up the bag. "For my shoes."

"No problem."

Mary stood right where she was, listening to the shop bell ring as he went out, watching him walk by the front window, moving much too quickly out of her line of sight.

When she turned for the back room, she found Margaret standing in the doorway.

She studied her friend's face for a moment, then

wrinkled up her nose. "You're looking really smug, Margaret, do you know that?"

Her friend beamed at her. "Go after him. Go after him right now."

"Oh, that's crazy. I can't do any such thing."

"Of course, you can."

"No. Now, let's drop the subject. Let's go ahead and take care of that order you've got back there."

Margaret made a low, impatient sound in her throat, but she didn't argue further. They went in back together and started going through the boxes, sorting things to hang on the racks, choosing which items to put on display.

They'd worked for about ten minutes when Mary realized she couldn't stand it. "Oh, all right." She smoothed her hair and straightened her glasses. "I'll be back in half an hour, tops."

Margaret had that smug look again. "No hurry. Take your time."

It was a three-minute walk to his storefront law office.

That secretary he'd told her about the night of the ball—the efficient and intimidating Mrs. Letterby— glanced up from behind an impressively tidy-looking desk when Mary entered the small, attractively furnished waiting room. "How may I help you?"

Mary experienced a distinct urge to whirl around and get of there. She ignored it. "I'm Mary Clark. I'd like to speak with Mr. Campbell."

Mrs. Letterby frowned and glanced down at her calendar. ''You have no appointment.''

Mary swallowed—but she didn't break. ''If you would please just tell him I'm here, I would really appreciate it.''

The secretary shrugged and picked up the phone. ''Mary Clark to see you. Yes. All right. Certainly.'' Mrs. Letterby hung up and rose from her chair. ''He says to show you right in. This way.'' She turned for the door a few feet behind her.

Mary just stood there, thinking, I'm to go right in. James said so.

The secretary paused with her hand on the doorknob. ''Ms. Clark? Are you all right?''

Mary blinked. ''I...yes, Mrs. Letterby. I am more than all right.''

He was standing behind a big cherry-wood desk when Mary entered the room. The secretary left them, pulling the door closed as she went.

Mary kept her spine straight, but she really would have liked to have had something to lean against. She felt more than a little weak in the knees. And her heart was a trip-hammer. Just bonging away in there.

Oh, could she do this? She prayed she wouldn't blow it.

They stared at each other.

He looked...happy. To see her.

That was good. That was a definite plus.

She sucked in a big breath—and the words were

there. More than there. They came pouring out, stumbling over each other in their eagerness to be said.

"Oh, James. I'm so sorry, I truly am. I shouldn't have run out on you that night, and I know it. But I've had this, well, I don't know what else to call it but a *crush*. An insane, impossible crush. On you. I've had it for months now, since you opened your office here and I noticed you walking by Margaret's shop. I would see you, every day, several times, just strolling by. So handsome, so sure of yourself. Just, well, a truly self-confident man. And then, I heard about you. Gossip, you know? About your parents and how you took care of your sister. And I, well, I really liked the things people said about you.

"Of course, I knew that a man like you would never look twice at someone like me. And you never did, until that one special night. And I…well, I just wanted to *save* that night, in my heart, in my memory. I never dared to believe there could ever be more."

James decided he couldn't stand it—the damn desk between them. He slid around it and he got to her in four long strides. "Mary…"

"Uh. What?" She blinked those gorgeous eyes.

He cupped her face in his hands and he whispered, *"Shy and wild, you came to me. I knew you, knew your secrets before you shared them, knew your heart that sang to mine…"*

"James." Her voice held wonder—and a touch of accusation. "You have been reading my mother's poetry."

He confessed, "I figured it out yesterday. I've been to the bookstore, bought all three of her books. And you're right. I *have* been reading. And, well, Mary, I have a question for you."

"A question…"

"Do you believe in love at first sight?"

She frowned at him, clearly unsure how to answer.

He stroked her hair, loving the silky feel of it, hardly daring to believe that she was really here, that he was touching her again when for two endless weeks he'd thought her gone forever from his life.

"Please, Mary. Tell me. Do you?"

She caught her lower lip between her pretty white teeth, thinking hard, then carefully began her answer. "Well, people do say that's not possible, don't they? I mean, there's *attraction* at first sight, certainly. But how can we really call it *love?* When you don't even *know* the person, when you aren't even—"

He went for broke. "I do, Mary."

She blinked again. "Hmm?"

"I do. Believe in love. At first sight."

"Uh. You *do?*"

"Since I first saw you, yes. I believe in it."

Mary felt it was only fair to point out the flaw in his logic. "But James, you saw me several times, before that night at the ball. And you didn't even know I was there."

"I was a fool."

Well, she couldn't very well argue with that. "Yes, James. You were."

"But now, I do see you, Mary. I see *all* of you, I swear that I do. You're here. You're real."

"Yes." She found she was smiling. "You're right, James. I am."

"Kiss me, Mary."

And she did.

And a month later, in June, they were married—at the Lone Star Country Club, of course.

FRANKIE'S FIRST DRESS
Ann Major

For my readers: The gate is always open
to those who come with love.

Chapter 1

Frankie Moore's hands flew off her steering wheel, and she shook her fists at the big, blue-white sky. Center stripes blurred crazily. Then her big tires hit the grooved edge of the shoulder that rumbled warnings to sleepy drivers, drunks and to girls who were as mad as hornets at tyrants who were ruining their lives.

When her tires hit grass, Frankie grabbed the wheel and swerved her pickup back onto the highway.

The things she did for the people she loved—especially for Aunt Susie!

"Not Vince Randal, though!" she hissed up at her rearview mirror as if there were a real person sitting up there who could hear her.

"It's really pushing it to demand I choose him to escort me to the debutante ball! I'll choose my own escort, thank you very much!"

"Okay, then—who, smartie-pants?" came a little voice.

The tall, golden-haired, impossible devil who sprang instantly to mind caused Frankie to shiver even though it was hot, very hot for May.

"No. Not *him!* No way!"

Not that Aunt Susie, who was the closest thing Frankie had to a real mother, had asked her such an impertinent question. Not that she would suggest that particular yellow-haired devil who swaggered around in tight jeans and cowboy boots like he thought he was a god. Not that Frankie would ever tell her aunt off, either. Aunt Susie had done so much for her. The last thing Frankie would ever want to do was crush her.

Frankie chewed at the sore place she made when she'd bitten her tongue during their heated discussion. Just the thought of that argument got her shaking again and caused her foot to fall heavily on the accelerator.

The speed limit sign outside of Mission Creek read fifty-five. She looked down. Her speedometer said eighty-five. Uncle Wayne's last admonition lit up in her mind like a neon sign.

"One more ticket—even a warning ticket—and no truck for you, young lady!"

With a sigh of regret, Frankie lifted her scarred boot off the gas pedal.

It was bad enough having to be a dumb old debutante. She couldn't endure the thought of suffering through such an ordeal on the arm of stuffy Vince Randal.

Aunt Susie's words rang in Frankie's mind. "If you aren't going to college, it's time you started thinking about settling down, about your future."

"I am thinking about my future. That's all I'm thinking about!"

"A smart, pretty girl should think about catching the right kind of man."

"Oh, please—"

"Why don't you just call Vince back?"

"I think I'll do all those errands you were fussing at me about instead."

"What about Vince?"

Frankie had chomped down on her tongue and then flung herself out the door.

This whole thing was crazy—Frankie Moore, tomboy, cowgirl, being fitted for a ball gown? Why, she couldn't even remember the last time she'd worn a dress. Or high heels. Bows and frills were for other girls.

Of course, there were those faded pictures on the piano of that guiless cherub with the big green eyes and mussed red ringlets reminding her of the times Aunt Susie had trussed her up in itchy outfits trimmed fussily with an over-abundance of lace and little seed pearls and lots of frilly bows. That was before Frankie had had a say of her own. But by the vast age of three, Frankie had been a pure tomboy cowgirl in her jeans.

Frankie didn't own a dress! Didn't want to either!

Being a debutante this season wasn't about *her*. It was about Aunt Susie, who was still a Houston girl at heart, a city girl who'd fallen for a rich cowboy. Aunt Susie hadn't had a clue as to how difficult life with her man in the south Texas desert would be for a society woman like her.

Saturday was a big shopping day in little towns like Mission Creek. Even though it was still early, as soon as Frankie hit the commercial section of the town, the traffic was bumper to bumper. She drove several blocks at ten miles an hour without seeing even one parking space. Then, as she was passing Coyote Harry's and was about to explode with impatience and give up by turning onto a side street, to her amazement, she saw two empty parking spots on Main Street. Right in front of Mission Creek Creations— Mrs. Margaret McKenzie's Little Shop of Horrors!

Her dreaded destination!

Frankie smiled. *Now be nice. Remember, nobody else in Mission Creek calls it that.*

Mrs. McKenzie had been running her fancy dress shop for thirty years. She'd dressed generations of debutantes. Much as Frankie dreaded being fitted for her ball gown, at least she'd get to see her friend, Mary Clark, who worked as a dress shop assistant.

After she parked, Frankie cut the engine and snapped her keys out of the ignition. A second or two later, she had her door open, and the warm south Texas breeze was whirling her shoulder-length red curls about her head like a mop. Not that she cared as she jumped lightly to the ground. She didn't care about her hairdo any more than she cared for makeup, clothes or boys—all the things Aunt Susie was always telling her a normal pretty, twenty-year-old girl should be thinking about.

Boys! Or rather men! Frankie got all shivery and shy at the thought of them.

More than anything she wished Aunt Susie would forget that Vince Randal, a young vice president with Mission Creek First Federal Bank and one of the town's most eligible bachelors, had started calling her.

Frankie had learned her lesson where men were concerned. "I'm not like *her*," she said aloud. And she wasn't referring to her aunt. She was thinking about her real mother.

An involuntary clutch of fear made her tremble as she remembered a grainy voice murmuring in the dark as a sinful mouth slid between her breasts. "There's nothing to be so afraid of, darlin'...."

She drew a swift breath and stopped the memory before it could take hold.

I'm not like her.

Most ranchers did their errands on Saturdays. Still, Main Street was way more congested than usual. Everybody seemed to be fighting for parking places. From the street, two warring horns blared.

"That's my space, buddy!"

Ignoring the man, a cowboy in a big, rusted red truck that was dangerously familiar swerved faster than Frankie could blink—straight at her own pickup.

Before she could jump out of the way, huge black tires spewed sharp bits of gravel against her scuffed boots. Hot blasts of engine air enveloped her. Not that the reckless driver in his Stetson shooting like a rocket into the parking space right beside hers, much cared.

"Hey!" she shouted. "Watch where you're going, cowboy."

The other driver, who'd lost out, jabbed a finger at the sky. Then he burned rubber as he roared away.

Quickly, she slammed her door and scurried up to the sidewalk.

Not that there was any need now. Mr. Macho had parked with deft precision and had left her plenty of space.

The cowboy got out slowly, uncoiling each long denim-clad leg one at a time. In the next instant his feral eyes climbed her skintight jeans, and she began to shiver. She didn't have to look at him to know his gaze lingered on her shapely thighs before burning higher to rake her T-shirt where it clung to her small, pointed breasts. She wasn't wearing a bra. She always told herself she didn't have enough up there to really need one.

Why hadn't she worn a bra?

This man with the whiskey-gold eyes made her feel stark naked and had her nipples rock hard.

"Matt?" On a shudder, she sucked in a hot, mortified little breath.

The sun was behind his broad shoulders and tall, wiry frame, so she couldn't see him all that well. He touched his hat with a tense brown fingertip, acknowledging her. She sensed that his dark lean face was as harsh and rigid as it always was whenever they chanced to meet. Even so, she could feel the heat from his wicked gold eyes lick her like flames, as she remembered...

"I'm not done with you. Not by a long shot...."

"What if I'm done with you...?"

Her cheeks reddened. He'd gone as white as if she'd punched him in the gut when she'd said that. Then his carved face, with those incredible knife-edged cheekbones hardened.

"You think you're too good for a Dixon, don't you? 'Cause I'm poor? 'Cause my daddy was a drunk? 'Cause my ranch wouldn't even be a good-size pasture to your uncle? You Lassiters think you're kings and queens of the county, don't you?"

"My last name is Moore, remember?"

She'd been slipping out of his arms, buttoning her blouse, and then running from him, stumbling in her panic to escape.

"I'm not what your aunt would call a good catch, am I?"

"I'm not trying to catch anybody," she'd yelled over her shoulder, stung.

He'd started his truck, driving up alongside her. "Hey, get in. I'll drive you home." When she'd kept walking, he'd braked, jumped out in front of her and held up his hands in mock surrender. "Hey...hey.... Sorry about the temper tantrum. Hey, I'm not some sex maniac either. It's two miles to your uncle's, for God's sake. Maybe BoBo Dixon was my daddy, but I won't touch you ever again. I swear it.'' He'd hesitated. ''Francesca, please just get in.''

He'd opened the door for her. She'd stopped walking, still not sure she could trust him. Then he'd smiled and said please.

They'd driven in tense silence to her ranch, but at the gate, he'd said in a low, low tone that had hurt somehow, ''I won't even talk to you, Frankie. Not unless you start it up. Understand? But if you do, you be careful, darlin'. 'Cause like I said, I'm not near done with you.''

What had he meant? That sex was like an appetite? That a girl wasn't special to him? That she was just like a meal in a life of many meals? That when he had gobbled his fill of one, he went on to the next?

Back on Main Street, Frankie chewed her lip and tried not to look at him. Matt took off his Stetson and awkwardly finger-combed his unruly golden hair. Maybe he felt bad, too. Maybe he was remembering that awful night, the things they'd done, the things they'd said. His dark face certainly had a reddish cast to it.

Matt Dixon. Why did his intense amber eyes burn her skin and make every nerve in her body tingle? His large hands fisted in his pockets. His wide shoulders were sort of hunched as if he felt uneasy around her, too.

Why did she still feel so mixed up about him? Why

couldn't she forget him? She'd spent that awful year at Vanderbilt trying to.

"What are you doing in town today?" he demanded, breaking into her thoughts.

She lifted her pert nose and stared down the length of it because once he'd told her not to look down her nose at him like he was a nobody and she was a queen. "I'm here to get fitted for my debutante gown."

His insolent, long-lashed eyes flicked to the sign above Mission Creek Creations. "Well, now that figures. Rich girl like you. You've got to bait your hook to catch yourself a rich guy. Somebody like Vince Randal, maybe?"

"I'm not out to catch anybody, Dixon."

"Not me, anyway. You made that clear."

"Not you," she agreed.

His nostrils flared above his perfectly carved mouth. *Oh, the things that mouth knew how to do.* She shivered. "Mind your own business, Matt Dixon."

"You ever wonder why you're still so mad at me, Francesca?"

"I could ask you the same question."

"But I know the answer. And so do you."

Her toes actually curled up inside her boots.

"How come you're talking to me today? And looking at me like that?"

"Like what?"

"Trying to start something—darlin'?" he whispered, luring her somehow with the pleasant rumble of husky sound.

In the end it wasn't the teasing innuendo in his deep baritone that sent her skittering into the dress shop for safety. It was the trill of excitement that coursed through her.

His harsh laughter boomed behind her.

She'd had a huge crush on him all through high school. Maybe because he was older and a loner and forbidden. Maybe because somehow because of her own mother, she'd understood about his no-good daddy and his alienation.

Maybe she was a rich girl, at least in his eyes. But her parents hadn't cared about her any more than his daddy had cared about him. They'd run off and left her with Aunt Susie, Uncle Wayne and Grandma Ellie, hadn't they?

What kind of parents did that? Or was it her? What was wrong with her? How come they didn't want her?

Matt Dixon was definitely not somebody her Aunt Susie approved of. She'd made that plain. He was five years older than she was and poor to boot. He came from a bad bunch, who were wild and no good, she said. That was another reason, Frankie, who'd been in one of her rebellious phases, had snuck out to meet him.

The things she'd let him do still shamed her.

Even as they still secretly thrilled her when she lay in bed sometimes, thinking about him. She was as bad as he was. Or maybe he just brought out the badness in her. Always, always he made her think about her real mother. Made her wonder…

No.

Frankie had to stay away from him.

For no reason at all, no sooner had she shut the front door, than she peeked out the shop window to see what he was up to.

He was leaning against the passenger side of his truck talking to a boy that looked about fourteen. Funny, that she hadn't even noticed he had a kid with him. Funny, how the only person on the busy street who held her attention was that ogre, Matt Dixon.

"So, the last debutante has finally showed up," said a sweet voice right behind her. "What's so interesting out there anyway?"

Frankie jumped as if she'd been caught with her hand in the cookie jar.

"Mary!"

Matt was still shaking a little from the encounter with the one young lady he always worked hard to avoid. Nevertheless, he shouldered his way past a knot of men just inside Luke Finnel's hardware store with a false air of nonchalance.

Frankie was so damned pretty. Even if she was a tomboy, who didn't dress right or ever do her hair. She was sexy as hell in those tight jeans and that T-shirt. And her hair—all those wild undisciplined red curls that made her look like she'd just climbed out of a man's bed. Even her small breasts were voluptuous.

Why couldn't she ever wear a bra? For him she

personified sensuality. He knew just how good she'd be if he ever got her in bed.

She took after her mother. *Princess* Heather.

Damn Francesca Moore and her blue blood. She didn't have to do one damn thing to get him hard and hot. He was mad as hell about it, too.

He headed blindly down an aisle. Why had he come inside, anyway? Where the hell was his list? He jabbed a hand in his shirt pocket. No list!

Why the hell couldn't he stop thinking about that sexy brat? And what possible use did he have for that other brat out in his truck, Lee. How the hell had he let Sheriff Jordan saddle him with a hellion for an entire week?

Not an hour ago, the sheriff had cornered him. "There's a new community service program. Small ranchers can get cowboys free...."

That had gotten Matt's attention. Until he'd figured out the sheriff was hell-bent on emptying his jail. Still, he'd let himself be strong-armed into meeting Lee, who hadn't even looked up when he'd said hi.

"No way," Matt had told Jordan out of the kid's earshot.

"It's either your ranch or jail."

"I've got enough problems of my own."

"Lee's fourteen. I don't have anywhere else to put him. He serves time. Or he does community service. Your choice. Besides, it's no secret, you could use the help."

"I don't need anybody's help."

"Like you said, you've got problems."

Somehow the sheriff had sweet-talked him into it.

"Hey, Dixon," said a hard, familiar voice behind him. "You're just the man I need to speak to."

"Vince—"

Matt's palms got sweaty and his heart raced faster. Vince Randal was his banker.

"About your daddy's old loans—"

'Not here," Matt whispered.

Vince lowered his voice, too. "You haven't answered my letters, Dixon."

"Haven't had time to go through the mail."

"Or my calls."

Matt jammed his hands in his pockets and rocked back on his boot heels. "Haven't had time to check my machine, either."

They stared at each other, each man pushing at the other with hard eyes.

"Call me. Monday. We need to talk," Vince said, relenting a little.

Matt nodded and turned away.

"Dixon, you friends with the Moore girl?" Vince called after him.

"I know her."

"Frankie's got the same bad habit you do. She doesn't return my calls either."

"Is that right?" Matt replied mildly.

"Did she ask *you* to be her escort?"

"What?"

Vince sighed with visible relief.

So, she *was* playing hard to get, trying to catch herself a rich one this time around. She'd damned sure hooked him with that game.

Matt had done everything he could think of to forget her, but she still crawled into his dreams, even when he was damn near dead with exhaustion. Just the sight of her on the sidewalk today had lit a raw fuse.

He wasn't rich enough. Or good enough. If he dated her openly, everybody would say he was after her money.

Maybe he was poor. Maybe he owed money on every cow, fence post and acre. But he was his own man, and he planned to stay that way.

What he'd better do was find another woman—fast.

Maybe tonight he'd go to the Saddlebag Bar. He'd pick up a girl and take her home. He'd forget about Frankie—once and for all.

Chapter 2

The white satin ball gown ballooned into the mirrored fitting room and crammed Mary and Frankie together into one tiny corner.

Mary was on her hands and knees behind Frankie, struggling with the hooks of Frankie's black lace merry widow.

"Ouch!" Mary said, shaking a bruised finger. "I hooked myself! Could you please quit squirming and just stand still."

Mary sucked her finger and then pushed her thick glasses higher up her nose.

"But it's so itchy." Frankie stuck out her tongue and jumped up and down. On an impulse she plucked a yellow and a red rose out of the vase on the low table and stuck them between her teeth.

"Frankie!" Mary plucked the roses out of her mouth and jabbed them back in the vase. "You're acting like a great big baby. Margaret left me in charge. If I handle you, she'll be so proud."

"You mean Witch McKenzie. So, even she can't stand her own little shop of horrors any more than I can."

The silver bells on Mrs. McKenzie's front door tinkled a warning.

"Shhh," Mary whispered. "Customers! Behave."

"What is this awful torture device anyway? It's way worse than a bra. It sucks in at the waist so tight, I can barely breathe." Frankie began flipping the cups of the black, boned corset contraption up and down, giggling rebelliously as she revealed her rosy tipped breasts and then covered them up again. "Now you see them. Now you don't. Not that I've got all that much to strut."

"Quit. They'll hear you!"

"I don't even have boobs. See." Frankie resumed flipping the black merry widow up and down again.

You've got big nipples. He'd said that.

Frankie swallowed at the hard lump in her throat. Just the thought of him made her stay still through the rest of the fitting, her only comment being that the voluminous white dress made her look like a red-headed marshmallow.

"You look like a princess," Mary said.

Frankie gasped. "You know better than to ever ever call me that."

"Sorry."

Only when Frankie was zipping herself back into her jeans and threading her belt through the belt loops, did both girls smile and relax again.

"See, that wasn't so bad," Mary said.

"It was torture. Sheer torture. Against all my principles. And the ball will be even worse. I can't wait 'til it's all over. Aunt Susie gave me this awful list of stuff I have to do. I've been putting it all off, hoping it would go away. But she really got on my case this morning, so I'm going to try to get everything done I can today. Then I'll just put this whole nightmare out of my mind."

"Until the ball," Mary said.

Frankie pulled out her list. "You know how every deb has to participate in some type of community service for twenty hours—"

"Laura is making cheesecakes for her church's cake sale."

"Well, Aunt Susie has it in her head that it would be good for me to work in the gift shop she runs for the hospital. She wants me to put on lipstick and do something ladylike for a change. She actually wants me to sell flowers and candy."

"What's wrong with that?"

"You know how Vince's mother is there, like, all the time—"

"So—"

"Well, Vince has been calling me."

"Vince? You and Vince?"

"No! That's what I'm trying to tell you! But Aunt Susie wants me to date him. She wants me to get to know Mrs. Randal better. And since Vince usually drives his mother to the hospital, I'd probably have to see him and talk to him."

"Vince is so cute."

"That's what Aunt Susie says. So, she should date him. Or maybe you—"

Mary blushed. "She's married to your Uncle Wayne."

"Which means she should let me lead my own life. She wants me inside the house, cooking and sewing and primping. Or working in a gift shop...selling flowers, chasing a man she thinks is a good catch. I want to be outside...or in the barn with Jez and the other animals."

"She only wants what's best for you."

"What she thinks is best. She and I are nothing alike. Everything Uncle Wayne and I love, she hates."

"She loves both of you."

"Yes. To distraction. She's always wanting Uncle Wayne to take her to a party just when he needs to be trapping cows or something else that's vital. She has no understanding of ranch work."

Mary picked up Frankie's list. "Oh! Look! She didn't note even half the stuff Laura had on her list that counts for community service."

"Just the awful ladylike things she wants me to do."

"Did you know that working on small ranches in

Lone Star County qualifies as community service this year?''

''What?''

''There's this cool new ranch program you can sign up for at the library.''

Frankie perked to attention.

''Because of the drought and all, a lot of the smaller, struggling ranchers can't afford to pay cowboys. So, some of the bigger ranchers thought volunteering to work for them would be a really valuable community service.''

''My aunt deliberately left that off! Because she knew—'' Frankie chewed on her thumbnail. ''Well, I'll show her. I'll just go over there right now and see about it.''

''What about the gift shop—''

''By the time Aunt Susie finds out I'm not working there, I'll have put in my twenty hours. What will she be able to say?''

''Plenty—knowing her.''

''I should have a little fun out of this dumb debutante nonsense, now shouldn't I?''

''Matt Dixon. I can't work for Matt Dixon.''

''The sheriff emptied out the jail,'' Louisa had explained. *''Every other ranch has got more cowboys, if you want to call those rough customers that, than they can handle.''*

''Dixon and I don't like each other much.''

''Too bad. Dixon really needs the help. I heard

*through the grapevine he could lose his place, that
Vince is pressuring him because Dixon hasn't been
making his payments. Remember how BoBo borrowed
all that money—"*

"Lose his ranch? Matt loves his ranch. He's so
proud, too."

"Exactly. Be a good girl and go help that nice boy
out. That's what community service is all about."

"I can't work for him."

"You're as stubborn as he is."

Reluctantly Frankie headed to the flower shop, only
to accelerate when she saw Vince's car parked in the
hospital lot. Then she couldn't believe it! She actually
turned down the rutted lane two miles short of her
uncle's ranch that led over the low water bridge
straight down to Matt's place.

Nobody seemed to be around when she pulled up
in front of his house. Used to be that when she snuck
over, he'd always been waiting for her at the gate, an
eager smile lighting up his handsome dark face.

She jumped out of her pickup and then shivered.
Matt's house looked dark and lost, set way back in the
trees under all those grapevines. He hadn't mowed
around the house lately either. Probably hadn't had the
time. Or maybe last year, he'd mowed it just for her.

The grass was nearly waist-high, and it rustled in
the warm wind as she walked toward the barn. But the
air smelled sweet—just like it did at home.

But this wasn't home. This was Matt's place. She
was crazy to come here.

Crazy.

And yet…

And yet she couldn't seem to stop herself. Somehow it was the only part of this debutante nonsense that made the least bit of sense.

When she got near his barn, the stench of urine nearly stopped her cold. But once inside, the acrid smoke from a cigarette bothered her a lot more than the odor of unmucked stalls. Then she saw a cigarette glowing orange in the dark. A long, bony brown arm lifted it sullenly.

"Matt?"

The shadowy figure didn't answer.

Her heart skittered, but she stood where she was. Slowly her eyes grew accustomed to the gloom, and she recognized the boy she'd seen in Matt's truck slumped on the floor beside a pitchfork he must have thrown down. The tip of the cigarette brightened again as he inhaled. She marched toward him and lunged for the cigarette before he could bring it to his lips again.

"What do you think you're doing—smoking in a barn?"

"Sure beats shoveling manure."

"Which is what you're supposed to be doing, am I right?" She threw the cigarette down in disgust, carefully stomping it out.

"I'm not *his* slave."

"Dixon's?"

The boy nodded, scowling. "I don't have to do what he says."

"You're from the jail, right?"

He slouched lower, his black hair dangling in a thick, greasy clump over his forehead.

"You want to go back there?"

"You gonna make me?"

"Maybe. Or…maybe I'll volunteer to help you clean up this mess."

"You from jail, too?"

"No. I'm a debutante."

"The annual Lone Star County Debutante Ball," he sneered.

"Believe me, it's every bit as awful as a jail sentence."

"So, what's a rich debutante doing in Dixon's lousy barn?"

The barn door rolled loudly. "Good question," thundered a voice vibrating with violence from the other end of the barn.

When Matt strode toward her, the boy hopped up with his pitchfork and vanished into a stall.

"Outside," Matt ordered as the pitchfork chinged across concrete.

Once they were out in the sunshine, Frankie felt safer somehow. He'd traded his town jeans for a soft, ragged pair that were faded to a shade that was nearly white. He wore a torn white T-shirt that was so tight it pulled across his massive torso. He seemed sculpted of solid brown muscle. All of a sudden it wasn't so easy to look at him, at least not if she wanted to breathe normally.

"So, what are you doing here, rich girl?"

"Don't call me that."

"Answer my question."

"Community service. Like your felon back there in the stall."

"Lee? He's all of fourteen and in trouble with the law. No family. He hasn't got a whole lot of other choices. You do." He hesitated. "I don't want you here."

"You need the help."

"I don't need anybody's help. Especially not yours. I'm doing just fine on my own, thank you very much."

"Then why did Louisa say Vince..."

His golden eyes flashed. "Don't you ever talk to Vince about me—understand?" His voice was rough.

"I wouldn't."

"'Cause you wouldn't want him to know what you were to me once—is that it?"

"You can think that if you want."

"I don't want your pity. What's between him and me has to do with my personal business—understand? I don't want your pity...or your help. Or your charity, or whatever else you think this is."

"I don't pity you. Maybe I came here...as...as a friend. Friends help each other."

"Friends? *Us?*" His gorgeous mouth curled. "Please." He looked away.

It hurt that he rejected the idea of her friendship.

"Okay. Maybe it wouldn't just be me helping you. Maybe you'd be helping me, too." When he frowned, she rushed on before he could argue. "I have to do community service to be a deb. I'd rather do ranch work than sell flowers, okay? Even if it means putting up with you. Your ranch was the only one with a vacancy in the program. I wouldn't have come here otherwise."

"I didn't sign up for any damn program."

"Well, then what's Lee doing here if you didn't?"

He didn't answer.

"Well, I'm here. Same as he is. And I'm staying whether you want me to or not."

When he took a step toward her, she backed up involuntarily.

He grinned. "You think so, huh?"

"So, just give me something to do."

"By God, maybe I will," he rasped, edging forward. Next his large brown hand clamped down on her arm, and he yanked her closer.

"What are you doing?"

"A long time ago, I told you I wouldn't touch you unless you started things up between us again. Well, you're here, aren't you, priming the old pump?"

"That's not why I came, and you know it!"

"What if I don't choose to believe you?"

He pulled her closer, snugging her body against a wall of hot male muscle encased in soft white cotton.

"Please, don't," she whispered raggedly.

"You're begging me to kiss you. Every time you look at me, you eat me alive with your eyes."

"I don't."

"How come you dropped out of college and came home? Did you miss me?"

"No! I just didn't like Vanderbilt. 'Cause I don't know what I want to do with my life, and college is a waste of time until I figure that out."

His fingers brushed a tendril out of her eyes. "I missed you. God, I missed you. I was glad you came home…even if you always avoided me." She could feel him shaking and realized how much the admission had cost him.

"You avoided me, too."

"You shouldn't have come over here," he said. "Not unless you want this." He moved a hand slowly up her arm and caressed her neck.

"I don't."

The heat from his open palms sliding up her throat to cup her chin burned even before he lowered his lips to hers. "Well, maybe I do."

"Quit acting like some caveman."

"I don't like how I feel and act when I'm around you any better than you do. But I can't seem to help myself."

"Neither can I…"

Her arms circled his neck, and she opened her mouth to his. When his tongue slid inside, her fingers curled into his thick golden hair.

His kisses were unhurried, yet his mouth and tongue caused intolerable waves of pleasure to wash through her. Soon she was so hot and tingly, she wanted more. So much more. She pressed her body tightly against his, mashing her breasts against his chest, rubbing her thighs into his.

Which was wrong, of course. Not that it felt the least bit wrong.

Still, she balled her trembling hands into fists and drew them down from his neck and then around his wide shoulders until she felt his shoulder blades. Flattening her hands and splaying her fingertips, she shoved as hard as she could against his massive chest. Her strength was puny compared to his. It was like trying to budge a granite boulder. When he resisted, she realized he could do whatever he wanted to.

"There's nothing to be so afraid of, darlin'—" His voice was husky, still aroused with desire. His tongue made another delicious foray inside her mouth.

"Oh, sweet heaven..."

Everything he did made her feel dizzy and helpless.

Even as her blood pulsed in an agony of need, she pushed harder. "We've got to stop this—now!"

He stiffened and slowly loosened his grip. Last of all he withdrew his mouth from hers and opened his long-lashed, golden eyes to meet hers.

White sunlight slashed across the knife-blade edge of his nose, across the carved planes of his proud, rugged face. Then he held up his hands in mock surrender and slowly backed away from her.

"Okay," he muttered hoarsely. "Have it your way, darlin'."

Gradually he banked the wild fires in his eyes. After a minute the only sign of his turbulent emotions was

the savage ticking of that telltale muscle along his jawline.

She watched it jump as he stood there in the shade
of his mesquite trees. A wind whispered across the
grasses, and she shivered. A loose shutter banged. His
ranch seemed so lonely. So did he. He was cutting her
out of his life as deliberately as he cut out the rest of
the world.

She wasn't used to this sort of deliberate, self-
inflicted solitude. At home the phone was always ringing. Aunt Susie was cooking, and the cowboys were
constantly banging in and out of the house. The cook
served tacos or beans or barbecue every weekday out
in the cookhouse for lunch. Aunt Susie was always
having other ranchers over for dinner parties at night.
Then there were the shopping sprees to town on Saturdays and church on Sundays.

Matt said nothing. He was standing very still. He
looked so alone—so lonely that her heart clutched.
Sunlight flickered behind the trees. She dug her nails
into her palms. Not that the pain brought her to her
senses. Involuntarily, she took a fatal step toward him
and stretched out to touch him.

"Go home...where you belong." His voice was
mild, but his lips were tight. "And don't come back."

"I could help you."

"That's not what I want you for. I want you
like all those men wanted your mother.... *Princess
Heather.*"

His words were like a blow out of the dark. Since

she hadn't seen them coming she couldn't ward them off.

"I'm not like her! I'm not! I'm…I'm like my Aunt Susie!"

He laughed.

"I am!"

"Everybody knows you're nothing like your silly Aunt Susie."

Suddenly Frankie saw a homesick little girl watching her golden mother on a yacht with the purple mountains of Turkey misting against the horizon. Her bikini-clad mother had been laughing at her daughter as she sat down on a strange man's lap and curled her body around his.

"I want to go home," Frankie had said.

Next Frankie saw the stacks of postcards in her bureau drawer.

Monaco.
Darling—I guess you've read by now—I married the prince… Italy…last week. Ha! Sorry there wasn't time to send for you. Ha!
Love,
                              Princess Heather.
P.S. Next summer when you visit me—you'll love him. Ha! Give your horse a kiss for me. Ha!

There hadn't been a next summer. Frankie hadn't seen her mother since.

"My mother's not like you think…."

But she was.

"She's not like anybody thinks!" Frankie persisted.

"Then why does she make all the tabloids?"

"Because she's so beautiful and admired...not just by men. She married a prince, didn't she?"

"You're running scared because you're like her. I want to be your first man. Then you can run off like she did and chase counts and princes."

First. The word cut as cruelly as a knife. As if she'd have many lovers. Counts? Princes? Was he out of his mind?

"I'm not what you think."

"Well, you don't belong here. Not on my place. Even if you aren't like her, what could a deb like you know about ranch work?"

"More than that boy in the barn, that's for sure! You let him stay! Why not me? I—I could supervise him. If...if it hadn't been for me, he would've burned your dumb barn down!"

"Was he smoking again?"

She nodded.

"Thank—" Matt bit back his words of gratitude. "I don't give a damn what you did! I know all I need to know about you. Bottom line—you're rich and I'm poor. You went to Vanderbilt, and then dropped out...to find yourself. I'm still working my way through night school at A & M in Kingsville on school loans. Hell, half the time I'm so tired I fall asleep in class. I made a C– in my last course 'cause I never have time to study—" He raked his hands through his hair. "Hell, what am I telling you for? You don't care."

"Maybe I would, if you'd stop being such a proud crybaby and let me!"

He colored. The nerve in his jaw jumped so furiously, she grew afraid for him. "Go home," he whispered.

"I—I came here today...because...because I—I stupidly wanted to be your friend!"

"What's it gonna take for you to get it—that's not what I want you for."

"You...you go to hell, Matt Dixon!"

"Go home," he said.

Fighting hot tears of shame and hurt, Frankie turned and ran.

Chapter 3

With flaming cheeks Frankie glared at her reflection in her bedroom mirror. But she didn't see herself. She saw a tall cowboy with yellow hair and narrow, golden eyes.

I'm not the girl you think I am, Mr. Know-it-all Dixon! I'm not.

Frankie was sitting on the very edge of her dressing stool yanking a comb through her tangled curls.

"Ouch!"

Gingerly she pulled the comb loose from the snarl of hair and shook out a sticker burr into her trash can.

Her heart raced and her eyes flashed as her thoughts turned back to Matt. She hated it when a person made her so mad she couldn't quit arguing with him in her head. Ever since Matt had run her off last week, he'd constantly popped into her mind. And always, she talked back to him big time.

She released a little rush of air and plucked a blade of grass out of her hair with an exasperated hand.

Why? Why couldn't she put him behind her? Why couldn't she stop trying to figure out how she could work for him instead of working at the gift shop?

Was he right about her, after all? Was she as man-crazy as her glamorous mother? Was she really a self-deluded, naïve wanton? Once she had sex, would she hop from man to man?

Just the thought of Matt thinking her so low had her trembling and itching to defend herself again.

She lifted her comb and shook it at her reflection.

''I'm not like her. I'm not,'' she croaked again.

You're doing it again.

For no reason at all she leaned down only to stare fixedly at the brass pull of her bottom drawer. One tentative fingertip on cool brass and she felt her control slipping. No sooner had she eased the drawer open an inch than her heart quickened in anxious little spurts.

Then the big leather-bound scrapbook resting on top of all the neat stacks of postcards stopped her cold.

''Courage,'' she whispered. Blinking back tears, she lifted the heavy album onto her lap. She had to say a quick little prayer before she could open it. And when she did, she flipped the pages so fast, they became a blur.

Even so the memories inside the book were such an assault, she slammed it closed so fast that a snapshot flew out, fluttering to her feet. Leaning down she saw the dreaded image of a slim, gorgeous blonde in a strange man's arms.

Her mother. No! She was Princess Heather now. Frankie didn't know who the man was. After all, there had been so many.

Frankie stared out the window. A mockingbird was jabbering fiercely with a squirrel. She watched the frantic bird hop higher and higher up the pink branches of a crepe myrtle tree. She felt just as desperate. With a long sigh, Frankie retrieved the picture and laid it down on her bureau. Then she spent an excessive amount of time smoothing it out. When it was perfectly flat, her eyes clung to the young, smiling blonde.

When she'd been younger, Frankie had thought her mother was the most beautiful woman in the world. She'd seemed like a dream mother, the perfect, exquisite fairytale mother. Aunt Susie had always told her how much her mother loved her.

"That's why she sends you all those presents and postcards and pictures."

Frankie had read the cards and thought that someday her mother would come to live at the ranch with her, that someday she would want her only daughter.

Frankie knelt and lifted a card from the drawer, reading it swiftly.

Cairo
Darling—
Having fun.
Ha!

It's hot though.
Ha!
Wish you were here.
Love you bunches,

                                        Heather

Always *Heather*. And now Princess Heather. Never Mother. The only reason Heather had married her father and stayed married to him for those six short months was to give her baby daughter his name. At least Heather wrote her and dutifully invited her to come to visit wherever she was for a week every July. Not that Frankie ever went anymore, not after that week in Greece.

Frankie's father had had four wives. He never wrote her at all.

"What can I say? He's a playboy," Aunt Susie had explained.

"And Mother?"

"She was always the most popular girl in school. Not that she studied. She was simply too beautiful."

"So are you."

"She was different. Her candle always burned a little too brightly. She liked to be noticed. What can I say? She wasn't meant to be a mother, and I was. Only I couldn't get pregnant." Aunt Susie's eyes had misted. "And she did. So, she gave you to me. There was no other solution. You're the only daughter I'll ever have. And Uncle Wayne, why he's better than ten fathers, isn't he?"

"Better than ten thousand. And Grandma Ellie...
She's wonderful, too."

"So you see, life has a way of working out...after
a few surprises. There's always a few curve balls in
any game."

Frankie replaced her mother's picture in the album
and stared at her reflection again.

The wide-eyed girl in the mirror with the smudge
on her nose in no way resembled the perfectly coifed
elegance of the overly made-up blonde in the photo-
graph. Why couldn't Matt see who she really was?

With a sad smile, Frankie reached up and plucked
another sticker burr out of her tangled red curls. She'd
fallen when she'd run from that javelina in the brush
after she'd accidentally surprised one of its baby javelinas. Wild javelinas made more attentive mothers
than...

Frankie puckered her dirty nose. Not only didn't she
look glamorous, she smelled bad, too. She didn't even
own a single bottle of expensive French perfume like
her mother wore. Her jeans, not designer jeans, but
discount store jeans, were torn and so muddy and
stank so foully of sweat and horse and barn, they
would take at least a couple of washings.

Quickly she began tearing them off.

When she was naked, she eyed her reflection even
more critically. No hourglass, movie star curves like
Princess Heather had! Frankie was long and slim, too
slim on top—that was for sure.

But you've got big nipples. Matt's voice had been raw and hoarse.

Just the memory of the hunger in his eyes made her nipples bead.

A chill shot through her. Maybe she was too skinny and too flat-chested. Somehow that devil still found her sexy.

Which was the problem. Sex was all he saw or wanted from her.

Who cares what he thinks? Put him out of your mind.

Instead, she caressed her breasts. Remembering the way he'd kissed them, gently circling her nipples with his lips, she moved her fingertips round and round in the same way.

."See how they perk up to attention," he'd whispered.

Hardly knowing what she did, she trailed her fingertips down her belly and traced the same path his lips had followed. She shivered a little and then yanked her hands away. It was no use. Her hands didn't feel nearly as good as his hot wet lips.

All Matt had to do was touch her to make her go achy and breathless.

She wanted his lips on her body again.

She wanted him again—plain and simple.

Only her feelings were way more complex than his.

She wasn't like her mother.

So—what was she like?

As always, questions like that confused and frustrated her.

When a knock sounded on her bedroom door, she jumped. In a flash, she grabbed the tail of her navy bedspread and ripped it from the bed, wrapping it around her waist.

Aunt Susie burst inside.

Groping to pull the spread higher, Frankie whirled indignantly. "I didn't say come in."

"You don't have a stitch on. Whatever were you doing?"

Touching myself the way Matt Dixon—

"This is my room! I—I was about to take a shower," Frankie spoke primly, hating herself when she blushed.

They stared at each other.

"You're up to some mischief."

No way could she confess her crush on Matt Dixon, of all people!

Her aunt came up to her and kissed the smudge on the tip of Frankie's nose. "I never could keep you clean when you were a little girl. I still can't. Promise me…promise me…that you won't tromp out to the barn in your ball gown to groom Jez."

They both laughed.

"You can't ride her in that dress, either."

"I know! I can't even breathe in it."

"You have the prettiest skin…so soft and smooth. And your hair. Youth—" Aunt Susie fluffed at the curls that fell over her shoulders. "All that glorious red hair. And that long, lean body of yours. You're so graceful, too. Why, you could be a model.''

"Don't be ridiculous. I'm a rancher! A cowgirl!''

"I never saw a girl that had so much and did so little with it. You don't even date.''

Frankie blushed. *No, but I have the hots for the next-door rancher you despise.*

"You're not going to be young forever.''

Frankie sighed. "We've had this conversation before, you know.''

Aunt Susie laughed. "Not that it ever does the least bit of good.'' She paused, her eyes glued to her niece. "Seriously, Diane Randal called and said you've only been in the hospital's gift shop once when you worked those two hours. I hate to pressure you, but you can't keep putting this off. You have to do your community service.''

Pulling free, Frankie notched her nose up rather defiantly. "I—I'm doing something else.''

Where had that come from?

"What?''

"Does it matter, so long as it qualifies as community service?''

"I suppose not.'' Aunt Susie admitted. "You do know how much all this means to me, don't you?''

Frankie nodded. "I suffered through all those boring etiquette lessons, didn't I?''

"But you yawned and never participated.''

Frankie sighed. "I'm sorry. This isn't easy for me.''

"Your season brings back your mother's and my

coming out season in Houston. Oh, how wonderful it all was to be young and beautiful, to have your whole life ahead of you.'' Aunt Susie smiled. ''You know, I really think it would be nice if you got a new hairdo at the country club's Body Perfect spa.''

''They'd make me look weird.''

''Just for the debutante ball. Oh, please. Please...''

''All right.''

''About the gift shop... You're sure you're doing something else—''

''Very.''

That settled it. Frankie had to go back to Dixon Ranch—tomorrow.

Not just for Aunt Susie.

But for herself.

For Matt too!

She had to prove to that stubborn hunk that she wasn't what he thought she was.

The screen door banged, and Matt sprang awake.

''Doesn't anybody around here wash the dishes—''

Frankie.

His heart lifted at the sound of *her* voice.

His sex hardened.

Relief flooded him. So—it wasn't broken. He couldn't resist touching himself down there—just to make sure.

He grinned and stretched. *Thank God.*

''So what if I forgot to wash them,'' came Lee's sullen rumble.

The kid had actually gotten up on time like he was supposed to. Maybe the sheriff was right about the brat after all.

"No time like the present to do them, then." Frankie's impertinent voice made Matt's heart skip a beat. "Where does the lazy slave driver keep the pancake mix anyway?"

Cupboard doors slammed so jauntily, Matt grabbed his head and rubbed his pounding temples. The lazy slave driver had a helluva headache.

What was *she* doing here? He'd deliberately driven her off.

Not that she'd been far from his mind—ever—not for one single minute. It was like she was a ghost—haunting him, and at the most embarrassing moments, too. Like last night when he'd tried to bed a new woman.

Only Frankie was worse than any ghost.

She was alive—a soft-skinned wanton with long slim legs that went forever. It hadn't helped that Vince had mentioned her again right after he'd called about his father's loans.

As if the pressure in his life hadn't been great enough already, every time Matt lay in bed lately, he'd wondered where Frankie was sleeping. Was she in Vince's arms or lying in her own bed, alone, just two miles down the road? Either image drove him crazy.

A damned debutante—Princess Heather's daughter. Did being a princess's daughter make her a princess, too? Any way you sliced the cupcake, Francesca Moore was way too rich for his blood.

"You are my sunshine..."

Matt's heart skipped lightly when she began humming.

Groggily he got out of bed and stumbled into the bathroom.

"My only sunshine..."

Because of you, Miss Moore, I tied one on at the Saddlebag Bar last night. Hell, I did my best to get laid. Didn't work out though.

When he'd started kissing, Sally—or was it Sarah?—Frankie had taken hold of his mind. Or at least his body. His appalling failure in Sally's or Sarah's bed had totally humiliated him.

Matt took a long, hot shower, lingering in the steamy cubicle deliberately, scrubbing in places, like the inside of his ears that he usually forgot about, soaping his hair twice. Then he shaved with a new blade. He slicked his wet hair back with a comb, spending way more time on it than usual. He grabbed his best jeans, the ones with the razor-sharp creases. It took him more than five minutes to choose the black shirt she'd once said he looked so cute in. He was jamming an arm through a sleeve when she laughed at something Lee said.

What the hell are you doing, Dixon?

Frowning, he tossed the shirt and jeans down on the floor. Leaning down, he yanked his dirty clothes from yesterday off the back of his chair.

No way was he dressing up for her.

You sure as hell want to, though.

On his way out, he stole a glimpse of his clean-scrubbed face and shining yellow hair. Catching himself again, he flushed.

He didn't give a damn what he looked like. He didn't.

The smell of pancakes and her merry singing drew Matt to the kitchen door like a siren's song. Once there his long legs seemed to lock up, and he stood paralyzed.

What was wrong with him? He felt as gun-shy and tongue-tied as a high school kid who was afraid to talk to a popular girl.

Matt swallowed convulsively. Was he going to cower behind the door forever? He had to throw her out. There was no other way.

Matt pushed the door open and charged into the kitchen like a bull on a rampage.

She jumped slightly. Then she whirled to face him, holding the spatula up in a defensive position. "You hungry?" she whispered in a voice that was as sweet as sugar and as soft as velvet.

His eyes devoured her slim body encased in jeans so tight she looked like she'd sewn herself into them. Her demure green blouse was buttoned all the way up her neck concealing those sexy breasts of hers. Lush fiery tendrils tumbled about her rosy face.

Hungry? Just looking at her did what Sally's kisses hadn't been able to do last night. *Hungry?*

Hell, he was about to burst inside his jeans. He wanted her so badly he wanted to tell Lee to scram, so he could take her in his arms and make love to her. Always, always she'd been so innocent and virginal, he'd had to hold himself back.

No kissing. No touching, Dixon.

He felt like he was going to fly apart if he didn't let go of some of what he felt. He wanted to kiss her and for her to kiss him back as she had sometimes when she'd forgotten to be afraid. Then he would strip her slowly, reverently removing each garment.

When she was naked, he would lick her everywhere.

Just the thought of her naked and his tongue exploring her made him so hot he wanted to grab her and push her up against the wall.

No kissing. No touching. No thinking about it either.

Maybe after he'd had her, he'd get her out of his system.

As if she read his mind, a telltale blush crept up her throat. "I meant—"

"I know." His stomach tightened. It was his turn to feel awkward. He looked away. "Smells good," he admitted almost wistfully.

"Want some pancakes?"

More than anything. Almost anything.

So, instead of ordering her off his land and out of his life, he swallowed. Slowly he dragged the chair beside Lee back from the table, scraping the legs across the wooden floor, scarring it some more.

"So, you washed the dishes, huh?" he said to Lee because it was easier to talk to him than to talk to her.

"Yeah." Lee swigged his milk straight from the carton. "She made me."

"How'd she do it, when I can't?"

"Said I couldn't have any pancakes."

"Syrup?" she said sweetly to Matt as she handed Lee a glass. "Use a glass," she whispered. "If you were a deb, they'd teach you not to drink like that in etiquette class."

The two of them laughed conspiratorially, and Matt felt a stab of jealousy.

That voice. That smile. That laughter—so easy and light.

She was so damned beautiful.

He liked the simple pleasure of waking up to her in his kitchen, too.

That rebel thought got him so hot and bothered he got really riled. His hand fisted around the plastic syrup bottle, squeezing it with such a vengeance that a geyser of golden goo shot onto his pancakes.

"Somebody's got a sweet tooth," she purred.

The first bite of her syrup-drenched pancakes was literally melting on his tongue when her slim hand placed a cup of coffee next to his tanned fingers.

When had anybody ever cooked him breakfast? He couldn't remember.

The white smooth hand beside his had not released his saucer yet. "Can I stay?" she whispered. Her low, vulnerable tone made him ache.

Lee dropped his fork with a clatter, causing Matt and Frankie to jump.

Then the kitchen got really really quiet.

''Sorry, guys!'' Lee whispered, growing self-conscious as the tension built.

Frankie was the first to turn away. Still, even with her back turned, Matt was keenly aware of her rigid posture, as she waited for his answer.

''She's a good cook. Better than you,'' Lee inter-jected. ''Why can't she stay?''

Matt lifted his coffee cup and sipped the hot, fla-vorful coffee, considering.

''How's the coffee?'' she asked.

''Perfect,'' Matt admitted.

''It's hazelnut,'' she said. ''Freshly ground this morning. I brought it from home.''

''It's fit for a princess.''

When she turned toward him helplessly, the mixture of raw pain and mute longing he read in her eyes ate him alive.

''Can I stay?'' she repeated softly.

His heart thudded.

''Can I?''

In a low voice calculated to reveal nothing, he said, ''Maybe...just for today.''

She edged closer to him, a smile fluttering at the corner of her pretty mouth. ''Maybe?'' she taunted. ''Just for today? I don't think so—you lazy slave driver.''

Then she laughed.

When Matt jerked his head up, he saw the sheen of new tears at the corners of her sparkling green eyes. He wanted to touch her face, to pull her close, to dry her tears with his kisses.

How she thrilled him! Suddenly life didn't feel so bleak or hopeless.

Not with a bellyful of the best damned pancakes inside him.

Not with her here.

Suddenly he laughed too.

"What's so funny?" Lee growled.

"Nothin'," Matt said, unable to stop staring at her.

"Ya'll are crazy."

"You're right about that," Matt admitted. Then to her alone he repeated himself.

"Just for today."

She saluted him with way too much relish.

Chapter 4

Just for today. Famous last words.

Matt rubbed his forehead, and then squeezed his eyes shut. When he opened them again, the column of numbers was as blurry as ever. The negative balance at the bottom slammed him like a fist in the gut.

Deflated, he sank back in his chair where he'd been sprawled half the night. Then with a frown he hurled himself away from his massive rolltop desk. Pitching the last ledger on top of the others littering the floor, he rolled his chair up to the desk again. Slowly, he opened his checkbook again and ran a callused thumb down the numbers.

"Damn."

He slammed the register closed. Next he grabbed the thick stack of unopened bills, put a rubber band around them and threw them into the top drawer.

What was the use? He'd juggled the numbers every way he could—to no advantage. He flung himself wearily to his feet, stretched his long arms. Then he stepped over the neat piles of cancelled checks that lay in little stacks all over the floor. Jamming fists into his pockets, he started pacing. His strides lengthened and speeded up.

He was still pacing when red rays spilled like feathers of flame into his office. Outside the leaves seemed on fire. He stalked over to the tall window and leaned on the windowsill.

She'd be here soon.

When he eyed the spot under a mesquite tree where she always parked, the muscle in his jawline began to throb. Not that he'd started getting up even earlier in the morning because he was eager to see her. Not that he ever listened for her truck when he did chores.

He wasn't a lovestruck fool for her. He wasn't.

The sky glowed orange. Soon it would be so hot and humid his shirt and hair would stick to his skin like wet glue. He loved the quiet and the stillness of the ranch, especially at this hour. Just as he hated the bustle and roar of cities. Even Mission Creek, especially on crowded Saturdays, gave him claustrophobia a lot of the time.

A mourning dove cooed. The vivid reds and golds that washed the mesquite branches and wild grapevines dangling outside his window made him think of the highlights that shone in *her* hair.

Red and yellow kill a fellow. That rule was supposed

to apply to snakes. Not to a beautiful woman with red and gold tresses like Frankie.

With a violent twisting motion, he shoved himself out of the red glare. He couldn't believe she'd been working for him here nearly two weeks.

Vince had called yesterday afternoon. "Matt, you've gotta come by the bank, so we can clean up these loose ends."

Matt had still been talking to Vince when the sheriff's big Suburban SUV had rolled up his drive and stopped right beside him.

"Think you can keep Lee a little longer?" the sheriff had hollered.

"Jordan, can't you see, I've got my hands full—"

Vince hung up.

The sheriff climbed out of his truck. "Lee's old man ran off...."

"Why'd you bother to ask me?"

"I knew you'd say yes."

When the sheriff drove off, Matt heard a sound at his kitchen window, but when he'd looked to see if she was there, the window banged shut.

Matt had gone into the kitchen and found Frankie in an apricot shirt and skintight jeans at the counter stirring a pitcher of lemonade.

Just having a redhead in his kitchen, in jeans like that, in his house, had been a powerful comfort. Even her air of nonchalance and the languid grace of her slim arm stirring the silver ladle through the lemonade had been mesmerizing somehow.

"What are you watching?" she'd whispered.

"What were you watchin'?"

"Nothing much. You…maybe."

She'd poured him a glass of lemonade, sliding a tall glass purling with condensation across the table. Briefly the tips of their hot fingers had touched and lingered. Only when she'd withdrawn her hand, had he lifted his glass to his mouth. Then he'd drunk two more tall glasses just to make her pour them, not speaking to her, yet feeling so easy with her, no words had been necessary.

"You're a good man…to keep Lee."

"Blame it on the sheriff. This whole thing's his doing."

"No. It's yours."

"Not mine. Yours. I couldn't have managed him… without your help."

She'd blushed, as uncomfortable with his praise as he always was with hers. But her butt had looked so good in those tight jeans, he'd lingered in the kitchen just to watch her walk around.

Being with her was the one bright spot in his life. The only difficult part of being so near her was the constant battle to keep his hands off her.

Despite those jeans, somehow he had.

Just thinking about her made him grin. She was hell on wheels.

That first day just to test her, he'd started her off by giving her way more than her share of the dirty work.

After their pancake breakfast, he'd stabbed a pitchfork into thick, dirty straw so hard, the handle had bobbed back and forth. "You probably think you're too good to muck my stalls."

"I'll have you know, I have my own horse—Jezebel."

"Why'd you pick a raunchy name like that for?"

"Who says I did, cowboy?" With some effort, she'd tugged the pitchfork out of the hay as defiantly as he'd jammed it in there.

"I bet she's a thoroughbred, too...just like her snippy mistress."

"Snippy? I'll show you snippy!" It was her turn to stab filthy straw, and she did it with even more vengeance than he had. "My point, Slave Driver Dixon, is that I muck Jez's stall out every day—a whole wheelbarrow full."

"Oh, really?"

Even though she was panting hard, she pitched the hay with more determination than ever. "Then I roll it to Aunt Susie's garden which is a long way from the barn. I can help deliver calves, too. I can haul feed."

Feed was a sore point. If the drought persisted, if Vince kept refusing to cut him some slack, he'd have to sell stock no matter how bad the cattle market was. That would be the end for him.

"I can't afford feed," he'd admitted aloud before he'd thought.

When she'd turned and caught his frown, he'd refused to look her square in the eyes.

"This ranch has belonged to Dixons for three generations. Not that it's much...by Lassiter standards."

Her face had softened. "Oh, dear."

Without the slightest hesitation, she'd gently leaned the pitchfork against the back wall and tiptoed to stand beside him in the gloom.

"I'm so sorry, Matt."

He'd turned his face away from her, crossed his arms defensively, and squared his wide shoulders—to shut her out.

When she'd placed a tentative hand lightly on his arm, he'd shaken free and strode several steps closer toward the door. Even so, for just a second or two he'd felt the warm imprint of every single finger through his chambray shirt.

He'd heard her footsteps, felt those warm, light fingers again. "You don't give up easily."

"Neither do you," she said. "Oh, Matt, you've done so much with this place, improved the livestock...the land, too. The way you worked with that tractor last Thursday...plowing all those mesquite roots out—"

"That won't matter now, will it? Not if your friend Randal has his way!"

Still, her words had brought a strange comfort that he was at a loss to understand. Usually he hated being pitied.

"Uncle Wayne is always talking about what a talented cattle breeder you are. About how you've worked so hard, made such a success.''

Her warm fingers and her soft voice that had filled with pride and wonder as she'd praised his accomplishments had warmed him somehow. He'd felt a glow inside that people like her and her uncle admired him. And that had scared him.

"I'm in debt up to my eyeballs, debutante. But you wouldn't know how that feels, would you? You've got money to burn on pretty dresses and deb parties."

She hadn't even flinched. "This place was a shambles when BoBo died. You had to pay off his debts. You've been going to school."

"There's no excuse for failure."

"Maybe you're too hard on yourself. My aunt has a saying—"

"Your aunt is the last thing from a real rancher."

"But she married one, and she's raised one."

"Is that what you think you are today—a rancher?" He'd looked away. "Please…"

"She says that life has a way of working out if we try hard enough. Although she does say it doesn't always work out how we think it should or want it to."

"What are you really doing here? Why do you keep coming back? You've served your time. Your twenty hours were up after the first two days."

He'd felt remorse when hot color had rushed into her cheeks because of the steel in his voice. Not that he'd apologize.

"Maybe I keep asking myself the same question.

You're not all that much fun, you know. You work from dawn to dark. You're anti-social...."

She had such beautiful, translucent, soft skin. So soft. His hand had itched to trace its satiny texture. But he'd known that if he'd succumbed, she would have run. Still, for an unending moment, he hadn't been able to tear his eyes from her face.

"I—I told you. I want to be your friend."

"A *friend?*" Why did she always have to ruin everything by saying that? The word had mocked the wild heat in his blood as well as the emotional turbulence in his heart. Suddenly he'd wanted her so much, her blushing beauty, her very nearness had been unbearable.

He'd peeled her fingers off his shoulders. "Get back to mucking—debutante."

"Will do—slave driver."

Matt stepped over the ledgers scattered all over the floor and fell back into his chair. Absently, he shuffled a month-old, thick stack of bills before he jammed them onto the spindle.

Frankie had stood up to him. He had to give her that. She wasn't quite the spoiled debutante or the delicate flower he'd imagined her to be. She wasn't a shallow princess like her high-living, amoral mother, either. She'd helped him deliver a calf in a sweltering barn. She'd ridden fence for him, too. She'd even helped him make repairs. Not content to be his helper and hand him his tools, she'd pounded nails until she'd pulled a muscle in her shoulder. And she was wonderful with Lee, who did most of his chores now without complaint—especially the supper dishes—but only if *she* asked him.

The transformation in Lee had impressed the hell out of the sheriff.

"You ought to marry her," Sheriff Jordan had said. "Maybe she'd work the same magic on you. 'Course it'd take her a spell—stubborn as you are."

"I'm not in her league, now am I?"

"Bed her. Hell, everybody knows she comes over here every damned day."

"Community service. Debutante stuff."

"Bull damn corn. Get her pregnant. Then she won't have a choice. That's why her mother married her father."

"That marriage lasted all of six months."

"Good—I see you've thought it through. A six-month marriage to her would bail you out of the mess your father got you in, boy!"

"Get your long nose out of my business, Jordan!"

"You'd better get on the stick, boy. Her aunt's campaigning mighty hard for Vince. Randal's got the hots for her, too."

"I said get."

His office windows were brilliant oblongs of red light now.

"Time to work, Dixon."

He knelt, intending to pick up the ledgers and put them back in the desk. But the morning quiet was broken by the roar of a big engine in his drive. He froze.

Something bright and metallic glinted from his window. A truck door slammed. He heard light running footsteps.

Matt dropped the ledger and jumped over the others. Then he raced to the front door to meet Frankie. She waited on the top step, tense and still, and as breathless as he was even though she smiled and pretended not to be.

As always she was as radiant as the new dawn. He banged the door open and stepped out onto his front porch. One glance down at the pink pearly softness of her mouth tightened every muscle in his body. Then the sweet warmth in her eyes made his heart do a somersault. He gripped the doorframe almost painfully and stopped himself from going any nearer.

"If I didn't know better, I'd think you were glad to see me, cowboy," she said, her voice fluttery and breathless.

Her face became a blur then, her eyes huge pools of sparkling green. Her hair turned to flame; her skin glowed.

Another pulse-hammering pause while he tried not to look at her.

Impossible. She was so damned beautiful. He bit his lip to keep from saying so. Compliments were way too dangerous.

So, instead he barked, "Who the hell did you ask to escort you to the debutante ball? Vince?"

Where had that come from?

"Better to attack—than to surrender?" Her quick laughter mocked him. "Would you care, cowboy?" She tilted her slim face back as if she thought she had him now.

"Maybe." He sprang from the door and stomped toward her. His voice was low and savage as he gently grabbed a fistful of hair and drew her slowly into his arms.

No kissing. No touching, Dixon. No thinking about it either.

When he hauled her closer, she didn't fight him. Instead, her emerald eyes caught fire, and she licked her lips as if deliberately moistening them.

"Do you know what you do to me, Frankie?" he muttered.

"I feel it, too."

"We've spent way too much time alone together lately."

"That's the same thing Aunt Susie says."

"What?"

"Seems Louisa has the whole town talking. You weren't on the program. Aunt Susie's mad at Louisa because she told me you were. Aunt Susie's mad as hops about me coming out here."

"Because she prefers Vince."

"How did you guess?"

"She wants you to marry well—same as she married well." An angry pulse throbbed in Matt's temple at the thought of Vince Randal.

"Jealous?" She batted her long lashes up at him. "No!"

She laughed. "You are too!"

"Damn your snippy hide! I've no right to be jealous!"

"Save your usual sob story. It's getting old."

"Sob story! That stings."

"My uncle's on your side," she said.

"Really?" He grinned at her in spite of himself.

"He says you're pulling yourself up by the bootstraps. He says you never ask for handouts the way BoBo always did. But Aunt Susie—"

"I don't give a damn what she thinks."

"She got really mad when I told her how handsome and determined you are. She said you never smile. I told her you had the most beautiful smile, but I agreed that you do need to smile more often. Like…like you did a while ago."

He flushed and ran his hand through his hair self-consciously.

"I want her to like you. Right now she thinks you aren't an integral part of the community."

"She's right, you know."

"But you could change."

"Frankie—"

"No—you listen. Just listen first. Grandma Ellie, who's hardly said a word for a month, got this really cool idea. She thought we…I mean Aunt Susie and Uncle Wayne and Grandma Ellie and I could throw a barbecue next week. She got me away from Aunt

Susie and said this could be a way to sort of get you in the swim of things.''

Don't you know me at all? I would hate being with all those debs and rich guys.

He started to protest. Then he clamped his teeth together. Frankie's eyes sparkled. She sounded so eager.

''Grandma Ellie hasn't been feeling so good lately, and when she's like that, we always sort of spoil her until she gets better. So, Uncle Wayne wouldn't let Aunt Susie argue with her about the barbecue...or even about you when she kept saying you're nice.''

''I'm really not much of a party person.''

''But Aunt Susie is, don't you see? So, if you cooperate, you could win her over. I know you could.'' Frankie was leaning toward him, smiling her sweet smile, taking his hand in hers.

''I've been acting so enthusiastic Aunt Susie's come around to liking the idea of all the debs and their escorts kicking up their heels on the Lassiter Ranch. And... I—I thought I'd bring you....''

''Me?''

She squeezed his hand. ''If you'd come.... After the party gets started and Aunt Susie is having fun. She could get to know you. We could prove to her once and for all that you can be an integral part—''

''Frankie, I don't know about this.''

Again she pressed his fingers. ''You work so hard. You deserve some fun. Oh, Matt, I do wish you'd come...as my escort.'' She released his hand and clutched his shirtsleeves. "I'm shy at parties too, same as you are. But if you were there—and…and… For all that Aunt Susie and I are so different, she's like a mother to me. I'd like her to get to know you better, and to realize—" She hesitated. "To realize how special you are to me."

Matt swallowed. Would Aunt Susie come to like him? Or to hate him? He said, "It won't work out the way you want it to."

"Maybe…maybe it could. Oh, please!"

He regarded her warily, but her shining green eyes soon worked their magic on him. "Oh, all right."

Her hands fell to her sides and she stood back a few steps from him. "So—the barbecue's why I can't stay and work today."

"What? You're not leaving…."

She nodded. "I've gotta go."

He stared at her distractedly. "But I thought—"

"I'm afraid I can't work for the rest of this week. Aunt Susie's got this super long list of things she wants me to do to organize the event. I have to get some fake silk palms and banana trees from Corpus. And then I have a fitting this morning. But I had to come over and invite you to the barbecue—first thing."

She took his hand again and pulled him into the darkest shadows of the porch. Then she stretched onto her tiptoes and whispered into his ear in a deep, throaty voice that mocked his. "I'm not done with you either, Matt Dixon."

"You sure about that?" His own voice was strangely hoarse.

She answered him with a light kiss. He closed his eyes when he felt the fluttery warmth of her lips claim his. Her mouth opened, inviting his tongue. His hands came around her waist to pull her closer. Gently he ran his hands through her curls.

"Francesca. Oh, Frankie. Frankie." He sucked in a gulp of air and clasped her closer. "I can't believe this!" He'd waited so long.

"Neither can I."

"What do you want?" he whispered. "How much? For how long?"

"What about you?"

All he knew was that he had to have her. That he'd take whatever she'd give him…and then he'd let her go when she was ready to move on to some rich guy—even if it was Vince Randal.

"I have nothing to offer a girl like you," he murmured thickly.

"Then why'd you say you wanted to be my first man?"

"Is that all you want? A thrill or two?"

"What's the matter with that? That's what you said you wanted, isn't it?"

"God, now you're using my words to torture me."

"If this is torture, don't stop."

His lips moved from her face down her throat to kiss the cotton that covered her breasts. "You smell like roses. You taste even better."

"You taste good, too."

His pulses were pounding when he clenched his fists and pulled away.

He closed his eyes on a shudder. "We'd better stop," he muttered hoarsely.

"W-why?" Her voice was halting as her mouth tried to nibble his throat.

"You said you had to go."

"Oh. Right." She paused. "My knees feel so weak, I'm not sure if I can even walk out to the truck." She laughed shakily. "Now is that any way to treat a girl?"

"Then I'll carry you."

She smiled impishly.

He shot her an answering grin. "When will I see you again?"

"The night of the barbecue—for sure. It's next Saturday at seven-thirty. When I think the time is right and Aunt Susie is prepared, I'll ride over on Jez and get you."

He put his arm around her and walked her to her pickup like she was his girl. Then he kissed her goodbye. When his lips touched hers, and she moaned, he grasped her more tightly. "God. I can't wait."

"You don't have a choice, cowboy."

She fluttered her fingers at him and waved goodbye.

"Is that your debutante wave?"

She laughed, blew him a kiss, and waved again.

He fluttered the ends of his fingers back at her.

When she was gone, he worked hard. He didn't quit

even after the sky was black and full of stars. After a supper of canned beans and ravioli, he went out to the barn, where he sat mending harnesses until he fell asleep on the concrete floor.

Matt watched the long black second hand jump as it circled the clock's face. It was nearly ten-thirty.

A branch scraped a windowpane, and he jumped.

"There she is." Matt sprang up and eagerly pushed the screen door open, only to stare vacantly at ten deer filing past the front porch and vanishing into the brush.

Damn it!

Matt stayed at the door for another long moment and rubbed his jaw where that muscle of his ticked so savagely. Slowly he closed the door and heaved his long body back down onto the couch beside his telephone once again. He raked his hands through his dark blond hair. Then with a scowl, he lifted the nearly empty bottle of scotch for another burning pull. There were dark shadows under his eyes; his shoulder muscles screamed with tension. No wonder. He was coiled as tight as a spring, ready to jump at the door or phone.

"She ain't comin'," Lee snorted in the sullen tone he'd resumed since Frankie had stopped showing up to cook him pancakes.

"I know that." Matt caught his breath on a growl. "But she oughta call."

"Not if she's dumped you. Maybe she doesn't like us anymore."

"Us?"

"What'd you do to her?" Lee whispered. "Did you do somethin'?"

"I don't need this. So, scram."

"You're just as pathetic as my old man."

Their eyes met and locked in mutual pain. Then Lee bolted upstairs.

Matt took another swig from the bottle. When he drained the last drop, he threw it at the wall just like BoBo used to.

Then, just like BoBo, he slammed outside onto the porch, banging the screen door behind him as hard as he could. How he'd hated that sound when he'd been a kid. He'd hidden outside the nights his daddy got drunk 'cause of that one time his daddy had chased him with a shotgun. He still kept a bunk in his supply shed.

The moon was full and bright, the air sweet with the smell of freshly mown grass. The barbecue had to be nearly over by now. Was Lee right? Had she changed her mind about introducing him socially to Aunt Susie and her set? Had she chosen Vince instead?

Why hadn't she called?

She doesn't like us anymore.

Raw hurt made Matt's temper flare. But what if something had happened to her? What if—

He had to call the Lassiters to check on her.

And have them tell him she was with Vince?

Matt swallowed. He had to make sure she was all right. He was stalking across his porch toward the screen door, when the ching of galloping hooves on his drive brought him to an abrupt halt.

A lone horse in a thick cloud of white dust snickered at him shyly.

Matt whirled. "Frankie?"

The horse pawed the drive.

"Frankie!" he shouted as he strained to see her in the darkness. "Is that you?"

The dust settled. He stared at the leather saddle. The skittish thoroughbred mare was riderless.

"Frankie! Oh, my God…"

He would have called to her again, but the realization that she'd fallen, that she could be hurt…or worse, got a grip on him. Her name died to a strangled croak. Purposefully, he strode down the walk toward the horse, stopping short just before the mare pranced nervously away.

His brain pounded. "Take me to your mistress. I've got to find her. I've got to help her. You're my only chance…Jez. Is that what she calls you, darlin'? Come here, Jezebel. Come, darlin'. Your mistress and I are *friends.*"

Jezebel lowered her head and as docilely as a lamb let him take the bridle.

He patted her and talked to her. Then he swung himself up into the saddle and dug in his heels, galloping into the dark.

"Oh, Frankie… Darlin'… You'd better be okay. 'Cause if you're not— If you're dead, I'll die, too."

Chapter 5

The moon and stars swam in a black sea just beyond the leafy pattern of the oak trees straight over her head. Cicadas sang from the nearby mesquite thicket. That's how Frankie knew it was still night and not morning yet. The cicadas shut up before dawn, so the birds could take over.

She swallowed on a convulsive breath, her hands clawing gravel and rocky ground. Her temples pounded every time she regained consciousness.

"Matt! Where are you? Why don't you come?"

She lay where she'd fallen. It wasn't just her head that hurt. Pain knifed up from her left ankle every time she moved it. That same foot was swollen so badly, she'd kicked her shoe off. She couldn't put even the tiniest bit of weight on it. She'd nearly fallen again when she'd tried to stand on it.

How long had she been here? Hours. Her brain felt fuzzy. She felt as if she were trapped in a weird dream. All she could remember was the coral snake spooking Jez.

What if *he* didn't come?

"Matt!"

Hot tears burned her eyes as she remembered the barbecue. Right before she'd snuck off to get Matt, Aunt Susie had sought her out and gushed.

"I can't believe this! What a wonderful party! What a wonderful surprise that you can be such a terrific hostess and a lady! I'm so proud of you, sweetheart."

She'd squeezed Aunt Susie's hand. "And I have another surprise—"

"What?"

"Something far more wonderful than the party."

"You look radiant. If I didn't know better, I'd think you were in love."

The powerful need to be with Matt surged through her. She yearned for him to find her with every fiber in her being. Was that love?

Oh, where was he? Why didn't he come? She'd left Aunt Susie and Uncle Wayne hours and hours ago. Way before sundown.

Frankie shut her eyes. The moon and the stars were snuffed out, and the bugs got quiet.

"Frankie! Oh, God, Frankie!"

She came awake slowly.

"Oh, God. You're alive!"

"I'm okay," she murmured in a sluggish voice that didn't sound like hers.

"Are you sure, darlin'?"

"I hit my head on a rock or something. And...and something's wrong with my left ankle, too. But I'm okay—now that you're here."

"I thought..." He winced and then refused to meet her eyes.

"You thought...I was with Vince?"

He hung his head and kept his eyes shut.

"Look at me," she whispered, staring at his long lashes that were dark crescents against his face.

He could only squeeze her hand against his lips for long, precious seconds.

"Oh, Matt," she sobbed. "There's only you. Don't you know that yet, cowboy?"

It was some time before he could regain his composure enough to open his eyes and gaze down at her. Then he knelt beside her and wiped the tears from her face. Gently and carefully he put his arms around her. "Tell me, if I hurt you."

"This isn't the first time I've fallen off Jez," she said shakily.

"She's pretty spirited...sort of like her mistress. I rode her over here. Oh, Frankie... Oh, God, darlin', I should have come looking for you earlier."

"Don't blame yourself. I should have called you before I saddled up. It was a stupid accident. Jez got spooked by a little bitty coral snake. You know the old saying...red and yellow—"

"Kill a fellow," he finished with a lame, guilt-stricken smile as he fingered her hair. "Hey, there's a supply shed nearby. Put your arms around my neck if you can, and I'll carry you over there."

"I'm kinda heavy."

"It's not too far."

And it wasn't. When they got there, he kicked one of the doors open. To her surprise there was a low bunk that even had clean sheets on it.

The mattress dipped when he laid her down.

"You said this was just a supply shed."

"Sometimes I come out here to think…away from the phone and all the other trappings of civilization."

A sharp shiver traced through her. Suddenly, the interior of the shed felt sweltering. Or was it just being in bed with him beside her that had her so hot?

"Will you be okay while I go get the truck?"

She clung to his arms. "Don't you dare leave me. I've been scared out of my mind for hours."

"I have to."

Clutching his sleeves, dragging him even closer, Frankie stared up at him, her heart in her throat. "No."

"Darlin', I can't carry you all the way back—"

"So, stay with me…here."

"What are you saying?"

She slid her hands up his arms, then moved them across the broad expanse of his shoulders, over his chest up to his warm throat. "I'm saying what I'm saying, cowboy." Shakily she unfastened the top button of his shirt.

"But you need medical attention...."

"Later. What I need...right now...and what I want...is right here...in this bunk with me. Now that I've found you, I'm not going to let you go."

His heart was pounding under her fingertips as she slid her hand down his throat and undid the second button.

"Frankie..." he murmured warningly. "You don't know what you're doing."

"Shhhh." Her hand moved inside his shirt. "You're so warm. You feel so good."

Quietly, he shifted a little closer to her on the bunk. Their hips touched, and his body heat fired her blood.

She held her breath. So did he.

"But you're hurt," he ground out hoarsely.

"If I was hurt as bad as you think, I couldn't feel this sexy, now could I?"

Still, he frowned, hesitating, too concerned for her to make a move.

"Don't argue, Rancher Dixon. Not with a spoiled debutante, who wants to have her way with you."

When he shuddered with suppressed longing, a wave of desire pulsed through her. "Do you have any idea how much I missed you this week? Aunt Susie kept me hopping with so much boring girl stuff, I nearly went crazy. Hair appointments. Menu changes. A pedicure. I wanted to be here with you. Instead I had to sit under hair dryers and have pins stuck in my bosoms until I wanted to scream that if they stuck me even one more time, I'd go to the ball naked.''

''I like your hair. And the makeup, too.'' He grinned down at her. ''And your bosoms best of all.''

She laughed. ''You said once that you weren't done with me yet.... So, why don't you finish what you started, cowboy?''

''I don't have a condom,'' he murmured against her ear. ''I have to protect you.''

''Isn't there some other way?''

He cleared his throat. ''Yes.''

His voice was oddly strained, as if he were short of breath all of a sudden. Her mouth felt dry and papery too. She licked her lips, wetting them for him.

''Kiss me,'' she whispered on a little prayer. *Make me like Mother. Just for tonight. Make me good at this.*

She closed her eyes. When he lifted her palm to his mouth and started in the center of her hand with his tongue and then his lips, her heart went mad. Then his lips blew kisses against her wrist and then higher up her arm, into the curve of her elbow. His mouth lingered at the hollow of her throat until she was breathless. Long steamy minutes passed before he finally got around to kissing her on the mouth.

He undressed her slowly, his big hands caressing her lazily.

''You're perfect,'' he marveled. ''Exquisite.''

''I'm too skinny.''

''Where? Show me where?''

"Up...there," she murmured shyly.

"You mean these?" He cupped her breasts, kissing each nipple.

"Too small."

"Perfect."

"Too—"

"Shut up," he ground out hoarsely as he yanked off his own clothes.

The moon bathed him in silvery warm light as he settled his powerful body on top of hers.

"You're beautiful," she whispered.

"So are you."

"Do it," she urged. "Just do it. I can't wait."

"Darlin', you made me wait." His hands traveled the length of her, from nipple to nipple and then down to her navel and then between her legs, where she was wet. "For years and years. You went off to Vanderbilt." She did a slow burn when his fingers parted those lips with tender care. "Now it's your turn to wait, darlin'. 'Cause waiting just makes it better."

She felt his hunger. When his body finally joined hers, even when he filled her on the brink of that first mutual explosion, there wasn't the least bit of pain.

She was a virgin.

She clasped him tightly. "So, I'm my mother's daughter after all."

"You're a natural," he whispered.

And he was right. She was both a lady and yet an animal, driven by instincts too powerful to deny, and yet caught up in the spell of her love for him, too.

They were like two wild creatures in the silvery dark woods. And yet they weren't. They were man and woman, drawn to each other by both body and soul.

When it was over, he wrapped her with his strong, brown arms and held her close. "I remember when you were in the first grade...how scared you were the first day of school."

"I came late and you showed me around—the great big sixth grader."

"You had the reddest hair I'd ever seen. I thought it was pretty. I wanted to touch it."

"You acted all gruff and grown-up. You barely said a word."

"I was probably trying to impress you. You were Wayne Lassiter's little ranch princess."

"Don't call me that."

He kissed her, and they made love again. The third time was best of all because they did it with their mouths. Again, some secret knowledge told her exactly what to do.

"Marry me," he whispered later when they woke up again in each other's arms.

"Why?"

"What kind of answer is that?"

"Why did you ask me—because we had sex and you think you should?"

He tucked a strand of hair behind her ear. "It's hot. That's what I think. And it's going to get a lot hotter." He got up. "It's almost dawn. I'd better get the truck."

It was only later that she realized she hadn't answered his question.

"So, this is what's really been going on!" Aunt Susie gasped as soon as Matt helped Frankie limp into the living room. "And...and I thought you were thrilled about the barbecue and the debutante ball.... I was so happy. Now I see I've been living in a fool's paradise."

Aunt Susie's green eyes bored holes through Frankie, which caused her to suck in a panicky breath. Only Matt's tall, tan frame slumped by the window near the front door of the big ranch house steadied her.

"You're as a pale as a sheet, girl. I can't believe you didn't at least call us from the doctor's office," Uncle Wayne said.

"We should have, sir," Matt admitted. "I was just too worried about her to think straight."

"So—you just drive up here, girl, and then hobble up to the door on crutches. I nearly had a heart attack when I saw you two." Aunt Susie's accusing green gaze shifted to Matt again. "What else happened to her...that her uncle and I should know about?"

Dizziness washed Frankie. "I don't feel too good, Aunt Susie. Dr. Jackson said I need to rest all day. To stay off my ankle."

"I'm glad it was you who found her, Dixon."

Uncle Wayne's deliberate calm voice sent guilt slithering up Frankie's spine. Her cheeks flamed.

"I'm glad she wasn't hurt worse," Matt muttered hoarsely. His dark face had flushed, too. He was staring out the window moodily, refusing to look at her now.

Did he already regret last night?

Oh, dear. What if he did…when she loved him. With all her heart.

Did he love her?

He'd asked her to marry him. But why? Because he'd felt he owed her? Was he finished with her now?

"What were you thinking of, girl?" Aunt Susie persisted, her tone increasingly alarmed.

"Susie, would you stop badgering her? She's hurt."

"I know she's hurt." Aunt Susie wasn't through, though. "What were you thinking? To leave the barbecue? To ride off on Jez like that?"

"I—I intended to surprise you." Frankie's voice was barely a whisper.

"Well, you did that all right. Showing up here at this hour—with BoBo Dixon's boy."

Matt stiffened.

"Girl, you've been a handful all your life. You ruined the barbecue last night. Now you probably won't be able to dance at the ball. Why can't you once, just once, ever be a proper girl?"

"I don't know. I was trying."

"Let her go to bed, Susie. We need to all calm down before we thrash—"

"Wayne! No! Not yet! Because I know what's really going on here. The whole town knows. I know why she ran off last night. Why *he* found her. I know everything. You spent the night with him, didn't you, Frankie? Just look at them, Wayne! They're both as red as beets.''

A thick silence fell over the living room as Aunt Susie stared from Frankie to Matt, neither of whom denied anything. ''I've tried everything to raise you right,'' Aunt Susie said. ''To keep you from ending up like your mother. Oh, I know her life seems glamorous. And sometimes I've been a little jealous. All that running around. All those parties. But it's best for a girl to marry the right kind of man. Not to fool around with the wrong kind, exciting as they may seem—at least in bed—and lose herself in the process.''

Matt uncoiled himself from the window. ''I'd better go.''

''Yes, you had,'' Aunt Susie said.

''Aunt Susie, no—''

''She's right, darlin','' Matt said.

''Darlin'?'' Aunt Susie snapped the word viciously.

''We were wrong,'' Matt whispered, his tone raw. ''I—I'm real sorry about all this, Mrs. Lassiter. I proposed marriage to your niece last night because I thought it was the right thing to do. Frankie, I retract my offer. I just asked you 'cause I thought I had to.''

The door opened and slammed.

''Matt—''

Matt was gone.

Frankie felt hot and clammy—scared and sick to the

core of her being. Well, she had her answer. He didn't love her. He'd only felt obligated to propose.

Still, she would have run after him, even thrown herself in front of his truck, but she could barely hobble.

"Oh, Aunt Susie, why did you have to ruin everything?"

"Me? Ask yourself that question! Oh, go to bed. Like you said, the doctor ordered you to rest. Do what you're supposed to—for once in your life."

Chapter 6

Tears shimmering in her eyes, Frankie clutched the phone to her ear.

Matt's harsh voice only compounded her misery. "Don't call me ever again."

Helplessly she dabbed at her face with the back of her hands. "But, Matt—"

"It was plain as day yesterday morning what your aunt and uncle think of me."

"You're not listening."

"No, you listen. They think I'm dirt, that I soiled your reputation. If they knew for sure how far this has gone, they wouldn't want me to marry you—even if I was fool enough to propose a second time."

"Just ask me," she whispered. "I'm the one who gets to answer that question. Not them."

"Correct me if I'm wrong—you didn't answer, did you, when I asked you that night?"

"Ask me again."

"No—Miss debutante. 'Cause I realized I don't want to marry you."

Because you don't love me. You just felt obligated. The same as Aunt Susie and Uncle Wayne felt obligated to adopt me.

The words hurt too much to even breathe aloud. "Please, Matt—"

He said nothing. Absolutely nothing.

She felt herself faltering. Still, she had to try. "All right. Then, I've got a question for you. Will...will you at least be my escort to the debutante ball?"

"Me? BoBo's no-good son? At your fancy debutante ball?"

"Please—"

"Are you out of your mind? Hell no. Your aunt loves Vince. Invite him, why don't you?"

"But—"

"You'll make a beautiful couple."

"But—"

"Stop chasing me, damn it. None of this would have happened if you hadn't come to my ranch and thrown yourself at me."

Stung, she could only gasp for breath.

He hung up.

"But, Matt, I love you—you, only you. I love..." Her voice died as the receiver slipped through her fingers to the carpet.

What was she going to do? How could she make him listen?

She couldn't.

Had she been right? Had he really only asked her to marry him that first time because he'd felt obligated?

Her aunt's brisk knock interrupted this unpleasant train of thought.

"Frankie! Are you dressed?"

"Come in."

Aunt Susie made her way over crutches, a pair of wadded thong panties and jeans as well as the bridle Frankie had meant to mend. Her aunt's eyes slowly circled the messy room before returning to Frankie's red, tear-blotched face.

"Well! What have you been doing—moping in here all by yourself?"

"Matt won't be my escort for the debutante ball."

"Well, praise the Lord. Why don't you call Vince, then?"

"Because I don't love Vince. Why can't you understand that?"

"But he's a perfect catch."

"For some other girl. Someone more like you," Frankie finished in the quietest of voices. "Not for me. I'm not like you. Why can't you understand that?"

Aunt Susie sighed as she bent over and scooped handfuls of clothes into the hamper. "All right. Let's forget about the barbecue and Vince. You're safe and sound. How's your ankle?"

"Much better."

"Good. We've got at least a dozen things to do in town this morning. Margaret called and said your gown is ready. And we need to schedule you to have your picture taken for the paper. Which means a hair appointment. Then there's your last etiquette class."

Frankie yawned.

"Couldn't you at least pretend to be a little bit excited about all this—for me?"

Frankie's eyes slid to her Aunt's disappointed face. "Yes, I can pretend. But that's all I do—pretend."

With difficulty she tried to shake off the sudden attack of nervous jitters that threatened her.

If I lose Matt, I'll be pretending for the rest of my life.

Still, she shot her aunt her most dazzling smile, and her Aunt Susie pretended not to notice that the false smile didn't reach her sad, glistening eyes.

"So—let's us girls have some fun," Aunt Susie said, determined to play along.

"Slow down, Frankie." Aunt Susie was grabbing at the yellow and red scarf billowing around her face. "You know what your uncle said he'd do if you got another ticket and I've got better things to do than to drive you everywhere."

"No cop will give me a ticket unless I'm at least ten miles over the speed limit."

"That's what you think...because you were doing nearly ninety when you got those other tickets."

Frankie lifted her toe, but just a little.

The heavy, silver-gray Mercedes convertible rolled easily under the two women. The top was down, but all the windows were up. Still, Frankie's red curls were whipping about her face.

Ever since they'd compromised by raising the windows, Aunt Susie had hunkered as low as possible in her plush, gray, leather seat, clinging to the corners of her red and gold silk scarf in a vain attempt to keep it from swirling off her elaborately set hairdo.

"The generation gap is real," was all she'd said when Frankie had lowered the black, canvas top.

Tall brown grasses, black-eyed susans and yellow daisies were whizzing past them on either side of the road.

"I can't believe how fast we got it all done—" Frankie said as she slammed on her brakes to avoid a large, green tractor hauling hay that suddenly pulled onto the road right in front of them.

"Macho, red-neck, cowboy sun-of-a-gun! Go back to driving school!"

"Frankie, you're the one who's going way too fast!"

"You just think that because he's going way too slow!"

Her foot tapped the accelerator impatiently, but a car was coming so she couldn't pass.

Frankie bit her lip and let out a sigh.

"Is that—*him?*" Aunt Susie muttered in a vehement undertone from under flapping silk tongues of flame.

Suddenly Frankie's fingers tightened on the steering wheel. She let up on the accelerator, and she felt herself blush with a thrilling mixture of sick confusion and heady adoration.

Matt. Oh, God, it's so good to see you.

Suddenly she realized that all day, she'd been looking for him—on the way into town, at the bank, even after she'd picked Aunt Susie up at the LSCC Body Perfect spa. She'd stared at every tall blond man in ragged jeans, at every red pickup truck on the road.

The car slowed to the tractor's crawl.

"Well, aren't you going to pass him?"

"There's a car coming."

The car flew past them, and still Frankie refused to pass.

Matt had taken his shirt off and tied it around his lean waist, white sleeves flapping back and forth. Completely absorbed, Frankie stared at his shining hair. Next she devoured the brown ripple of muscles on his glistening back.

He had been on top of her, straddling her, and she had clutched that back at his every powerful stroke. His skin had been warm and wet with perspiration then, too.

"You can pass him now," Aunt Susie offered a little too helpfully.

"Back seat driver!"

"Front seat," Aunt Susie corrected.

When Frankie pulled slowly along beside him, Matt glanced her way and reddened with shock when she smiled. Instead of smiling back, his lips thinned.

When she held up her right hand, fluttering her fingers at him gaily, he flushed a deep, dark shade of purple and turned away, rudely clenching his steering wheel.

She tapped the horn and kept waving. His broad brown shoulders hunched forward. She jammed her fist on the horn and didn't let up. Not that he so much as glanced her way again.

"Frankie! For God's sakes! There's a car coming!"

Pulling ahead of him, she slowed the convertible to a speed even slower than his crawl, driving at this snail's pace all the way to his own turnoff, almost stopping there, forcing him to brake, too.

"Frankie!"

She inched forward, so he could make the turn.

Only when he disappeared from her rearview mirror did Frankie stomp down on her accelerator again. She drove ninety all the way home.

As soon as she got home, she called him.

"Matt—"

"Darlin', this has got to stop."

"I love you."

He hung up on her.

"You tell your Aunt Susie next Monday. Three o'clock on the dot."

One minute Sam Jenson was explaining to Frankie

when he'd have her proofs ready. In the next, all she saw or heard was the tall man in crisply pressed jeans and his best Stetson on the opposite side of the street.

"Matt..."

She leaned forward on the counter to get a better look. Unused to her long manicured fingernails, she dropped her pen. Not that she noticed.

Jenson caught it before it rolled off the edge of the counter. Not that she noticed that either.

All she saw was Matt's long body as he dragged each scarred boot forward in that slouchy, sullen way that meant he had no enthusiasm for the task ahead of him.

Then she read the shiny gold letters that spelled Mission Creek First Federal Bank above the revolving doors and let out a forlorn little cry.

"Something wrong, girlie?" Mr. Jenson demanded.

"Monday," she whispered, her voice sounding a little shrill even to her own ears. "Monday will be just fine."

Then she stumbled blindly for the door.

"Your pen, Miss Moore. You forgot your—"

"Keep it. I—I just remembered I've gotta see about Uncle Wayne. Right now! I—I just forgot...all about him. See, he's got that bank board meeting this morning." Why was she babbling?

"Same as he always does."

"Well, I was supposed to pick him up because his SUV is in the shop to get a new battery...." She didn't have to explain herself to Mr. Jenson, of all people, but she couldn't seem to stop talking.

"Simmer down, little lady. The board never gets done this early."

Indeed, Uncle Wayne was the last errand on Aunt Susie's list, not the next item.

"Just the same I feel like I've got to see about Uncle Wayne right now! What if the meeting lets out early? I wouldn't want my darling uncle to have to wait, now would I?"

"Was that the Dixon fella you've been working for I seen going in the bank a while ago? Maybe to see about his daddy's old loan?"

"I—I wouldn't know."

"You know the whole town wants to know what's going to happen to that boy if he loses his ranch after all his hard work?"

"Really?"

She pushed the door open and flung herself outside.

Matt glanced up, his gaze drawn to the slim woman in the jade green sundress with a mane of shockingly bright hair high-stepping it saucily in her strappy green sandals through the revolving doors straight toward him. His lips thinned. As quickly as he looked up, he lowered his gaze. But not in time.

Already his heart was pounding, and his throat was dry. A wave of heat crawled up his collar.

Frankie in that slip of a dress...more like a night-gown than a dress. The silken stuff clung to her legs and breasts and narrow waist. It was so short it revealed way too much of her long, shapely legs.

Even though he'd looked away the second he'd seen her, the image of her had burned into his brain. All that hair. Today those glorious red silk curls were restrained by a demure bow at her neck that somehow made her look even sexier.

Yesterday when she'd driven so slowly in front of him had been sheer torture. Then when she'd called him, her velvet voice saying those three hellish words had made him sweat.

Oh, God.

Just watching her hair fly loosely in the wind as she drove had made him remember how the stuff felt coiled around his hand. But seeing her like that with her aunt who despised him, knowing she was forbidden, knowing that she was deliberating teasing him with her beauty had made him mad too.

Why couldn't she play fair?

The minx pranced across the bank toward him and said, "Hi," just as casually as you please.

"Hi," he said edgily, too aware of the other men watching them. "Now get...before people get the wrong idea!"

"Or maybe the right idea, cowboy!"

"Quit! You know how gossip spreads!"

She batted thick, mascara laden lashes. "Maybe I want to light a fire or two."

Then she plopped down beside him, so close her

thigh touched his, burning him up with her body heat and her perfume that smelled like roses.

"What the hell are you doing in here in that dress? You couldn't look sexier if you were prancing around stark naked."

"Oh, so you like it?" She smiled. "I hoped you would."

"And all that makeup? Did you fall in a vat of perfume or what?"

"Just call me a before-and-after advertisement for the country club's Body Perfect spa."

"On you it's overkill."

"Well, if you like it, cowboy, maybe it was worth the fortune it cost my Aunt Susie."

"Is this little show for Vince?" he whispered. "Did you come here to ask him to be your escort?"

"I asked you to be my escort to the ball, remember? The offer's still open, cowboy."

"No way," he growled.

Her voice softened. "Matt…"

Because the eyes she turned on him were so glassy-bright, he almost softened. What if she cried?

Then Vince, whose secretary had told Matt he'd have to wait, stormed out of the boardroom and waved to her. "Do you need something, Frankie dear?"

Dear. Rage engulfed Matt like molten lava as she glanced in confusion from Matt to Vince.

"I—I…"

"Go ahead. Ask him, why don't you?" Matt said. "Hell, we both know it's over between you and me."

He flung himself to his feet. His boot heels clicked so furiously on the marble floors, all heads turned to watch him. Then he slammed out of the bank, leaving the revolving doors spinning behind him.

She caught him just as he was about to open the door to his rusty, red pickup.

"You've got to be the most stubborn, impossible man in the whole world," she sobbed.

"What about you? What kind of girl won't take no for an answer?"

"What do I have to do?"

The livid pain in her wet green eyes broke his heart and made him want to devour her. Her red mouth was so moist and sexy; he licked his dry lips and tasted like dust.

"If you know what's good for you darlin', you'll get. And fast."

"I—I know what's good for me." She hurled herself into his chest. "Kiss me, you big idiot. Kiss me."

"A kiss won't solve it, darlin'."

She fused her body to his. In the next instant his entire being pulsed like a red-hot volcano about to blow. Then her hands clasped his lean waist and clung, snugging her hips against his.

"You want me," she whispered shakily. "You do. I know you do. Don't be such a coward. Say it."

Uncle Wayne stepped outside onto the sidewalk along with Vince, their eyes on Jenson, who had stepped outside his photo shop across the street.

Frankie squirmed her hips a little more, probably to get the whole gang, especially Matt, really riled.

"Don't you dare fine-tune it, Frankie."

She wiggled harder.

"By God..."

Her uncle and Vince and Old Man Jenson blurred. There was only Frankie, her red hair blowing against his cheek, the smell of roses, and the scent of her skin too, seeping inside him. His hands ran up and down her soft arms.

"I don't give a damn who's watching us," he muttered thickly.

"It's about time you came to your senses, cowboy."

"No man alive could stop himself from taking what you're offering."

"So take it," she teased. "Did I ever tell you that one of my big big faults is that I'm impatient?"

Matt's arms closed possessively around her. Then his mouth came down, branding her with a searing kiss that went on and on. She parted her lips, so his tongue could ease inside. One taste, and they melted into each other as if they were one.

His hands wound red curls through his fingers. "You feel so good."

"Do I?" she whispered.

"Why does it have to be this good with you?"

"It just is. Like you said, I'm a natural."

"I wish we were alone on my ranch. I'd strip you. I'd have you, just one last time."

She moaned. "I love you, too," she whispered.

I love you.

The immensity of those words washed over him.

"You don't mean that."

The flush on her cheeks was rising. "What if I do?"

"You'd come to despise me in time, same as your aunt and uncle do."

"Shut up and just kiss me," she sobbed.

He bent obediently. She was so delicious, so smooth, and soft, and warm—so perfect, so dear. It was a long while before he could end the kiss.

Only when he felt as hot as a kettle ready to boil over did he tear himself away.

"Damn it to hell—you boy-crazy, man-chasing debutante! Stay away from me!"

Every muscle in Matt's body ached as he lifted the pitchfork and tossed manure into the wheelbarrow. He should have Lee doing this, but Lee had wanted to go fishing with his new friends, so he'd let him. The sheriff said it was good the way the boy was making friends with the right crowd for a change and that Matt should encourage this. He'd said he'd located the boy's aunt, who was considering taking Lee on a permanent basis.

Matt had thrown himself into his work all day in an attempt to forget kissing Frankie in broad daylight on Main Street. Gossip was a reality of small town life. Now everybody knew there really was something between Wayne Lassiter's ranch princess and BoBo

Dixon's loser son. Frankie's reputation was bound to suffer.

Maybe the town would forget about the kiss in time. But would he?

His mouth still burned from her lips. He could still taste her on his tongue. He didn't want to work. What he wanted was Frankie—in his bed, in his life—forever.

He dropped the pitchfork in disgust and stomped outside the barn so he could stand in the breeze and cool off. Not that so much as a breath of air stirred the trees. The sun was sinking, reddening the sky to the exact shade of Frankie's hair.

Would he ever forget her? Would he forget how wonderful it had been to have her here, working beside him? Would he ever find another woman who thrilled him in bed as she did?

He didn't think so.

What if it didn't rain? What if Vince really went through with the foreclosure?

What if he lost the ranch, too?

So what? Hadn't he always been alone?

But Frankie had come; she'd changed him with her sparkling eyes and eagerness, with her belief in him. Almost, almost she'd made him believe a woman like her could love him, could be proud of him. Him—BoBo Dixon's boy....

Matt squeezed his eyes shut. His head throbbed.

How does a fighter learn to be a quitter?

It was time to move on. Time to run. Time to give

up. Time to let go of his dreams. Most of all it was time to let go of Frankie.

Matt dropped down into the dirt and propped his forehead against his knee. What he wanted was to hold her in his arms one more time, to make love to her violently even if theirs was a love that could never be.

Tears stung his eyelids. But he didn't cry.

Not right then anyway.

Chapter 7

Even though it was a warm Saturday near the end of May, it felt more like Christmas Eve. People in Mission Creek were as excited as children waiting up for Santa Claus. After all, tonight was the night of the annual Lone Star County Debutante Ball.

Everybody was thrilled—everybody except Frankie. She'd locked herself in her bathroom to get away from Aunt Susie, who was driving her crazy by dashing into her bedroom every five minutes.

"The ball's not supposed to start for three hours, Aunt Susie."

"I just can't wait to see you in that dress."

"Okay. I'm going to bathe. And get ready. Just for you."

Frankie's heart was pounding heavily as she

sponged herself with a coarse wash rag. How she dreaded walking into the ball—alone.

"Your Uncle Wayne and I will be with you, sweetie."

Damn it to hell—you boy-crazy, man-chasing debutante! Stay away from me!

How would she stand it…without Matt?

Frankie lingered in the warm sudsy water, her unhappy thoughts drifting to no purpose. She couldn't make herself get out of the tub and get ready.

Better to shrivel up like a prune.

She felt lost and insecure, more so than when she had first come home from Vanderbilt, and everybody had asked her what she planned to do. Slowly she'd realized she was a rancher at heart. Then she'd fallen in love with the proud rancher next door.

If she couldn't have Matt, what would she do with the rest of her life?

According to Aunt Susie her future didn't matter. What mattered was the ball tonight and that the show had to go on. To Frankie, her designer ball gown that hung on her closet door was a big puffy monster about to eat her alive. The long white limousine that would arrive promptly at seven spelled doom.

Vince had called an hour ago to say he had his tuxedo ready.

"Just in case you change your mind and need an escort."

"No, Vince, that wouldn't be fair to anybody," she'd whispered brokenly.

Somehow she would dress and survive this ordeal—alone.

Mary had called from Mission Creek Creations. "Everybody, simply everybody, is talking about *the kiss.*"

"Not Aunt Susie or Uncle Wayne."

"That's funny."

"Not really."

But it was strange, how quiet Uncle Wayne had been when he'd finally driven in from Mission Creek so late this afternoon.

Not so strange. He was probably still too furious to face her. Uncle Wayne was like that. Unlike her more volatile Aunt Susie, he preferred to cool down before he confronted Frankie when she displeased him.

"So—everybody's talking about the kiss."

"I wish I could have seen it," Mary said.

"Well, I can't forget it, either."

Just remembering, Frankie touched her lips with her wash rag, sucking on the rough terry cloth that oozed bath water. His mouth had felt so good. It had been ten times better than any kiss she'd ever had before. All that suppressed fire…and longing and need and fury. His lips had gobbled her.

He still felt something for her. She knew he did.

What if I went over to Matt's one more time?

Frankie sprang out of the tub. Without bothering to towel herself off, she pulled on the same jeans and blouse she'd worn all afternoon. To protect her stupid hairdo, she covered the piles of curls with the red and gold scarf her aunt had left for her to use, insisting she wear it just in case she went outside before the ball.

Knotting the silk beneath her chin, Frankie tiptoed out the back way and ran lightly through the trees to the barn to saddle Jez. Then she galloped off toward the Dixon place in feverish anticipation. Only when she got to Matt's house and jumped off Jez, his truck was gone.

Despair closed over her. His empty house seemed about as inviting as a tomb. As she forced herself to walk his fence line, all was ominously silent. Not a single bird, not even a cicada sang from the dense underbrush. It was hot too, and sweat began to trickle down her neck under the scarf. She wanted to yank it off, but she remembered her promise to her aunt.

She called to Matt, but he didn't answer. Finally, she moved like a dreamer through that still white heat toward his barn. Inside, it was dark and dank, and there was no sign of anybody.

She retraced her steps to his house, dragging herself up the stairs to his porch. After knocking and waiting, she cautiously pushed the screen door wider before tiptoeing inside. The kitchen was neat; the dishes stacked by the sink.

A brown manila bank envelope had been ripped open with a knife, spilling its contents all over the kitchen table. Her heart slammed as she unwadded several long, crisp sheets and realized what they were.

Foreclosure papers.

The house seemed too quiet. Growing more frightened by the second, Frankie stumbled down the hall into Matt's bedroom where she found suitcases piled on his bed. Dropping the foreclosure papers, she screamed. Then she began to sob.

"Don't leave! You can't give up! No! Matt! No!"

She dashed outside the house again, some part of her refusing to believe he was gone despite all the evidence. She yelled his name over and over again until she became too hoarse to do so. But it was no use. He didn't answer.

He was gone.

Outside, she sank down on the bottom step of the porch and wearily folded her head upon her knees. The lawn had been sheared too close to the ground and was brown, the St. Augustine dying as everything else would if Lone Star County didn't get rain pretty soon. Even the squat oaks near his house and the straggly mesquite with their draperies of vines looked bedraggled.

Not a breath of air was stirring. It was so hot, she forgot her promise and took her aunt's scarf off and ran her fingers through her stiff hairdo.

Without Matt, the house, his ranch, indeed the whole world seemed desolate and soulless.

He was gone, and he hadn't thought enough of her to even call and say goodbye.

Damn it to hell—you boy-crazy, man-chasing debutante! Stay away from me!

Did he hate her? Oh, why had she thrown herself

at him in the square? Had that last humiliation been too much?

After a long time, she forced herself to stand up. She had to get ready for the ball. After all the show, and that's all this elaborate farce of a ball was now, had to go on.

"Oh, Wayne! Just look at her!" Aunt Susie gushed running toward the stairs to worship at the feet of the beautiful goddess hovering above them.

Frankie colored. The vision in shimmering white satin that had stared back at her from her bedroom mirror had been way too glamorous for her tomboy comfort zone. Surely that bewitching creature with the glitter in her hair had nothing to do with the real girl, whose heart felt heavier than stone.

With one hand Frankie was lifting her long ball gown, so she wouldn't step on the hem and trip. With the other, she clung to the railing because her left ankle was so wobbly on high heels.

"I feel like I'm on stilts."

"You'll get used to them."

"I'm going to kick them off just as soon as I get to the country club."

"Don't you dare!"

Uncle Wayne's black eyes lit up. "Wow!" For a long moment he just stared up at her, too stunned to say another word. "Wait till—" He seemed to catch himself. "Let me get my camera!"

Always an enthusiastic photographer, he snapped at

least a dozen shots. Afterwards when she was a little blinded by all the flashes, Frankie's fingers played nervously with the voluminous satin folds of her gown. She gasped when her hand slipped inside a secret pocket and her fingertips closed over a little envelope hidden there.

Drawing the white rectangle out, she wobbled over to the window. Turning her slim back to her aunt and uncle, she opened it.

Two velvety rose petals fell out on her palm—one red, the other yellow.

Puzzled, she flipped them over, stroking their velvet softness.

The note inside read, "Yellow is for friendship, red is for love."

"There's your limo!" Uncle Wayne shouted.

A ridiculously long white limousine with black-tinted windows rolled up to the front of the sprawling ranch house.

Frankie scarcely heard her uncle. Nor did she glance out at the dreaded limo. Instead, her hand was closing around the soft petals as she pressed them to her heart.

"Matt. All I ever wanted was your friendship and your love."

Did Witch McKenzie have special powers?

Quickly, softly, Frankie said a little prayer. Then she kissed each petal and carefully put them back into the envelope, which she slipped back inside the secret pocket.

Her aunt pressed her elbow. "It's time to go, Frankie!"

Frankie swallowed, merely nodding, letting herself be led like a doll through the door into a glimmering twilight where cicadas and night birds sang in raucous chorus.

"Your glass coach awaits, Cinderella," Aunt Susie called gaily.

If only this were a fairy tale and her very own Prince Charming awaited her.

But tonight was merely an ordeal she had to face alone.

The first of many.

Just the sight of the stretch limo caused Frankie's temple to throb searingly.

Then the limousine door opened.

"Go on, dear. Get in. We don't want to be late."

Frankie, feeling a hopeless, overwhelming bottomless despair let herself be pushed listlessly forward. She felt weak. Her eyes blinked rapidly. Her stomach knotted. For courage she slipped her hand inside her pocket and clutched the little envelope that held the little rose petals.

She couldn't believe what happened next.

Matt got out of the limousine.

He looked too elegant for words in his black tuxedo. Broad-shouldered, tall, he held a corsage made of yellow and red roses in his hand.

Not that there was anything elegant or pure about his whiskey-gold eyes that burned her. Gradually, the hard planes of his face softened into an expression that held infinite tenderness.

Her fingertips crushed the little envelope that contained the yellow and red rose petals that were the same colors as Matt's corsage.

Friendship and love.

Maybe Witch McKenzie *did* have powers. Maybe... maybe Frankie Moore was going to have her fairy tale and her very own Prince Charming after all.

"Matt... You're here. You're...really here."

Just as she was about to run to him, fingernails dug into her elbow as Aunt Susie tightened her grip.

"There's some mistake," came Aunt Susie's querulous tone.

"No mistake," Uncle Wayne said. "The Dixon boy and I had a long talk this afternoon. He's a talented rancher, a good man. He's just what we need around here."

"Around here?"

Frankie barely heard them.

"What are you saying, Wayne?"

"Someone to carry on...after we're gone, Susie Lou."

Their tense voices came and went like static on a radio Frankie wasn't really listening to.

"The ranch? Is that all you ever think of?"

"I love you too, Susie Lou," Uncle Wayne placated. "Same as Dixon loves Frankie. But the ranch doesn't belong to us. It belongs to the generations— to them."

''Them?''

''Are you blind? She's found her cowboy—same as you did at your coming out ball.''

''That's what you think?''

He nodded. ''Kiss me, baby.''

''Later, you big lug. You'll mess up my lipstick.''

''To hell with your lipstick. Anyway, just think, now you get to plan a wedding.''

Aunt Susie kissed him.

Frankie was tearing loose from them, running, running straight into Matt's strong, waiting arms.

''Darlin','' he said, taking her hand in his, pulling her close. Then they just stood there for a long time, her breasts heaving against the wall of his chest, each marveling at the other, neither of them able to speak, so great was the depth of their emotion.

Slowly he lifted the corsage out of its plastic container and slid it onto her wrist.

Tears, swift and hot, came before words. Frankie bowed her head a moment, then raised it when she felt his hand on her cheeks brushing the dampness away.

''Don't cry,'' he said gently. ''I'm not worth it.''

''You...you're worth everything.''

''That's what your uncle said.''

''Uncle Wayne?'' The red and yellow roses blurred.

''He came by my place this afternoon, tore up the bank foreclosure papers.''

''He did?''

''Said he was having a hard time too, that ranching was like that, even for the big players like him. Said

I had to see myself as a winner, to be one. That... that's how you saw me.'' He paused. ''That if I was a loser, you wouldn't love me so much.''

''He said all that?''

''And a helluva lot more. After he made me realize I'm no quitter, he drove me into town and got me fitted for this damn tux.''

''You're not here...you didn't buy the roses... because he made you feel...feel obligated?''

''Is that what you think, darlin'?'' Gently he lifted her chin and feathered warm, sweet kisses against each damp eyelid.

''I can't believe you're really here,'' she murmured. ''It's like a fairy tale.''

''There's more.'' Matt slid his hand inside his pocket and pulled out a black velvet box. ''Open it,'' he whispered, handing it to her.

She popped the lid and gasped when she saw the small, but exquisitely perfect diamond winking up at her. Clumsily, he lifted the ring out of the box. Taking her hand, he pushed it up her finger.

''You told me to ask you again,'' he said.

She stared at his ring twinkling on her finger. Hardly daring to breathe, she said, ''I'd rather hear three little words first.''

''Oh, Frankie, I love you.''

''I love you, too. I have for years and years. Maybe ever since the first grade.''

''Me, too.''

''Only I was scared.''

"Me, too,' he repeated. "Every bit as scared as you. Scared I wasn't good enough, scared I couldn't ever measure up to someone as classy as you."

"Oh, Matt, I'm not some high-classed snob...or a princess. I'm just like you—a rancher. Really, I am. And there's something else. All my life I've wanted to be loved—just for me. Not because of some obligation. I always felt my aunt and uncle had to raise me."

"They love you. Your Uncle Wayne went on and on about how great you are and how lucky we all are to have you. When will you ever figure that out?"

"But you? Are you sure you really love me—just for me?"

"Yes, darlin'. With all my heart."

"And...are you my friend too, Matt?"

"There's that bad word again." He smiled at her. "Your friend? Yes—if I can be your lover, too."

"Oh, Matt. You already are."

His arms wrapped her so tightly, she grew dizzy. Then he bent his head against hers and went on holding her as if she were very precious to him. A long time later, he sighed. Then his lips found hers again.

"Well?" he whispered. "You never did say whether or not you'd marry me."

She felt a thrilling happiness. "Oh, yes. Yes! Yes! The sooner the better!"

"What's the hurry?" he demanded, his own voice gritty with desire.

"I guess I'm too much like my mother after all. I

keep thinking about what happened in the shed together. And I want to do it again and again.''

"So do I. For the rest of our lives. I can't live without you, you know. I tried and it damn near killed me.''

"I know what you mean,'' she agreed, laying her head close to his heart.

"The last few days we've spent apart have been the longest in my life. Oh, Frankie, I love you.''

"Not nearly as much as I love you—slave driver.''

"God, I want to make love to you.''

"We've got a whole lot of dancing to get through first.''

"How's your left ankle?''

"Fine. Everything is wonderful now that you're here.''

He clasped her tightly, burying his face in her hair, breathing in the scent of her.

Frankie started laughing. All of a sudden she knew that she wasn't going to have to pretend she was having fun tonight. She really was going to be the happiest debutante at the ball.

Frankie and Matt, their bodies glued together, whirled round and round beneath the glitter of the country club chandeliers. Her bare feet skimmed lightly over the parquet floor, following his lead easily.

"How's your ankle now?'' he whispered, staring down at her with brilliant, golden eyes.

"Never better since I lost those high heels. Hey, I didn't know you could dance. I kinda like this debutante stuff.''

''Me, too.'' He kissed her hair. ''Hey, I didn't know you'd look like a real princess in a dress. I'll dance more often—if you'll wear a dress.''

''Deal.''

''Lipstick, too?''

''Now you're pushing it.''

''No, the fancy hairdo would be pushing it.''

They both laughed.

''Lipstick, too,'' she promised. ''I'd do anything, anything to make you happy. You're awfully handsome in that tuxedo.''

He groaned. ''More formal balls?''

''You've got to admit, we're having a lot of fun.''

''Just because we're together.'' He smiled down into her upturned face. ''We're going to have all kinds of fun...just because we're together.''

He whirled her toward the tall French doors that opened onto a series of terraces overlooking the pool, tennis courts and golf course. Folding her hand in his, he pulled her outside into the glimmer of moonlight and stars that reminded Frankie of the night they'd first made love.

Matt bent his head to hers. Eagerly her lips met his and clung.

''Each kiss just gets better and better,'' she said when he finally let her go.

''We have a lot to look forward to then. A whole lifetime of kisses that get better and better.''

They kissed again and then again, just to make sure.

A smile curved her mouth. ''See, I'm right about

the kisses getting better. Do you know what we've got to test next?''

''I can guess.''

''Tonight? After the ball?''

His amber eyes flared. His arms tightened. ''We'll make love until dawn.''

''Promise?''

He squeezed her hand. Then he slowly brought it to his lips and began to kiss her palm exactly as he had in the shed. With his tongue, he laved each finger. ''I want to kiss you like this all over.''

''Careful. You're provoking my mating instinct. I did promise Aunt Susie I'd pretend to be a lady.''

''You're very much a lady—especially in my bed.''

The silver moon wrapped the lovers in its magic glow and made them feel that they were the only two people in the world.

Matt crushed her to him, his arms circling her slender waist. ''Kiss me, sweet angel.''

Their lips met. She threaded her fingertips in his bright hair. Soon his breathing was harsh and rapid. It was a long time before he could bear to stop kissing her and lead her back inside the crowded ballroom on his arm.

''I'm the happiest debutante here,'' Frankie said. ''Because you're here.''

''Can I have this dance?''

''And many, many more.''

* * * * *

*Don't miss the next story
from Silhouette's*

LONE STAR COUNTRY CLUB:
STROKE OF FORTUNE

*by Christine Rimmer
Available June 2002
(ISBN:0-373-61352-0)
Turn the page for an excerpt
from this exciting romance...!*

Chapter One

The two golf carts reached the ninth tee at a little after eight that Sunday morning in late May. Tyler Murdoch and Spence Harrison rode in the first cart. Flynt Carson and Dr. Michael O'Day, the blind fourth they'd picked up at the clubhouse when Luke Callaghan didn't show, took up the rear.

It was one of those rare perfect mornings, the temperature in the seventies, the sky a big blue bowl, a wispy cloud or two drifting around up there. Somewhere in the trees overhead, a couple of doves cooed at each other.

When the men emerged from under the cover of the oaks, the fairway, still glistening a little from its early-morning watering, was so richly green it hardly seemed real. A deep, true green, Flynt Carson thought. Like Josie's eyes...

Flynt swore under his breath. He'd been vowing for nearly a year that he'd stop thinking about her. Still, her name always found some way to come creeping into his mind.

"What did you say?" Michael O'Day pulled their cart to a stop on the trail right behind spence and Tyler. "I think I caught the meaning, but I missed the exact words." He slanted Flynt a knowing grin.

Flynt ordered his mind to get back where it belonged—on his game. "Just shaking my head over that last hole. If I'd come out of the sand a little better, I could have parred it. No doubt about it, my sand wedge needs work."

Michael chuckled. "Hey, at least you—"

And right then Flynt heard the kind of sound a man *shouldn't* hear on the golf course. He put up a hand, though Michael had already fallen silent.

The two in the front cart must have heard it, too. They were turning to look for the source as it came again: a fussy little cry.

"Over there," Spence said. He pointed toward the thick hedge that partially masked a groundskeeper's shed about thirty yards from them.

A frown etched a crease between Michael's black eyebrows. "Sounds like a—"

Spence was already out of the lead cart. "Damn it, I don't believe it."

Neither did Flynt. He blinked. And he looked again.

But it was still there: a baby carrier, the kind that doubles as a car seat, tucked in close to the hedge.

And in the car seat—wrapped in a fluffy pink blanket, waving tiny fists and starting to wail—was a baby.

A baby. A baby *alone*. On the ninth tee of the Lone Star Country Club's Ben Hogan-designed golf course.

"What the hell kind of idiot would leave a baby on the golf course?" Tyler Murdoch asked the question of no one in particular. He took off after Spence. Flynt and Michael fell in right behind.

Midway between the carts and the squalling infant, all four men slowed. The baby cried louder and those tiny fists flailed.

The men—Texans all, tall, narrow-hipped, broad-shouldered and proud—stopped dead, two in front, two right behind, about fifteen feet from the yowling child. Three of those men had served in the Gulf War together. Each of those three had earned the Silver Star for gallantry in action. The fourth, Michael O'Day, was perhaps the finest cardiac surgeon in the Lone Star State. He spent his working life fighting to save lives in the operating room—and most of the time, he won. Flynt's own father, Ford Carson, was a living testament to the skill and steely nerves of Dr. O'Day.

Not a coward in the bunch.

But that howling baby stopped them cold. To the world they might be heroes, but they were also single men. And childless. Not a one knew what the hell to do with a crying infant.

Another several edgy seconds passed, with the poor kid getting more worked up, those little arms pumping wildly, the fat little face crumpled in misery, getting very red.

Then Tyler said, "Spence." He gestured with a tight nod to the left. "I'll go right. We'll circle the shed and rendezvous around the back. Then we'll check out the interior."

"Gotcha." The two started off, Tyler pausing after a few steps to advise over his shoulder, "Better see to that kid."

Flynt resisted the urge to argue, *No way. You deal with the baby. We'll reconnoiter the shed.* But he'd missed his chance and he knew it. He and Michael were stuck with the kid.

Michael looked grim. Flynt was certain his own expression mirrored the doctor's. But what damn choice did they have? Someone had to take care of the baby.

"Let's do it," he said bleakly, already on his way again toward the car seat and its unhappy occupant.

As his shadow fell across the child, the wailing stopped. The silence, to Flynt, seemed huge. And wonderful, after all that screaming.

The baby blinked up at him. A girl, Flynt guessed—the blanket, after all, *was* pink. Her bright blue eyes seemed to be seeking, straining to see him looming above her. And then she gave up. She shut those eyes and opened that tiny mouth and let out another long, angry wail.

*Silhouette presents an exciting
new continuity series:*

**When a royal family rolls out the red carpet
for love, power and deception, will their
lives change forever?**

The saga begins in April 2002 with:

The Princess Is Pregnant!

by Laurie Paige (SE #1459)

**May: THE PRINCESS AND THE DUKE by Allison Leigh
(SE #1465)**

**June: ROYAL PROTOCOL by Christine Flynn
(SE #1471)**

Be sure to catch all nine Crown and Glory stories: the first three appear in
Silhouette Special Edition, the next three continue in Silhouette Romance
and the saga concludes with three books in Silhouette Desire.

And be sure not to miss more royal stories,
from Silhouette Intimate Moments'

Romancing
the Crown,

running January through December.

INTIMATE MOMENTS™

presents:

Romancing the Crown

With the help of their powerful allies, the royal family of Montebello is determined to find their missing heir. But the search for the beloved prince is not without danger—or passion!

Available in June 2002:
ROYAL SPY
by Valerie Parv (IM #1154)

Gage Weston's mission: to uncover a traitor in the royal family. But once he set his sights on pretty Princess Nadia, he discovered his own desire might betray *him.* Now he was determined to discover the truth about the woman who had grabbed hold of his heart....

This exciting series continues throughout the year with these fabulous titles:

Available only from Silhouette Intimate Moments at your favorite retail outlet.

 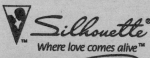

Silhouette®
Where love comes alive™

Visit Silhouette at www.eHarlequin.com

SIMRC6

Silhouette Books is proud to present:

Going to the Chapel

**Three brand-new stories
about getting that special man to the altar!**

featuring

USA Today **bestselling author**

SHARON SALA

*It Happened One Night...*that Georgia society belle
Harley June Beaumont went to Vegas—and woke up married!
How could she explain her hunk of a husband to
her family back home?

Award-winning author

DIXIE BROWNING

*Marrying a Millionaire...*was exactly what Grace McCall was
trying to keep her baby sister from doing. Not that Grace had
anything against the groom—it was the groom's arrogant
millionaire uncle who got Grace all hot and bothered!

National bestselling author

STELLA BAGWELL

*The Bride's Big Adventure...*was escaping her handpicked
fiancé in the arms of a hot-blooded cowboy! And from the
moment Gloria Rhodes said "I do" to her rugged groom, she
dreamed their wedded bliss would never end!

Available in July at your favorite retail outlets!

∇ Silhouette®
Where love comes alive™

Silhouette Books presents a dazzling keepsake collection featuring two full-length novels by international bestselling author

DIANA PALMER

Brides To Be

(On sale May 2002)

THE AUSTRALIAN
Will rugged outback rancher Jonathan Sterling be roped into marriage?

HEART OF ICE
Close proximity sparks a breathtaking attraction between a feisty young woman and a hardheaded bachelor!

You'll be swept off your feet by Diana Palmer's BRIDES TO BE.

Don't miss out on this special two-in-one volume, available soon.

Available only from Silhouette Books at your favorite retail outlet.

Where love comes alive™

Where Texas society reigns supreme—and appearances are everything!

A sexy and sophisticated 12-book continuity from Silhouette Books in which provocative romances and heartwarming tales create larger-than-life Texas stories.

Save 50¢ off

your purchase of any Silhouette®
Lone Star Country Club title

Visit us at www.lonestarcountryclub.com
LSCC6/02-50¢COUPCAN
© 2002 Harlequin Enterprises Ltd.

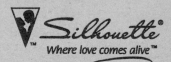

LONE STAR
LSCC
COUNTRY CLUB
EST. 1923

Where Texas society reigns supreme—and appearances are everything!

A sexy and sophisticated 12-book continuity from Silhouette Books in which provocative romances and heartwarming tales create larger-than-life Texas stories.

Visit us at www.lonestarcountryclub.com
LSCC6/02-50¢COUPUS
© 2002 Harlequin Enterprises Ltd.

Silhouette®
Where love comes alive™

Three bold, irresistible men.
Three brand-new romances by today's top authors...
Summer never seemed hotter!

Sheiks
of Summer

*Available in August
at your favorite
retail outlet!*

"The Sheik's Virgin" by Susan Mallery

He was the brazen stranger who chaperoned innocent, beautiful
Phoebe Carson around his native land. But what would Phoebe do when
she discovered her suitor was none other than Prince Nasri Mazin—
and he had seduction on his mind?

"Sheikh of Ice" by Alexandra Sellers

She came in search of adventure—and discovered passion in the arms
of tall, dark and handsome Hadi al Hajar. But once Kate Drummond
succumbed to Hadi's powerful touch, would she succeed in
taming his hard heart?

"Kismet" by Fiona Brand

A star-crossed love affair and a stormy night combined to bring
Laine Abernathy into Sheik Xavier Kalil Al Jahir's world. Now, as she
took cover in her rugged rescuer's home, Lily wondered if it was her
destiny to fall in love with the mesmerizing sheik....

Where love comes alive™